Just One Drop

Quinn Loftis

Acknowledgments:

First I want to thank God for blessing me with a creative spirit. He has blessed me beyond measure. I also want to thank my husband for all his support, for the teasing that he gives me for writing teen paranormal romance. I like to remind him that at least he's never bored being married to me. I also want to thank a friend who has been a blessing to me, Melinda Senter, for her help in the creative editing. Her wicked sense of humor and eye for details has truly been a help. I also want to thank her for the beautiful cover art she has created for me. I want to thank Rachel Carr for being a fantabulous editor. I have been so blessed to get to know Rachel and her help has been invaluable. Thank you also to Jennifer Nunez for also editing and encouraging me to keep writing. Thank you to all my beta readers and reviewers. I cannot express my thanks for all your feedback and help. Finally, most important in many ways, thank you to everyone who has taken a chance on an unknown, self published author and purchased my book. Thank you for the reviews good and bad. Thank you for taking your valuable time and spending it with my characters and their story.

Chapter 1

"Jen, you are not going back to the states so quit trying to pack your damn clothes," Sally growled. She intercepted Jen and snatched the pants she was carrying to an open suitcase, which lay haphazardly across the large four poster bed. Jen steadily ignored her and did an about face   to the closet to grab more of her clothes.

"Would you please just talk to me? Please?" Sally's voice was beginning to take on a high-pitched whine.

"Oh, good grief. For the love of healthy ears everywhere, quit your belly aching," Jen snapped, the clothes in her hands growing more wrinkled by the second. "Sally, there is nothing to talk about, okay? It is what it is."

Sally threw her hands up in the air as she exhaled loudly. "No, it is not what it is, whatever the hell that means. It's a whole freaking lot more complicated than 'it is what it is'." Sally was beginning to get desperate, and although when Jen started this little stunt Sally thought that throwing her suitcase out of the window might be drastic – yeah, not so much anymore.

As Jen continued to throw clothes into the suitcase, Sally decided that desperate times called for desperate measures. She went over to the window and pushed it open. Without much grace, she managed to push the screen out and didn't blink when it tumbled down the side of the three story mansion. Jen was still in the closet when Sally picked up her suitcase and began carrying it toward the open window.

"Put the suitcase down, step away from it slowly, and nobody gets hurt," Jen ground out as she came out of the closet.

"I'm sorry, Jen, but I can't let you leave. So I'll risk your wrath and do whatever it takes to keep your cranky, sulky, continually pissed off butt in Romania."

Jen took a step towards Sally and the suitcase that was now teetering dangerously on the ledge of the open window.

"Back the hell off, Jennifer Adams." Sally tilted the suitcase back as if to let it fall. Jen continued to take slow, measured steps towards Sally, thinking that her usually mild mannered friend wouldn't dare let go of the suitcase…She was wrong, so very wrong. Sally didn't just let go of the suitcase, she gave it a huge shove just as Jen lunged to grab it. Sally jumped back, slapping her hands over her mouth. She was nearly as surprised with herself as Jen was.

"What…how… why," Jen sputtered as she stared at Sally incredulously. "You bitch," she finally managed to spit out.

"It's for your own good, Jen. Really it is," Sally told her, backing away from the fuming Jen.

Jen leaned out the open window and saw the fate of her now scattered suitcase and clothes. She looked back at Sally, still shocked that her friend had pulled such a stunt. Shaking her head, she turned and headed towards the door of the bedroom.

"Where are you going?" Sally asked.

"Out," Jen growled as she pulled the door open.

"At least take a coat. It's cold out!" Sally yelled at Jen's retreating form.

Sally stood and stared. She didn't know if she had done the right thing, but she knew that Jen didn't need to leave. Sally couldn't explain the feeling, but something in her said that something bad would happen to Jen if she left Romania right now. She didn't try to examine the feeling; she just accepted it for what it was…for now.

Jen stormed down the long staircase, taking two at a time, all the while hoping she didn't pass anyone so she wouldn't have to talk. Once on the ground floor she made a right and headed down a long hallway. She passed the library, a sitting room, and the entertainment room before finally arriving at her destination. Without knocking, she threw the door open and walked inside.

"Jen, what can I do for you?" Vasile asked as he looked up from his desk.

Before she answered she shut the door behind her. Then, taking a deep breath, she turned back to Vasile.

"I can't stay here."

Vasile didn't look surprised at her admission and he didn't respond. Instead he waited for her to continue.

She took another deep breath and let it out slowly. "Look, I know you know what Dr. Steele told me about my blood results. Regardless of that, I can't change how I feel about a certain wolf. I can't change the fact that, wolf blood or not, I'm not his mate, and said wolf wants nothing to do with me. How do I know this, you ask?" Jen continued before Vasile could say a word. "Because he just up and left. Not so much as a 'see ya later, Jen', 'take care, Jen', 'goodbye, Jen', 'have a nice freaking life without me, Jen',"

Jen slapped her hand over her mouth, embarrassed that she had spilled all that to Vasile. She knew the only reason she was discussing this with Fane's father was because she was desperate to get away from this place. To get away from the only man – she'd come to realize over the past couple of months – that she loved. After Dr. Steele revealed to her that she had a minute, very minute amount of werewolf blood in her, she had thought that maybe there was a chance for her and the fur ball. That hope been quickly doused when said fur ball up and disappeared. A week after Jacque and Fane's ceremony, Decebel had gotten in his Hummer and, without looking back, driven away from the pack mansion. And 62 days, 4 hours, and 22 minutes later he still hadn't returned. *But who's counting?*

"Didn't you just turn eighteen, Jen?" Vasile asked her.

Jen looked a little confused at his choice of response. "Umm, yes. I believe that loud racket you heard a couple of weeks ago was Sally and Jacque's idea of a birthday party. What does that have to do with me leaving?"

"If you are eighteen, Jen, you are an adult. I can't make you stay here. If you want to leave, if you really think that is the best thing for you, then you can go. I will allow you to use the pack plane to get back to the U.S. if that is truly what you want," Vasile explained.

Jen cocked her head to the side, eyes narrowed at the Alpha sitting calmly in front of her. "Just like that? No trying to convince me to stay, or telling me not to give up, or yada yada yada bull crap?"

"No 'yada yada yada bull crap'," he agreed.

"Huh, okay then. Let's do this," she stated.

"Now?"

"Yes, now. Is that a problem?"

Vasile picked up the phone, never taking his eyes off her. "Sorin, could you please come to my office?"

Jen took a seat in one of the chairs in front of Vasile's desk. Resting her hands on the chair arms, she couldn't keep her legs from bouncing up and down as she waited for Sorin to arrive. Vasile didn't say anything while they waited and that was just fine with Jen. She didn't want to listen to any more reasons about why she should stay. She heard the door open and close, and then Sorin stepped up beside her.

"What can I do for you, Alpha?" he asked Vasile.

"Jen has decided that she wants to go back to the U.S.," Vasile began, and to Sorin's credit he didn't so much as flinch in Jen's direction. "Could you please arrange for the plane to be ready? Get her things, drive her to the air strip, and make sure she gets on the plane safely."

"Of course." Sorin answered as if Vasile hadn't just told him Jen was leaving only two months after arriving.

As Jen stood up, she stopped Sorin from leaving with a hand on his arm. "Please, it's not necessary to get my things." Sorin started to object but Jen cut him off. "Really, I'm good to go. Right now." She turned to Vasile, looking for some sort of confirmation that this was okay. After a moment of looking into her eyes, Vasile turned to Sorin and nodded once.

As they began to walk out of the office, Jen turned back to Vasile. "You won't tell anyone, will you? I mean, will you let me call them once I get back to the States?"

Vasile smiled gently. "I won't say a word."

She let out the breath she had been holding. "Thank you."

Jen sat in the passenger side of yet another Hummer, wrapped in a parka Sorin had grabbed. "What is with you wolves and Hummers?" she muttered grumpily.

"They do well in this climate," Sorin answered, never taking his eyes from the road.

Jen glanced at him briefly, then looked out the passenger window. Her mind wandered to a certain tall, dark, gorgeous werewolf that she so desperately wanted to see, yet longed to stab in the hand with a butter knife at the same time…funny how that temptation seemed to apply only to him.

Vasile waited until he heard Sorin pull away from the driveway before picking up his phone again. "I need to speak with you." He listened to the voice on the other end. "No, not necessarily right this minute, just in the next hour would be good." Ending the call, he immediately dialed another number and waited for an answer, a voice came on the line. "Stall," was all he said.

Vasile leaned back in his chair, folding his hands in his lap. He shook his head as he chuckled. Alina was going to scold him for meddling, as she would call it, but he was Alpha. It was his job to meddle, and he was good at it.

Chapter 2

An hour and a half later…

Fane held up the piece of paper his father handed him. He looked at his father, then back to the paper in his hand. "You want me to tell my mate that you waited an hour and a half to inform me that her best friend left to board a plane headed back to the States?" Fane growled.

"I did not wait. I called you the minute she left. You didn't arrive for an hour and a half," Vasile answered, completely unruffled by the growl in Fane's voice.

"With all due respect, Alpha, you could have mentioned the reason you wanted to see me."

"No, I couldn't. I told Jen I wouldn't *say* a word," Vasile emphasized.

"Jen didn't catch that little loophole?" Fane asked, his eyebrows raised.

"Don't you think you ought to tell your mate what's going on? I don't know how much longer Sorin can stall the plane before Jen figures out something is going on."

Fane's head snapped up at his father's words. "She hasn't left yet?"

"Do you honestly think I would let her leave?"

"Luna, I need to speak with you. Could you please come to my father's office?" Fane sent Jacque his question through their bond. It had become so strong since their mating that she was a constant presence and comfort in his mind.

"Why do I hear worry in your voice, wolf-man?" Jacquelyn asked him suspiciously.

Without answering his mate, he glared at his father. "I will get you back for this, Alpha. Just to warn you ahead of time."

Vasile winked at his son. "A little lesson in dealing with conflict with your mate will be good for you."

Fane looked at his Alpha in amazement. "Father, you do realize who I'm mated to, right?"

Vasile cleared his throat. "You do have a point there." But he still offered no apology for his nonchalance in the matter.

The door to the office flew open as a frustrated looking Jacque stormed in with a worried looking Sally right behind her.

"What's going on, Fane?"

"First, it's not as bad as it sounds," Fane began.

Jacque held up her hand to cut off her mate. "Spit it out, fur ball."

"Sorin took Jen to the pack plane to fly back to the States."

"WHAT!" Jacque and Sally yelled at the same time, causing both wolves to grimace in pain because of their sensitive hearing.

Jen sat on the plane, drinking the second Coke Sorin had brought her while she waited for the runway to be cleared. Apparently, December in Romania got icy. Go figure. She didn't really care about the runway or the plane being ice-free, she just knew that the longer she sat here, not in the air, not moving towards North America, the more nervous she became that she would be discovered by her two neurotic best friends who she knew meant well, but didn't get why she had to leave.

Everyday Jen woke up hoping that she would go downstairs and find Decebel; she went to bed every night wondering why he left. She had no idea if he knew about her wolf blood, and she was to the point that she didn't want to care. *Easier said than done*, she thought. Why couldn't she fall in love with a normal guy, someone who didn't go furry at will? *No. That would be too stinking easy.*

She leaned her head back and closed her eyes. Her mind wandered back to the night of Jacque and Fane's bonding ceremony. Her life forever changed when Dr. Steele had explained that the blood test she had run on Jen after the car wreck had come back abnormal. Abnormal as in not human. Jen remembered feeling like the walls of the room were closing in on her.

"What do you mean, 'not human'?" she had asked Cynthia.

"You have werewolf blood. Though it is a very minute amount," Cynthia had answered.

Sally'd been sitting next to her, and her reaction had been what Jen wanted to say: "SHUT UP." Sally yelled this, causing everyone around them to stop and stare. Jen hadn't really noticed. The only thing she'd been able to focus on was a certain wolf who had been eyeballing her all night.

"What does that mean, exactly?"

"It means that somewhere in your family, generations ago, was a werewolf." The doctor seemed baffled by this. "I don't even know how it's possible unless all of his descendants mated with humans and the bloodline gradually diluted."

Jen and Sally had listened to the doctor explain that maybe something as traumatic as the accident had triggered the very dormant gene – perhaps that was why her wounds had healed so quickly. Jen asked if she thought she would develop any other werewolf characteristics. Cynthia felt that since Jacque hadn't, and she was half-were, that Jen was in the clear. But she truly didn't know what it would mean for Jen or her future. "You are the first dormant I have ever met," she told Jen.

For two months after learning about the werewolf blood that lay dormant in her blood, she had been constantly watching for any other wolf-like attributes. The only thing that she felt was different was that she could sense emotions. Well, strong emotions to be exact. She didn't really understand it, but she could almost *smell* them and each emotion smelled differently. Jen mentioned it to Sally and Jacque and they both had wanted her to go to Dr. Steele. She never did.

Jen heard a car door slam, which brought her back to the present, to the wonderful fact that she was sitting in a plane, a plane that would take her away from all this werewolf stuff.

She tapped her foot impatiently and drummed her fingers on the arm of the seat. "What could possibly be taking so freaking long," she said to the empty plane. With an exaggerated huff she undid the seat belt and stood, tired of waiting. It was time to take things into her own hands.

She looked out a window and her breath froze in her lungs at the sight. Where there had only been one black Hummer, now sat two. *No way*, she thought. *It's not him. Vasile has, like, a million black Hummers*. She had long ago decided it was a wolf thing.

Jen stepped back from the window, taking some slow, deep breaths. She closed her eyes and tried to regain her bearings. *I got this.* Finally ready, she walked towards the exit sign.

To what, she didn't know.

Chapter 3

"Don't you think you should call him?" Jacque asked Fane as they walked out to the car, moving slowly, trying not to slip on the snow covered ground. Fane opened the passenger door for Jacque but she didn't get in. He realized she wasn't moving until he answered all of her questions.

"My father will be the one to decide if Decebel should be called."

"That's not good enough," Jacque growled. "Not when it's *my* friend making possibly the biggest mistake of her life." She turned and, holding her arms out for balance on the slick ground, headed back into the mansion.

Sally stood next to Fane, her arms folded around her waist in an attempt to ward off the cold. She watched her friend leave. "She's going to tell your father what he should do, isn't she?"

"I keep telling her it's going to bite her in the butt one of these days."

Jacque pushed the door to Vasile's office open without knocking. Alina stood in front of Vasile's desk and Jacque stopped beside her.

"Don't mind me. Carry on," Jacque said to them when they both stopped talking to stare at her.

"Did the concept of knocking somehow diminish when you left your country?" Vasile's eyebrows were raised.

"I apologize, Alpha, but it's important," she answered and was proud when her voice came out without wavering.

Alina wrapped an arm around Jacque's shoulders. "What is important?"

"I think Vasile should call Decebel and tell him to go talk to Jen. I think Jen would listen to him," Jacque explained.

"What would lead you to believe that Jen would listen to Decebel?" Vasile asked. "It was my understanding he was the reason she was leaving."

Jacque's jaw dropped open. "She told you that? She actually told *you* about how she felt about *him*?"

"Well, not in so many words, but I saw how she looked at him at your ceremony. There is only one reason a woman looks at a man like that." Vasile winked at his mate.

"Vasile, quit torturing your daughter-in-law," Alina admonished. "Go on and tell her."

"Tell me what?" Jacque asked eagerly.

"I called Decebel just after you left my office."

"You did?" Jacque asked as her brow furrowed. "What did he say? Is he going to go and get her? Did he care at all?"

"Slow down, little one." Alina chuckled.

Vasile stood from his desk and walked around to Jacque. "I can't speak for Decebel's feelings. Although, the snarl he let out when I told him Jen was leaving would lead one to believe he felt something for her. And yes, he is going to see her. Hopefully Sorin can continue to stall the plane without Jen getting suspicious."

"Crap," Jacque whined. "She's probably already snuck off the plane and decided to swim to North America. This is Jen we're talking about. She's suspicious of everything."

"I would advise that you three stay here and let Decebel handle this for now," Vasile said soberly, making it clear to Jacque that it was really more of an order.

Jacque nodded and left his office in search of Fane and Sally. They were where she'd left them, standing next to the car.

"Well?" Sally prompted.

"He had already called him," Jacque told them.

"There is a reason he's Alpha," Fane teased.

"Yeah, yeah. Soak it up, wolf-man," Jacque said, narrowing her eyes at her mate. "Your dad advised that we stay here and let Decebel handle it."

"So he's going to get her?" Sally's eyebrows rose in surprise.

"According to Vasile."

"If I could be a fly in that plane..." Sally said as she rubbed her hands together.

"I know, right?" Jacque agreed.

With her mind made up, Jen quickened her steps towards the plane exit. She grabbed the handle, yanked it open, and walked into a solid wall.

"Ummph" Jen grunted, then froze. She knew that smell. *Great*, she thought, *there I go with the smell thing again*. But she did know that smell: woodsy, spicy, and male. A very, very pissed off male. She took a step back and slowly raised her chin to look up into the face of the wolf whose memory had haunted her for the past two months.

"Going somewhere, Jennifer?" Decebel asked, eyes narrowed and lips drawn tightly.

Jen stared up into glowing, amber eyes. She couldn't speak, couldn't move, and at this point even breathing seemed to be too much for her body to ask of her. The spell was broken when she heard Decebel growl and realized that she was staring him straight in the eyes. His wolf would see that as a challenge. She took a step back but, challenge or no, did not avert her eyes. Slowly, the anger and hurt that plagued her came rushing back in, flowing through her numb body, giving her life and the ability to speak again.

"As a matter of fact, I am going somewhere. Not that it's any of your business." Jen raised one eyebrow as she folded her arms across her chest. "So if you would kindly leave, I can be on my way." Jen couldn't believe the pain that pierced her heart as she told Decebel to leave. It took everything she had not to flinch at her own words.

Undeterred by Jennifer's haughty attitude, Decebel stepped into the plane. And unless Jennifer wanted his chest pressed to her, made her take another step back.

"I have to disagree with you. I consider it very much my business when it concerns you."

Decebel watched the emotions play across Jennifer's face, so transparent to him. He waited for her to respond, knowing it would be quick-witted and sharp, one of the many things he admired about her. She did not disappoint.

"Funny that," she began. "If I'm so much your business, where have you been for the past two months? If I am so much your freaking business, then you must have a phenomenal excuse for not even coming to my eighteenth birthday party." Jen couldn't hide the hurt behind her words. She ducked her head, biting her lip to keep from crying. It didn't work.

Decebel took a step forward, drawn to her for reasons he didn't yet understand. All he knew was that standing there seeing her hurt was unbearable to him. He placed his fingers under her chin and raised her face to look into her tear-filled eyes. In that moment he was in a different time and place. He looked into a face with green eyes, not blue. A face with dark chocolate locks framing it instead of blonde. He watched as he held her fragile body in his arms, her life draining away. He held on until her form was still, only a shell left to wither from the earth.

"Decebel." The sound of Jennifer's voice brought him back to the present, but the memory of that lifeless body reminded him what happened when he cared about someone, what happened when he was unable to keep those he loved safe. He dropped his hand from her chin and took a step back, not missing the hurt that flashed across her face.

"You are my business because you are my prince's mate's best friend. As Beta it's my job to keep you safe," he answered his demeanor suddenly much more formal.

"Well, I'm relinquishing you of that *job* by leaving. So no worries, Dec. I'm perfectly capable of sitting on a plane by myself." Jen turned to go back but didn't get far before she felt a strong hand close around her arm. Decebel turned her to face him and she could see emotions running across his handsome face. For the life of her she didn't know what they were.

"You aren't leaving, Jennifer. Jacque needs you and Sally right now. For some reason I thought you weren't the type of friend to bail on those who depend on you." Decebel figured the easiest way to get Jennifer to cooperate would be to piss her off and present her with a challenge.

Jen jerked her arm from Decebel's grasp. She pulled her shoulders back and stood up as straight as she could. Then she took a step forward and he swore that there had to be steam coming off her skin. She jammed her finger in Decebel's chest as she glared at him.

"First, you don't know a damn thing about me so don't you dare tell me what kind of friend you think I am. Second, I would never, ever bail on one of my friends. Unlike one furry canine that I know, I don't take off without dealing with whatever my friends need. Jacque knows I need to go back to the States. She has Fane and Sally."

"Is that so?" Decebel challenged.

"Yes, Cujo. That is so." Jen's jaw jutted forward as she ground her teeth together.

"If Jacque is so understanding, then why did she go to Vasile to have him call me to come get you?" The look on Decebel's face when he finished talking was that of a cat who had just caught a little birdie. He watched as Jennifer's jaw dropped open at his words. He stood silently and let the information set in. Finally, she looked up into his eyes again – the only one other than his Alpha allowed to get away with it – and rubbed her hand over her forehead.

"Is that why you came, because Vasile sent you?"

Decebel could tell that his answer had the ability to crush her and possibly push her away, making it easier to keep his distance. He stared into her blue eyes, eyes that pleaded with him for the truth, painful or not.

"Vasile called me." Jennifer's face fell, so Decebel continued quickly. "But he did not order me to come get you."

Her head snapped up at his words, her eyes searched his face for any hint of a lie. Decebel was sure she would ask why he came but instead she took a deep breath. She suddenly looked tired, defeated.

"Fine, I'll stay. But not because you said I have to. I'll stay for Jacque." Jen went to step around Decebel and head out of the plane exit. As she pushed the door open and felt the cold December air and the sun on her face, she turned back to the wolf who watched her silently. "I'll stay, but you need to make sure you stay out of my way. I don't need you thinking I need a big brother to watch over me and tell me what to do, so don't." She stepped out of the plane and the crisp, frosty air burned her lungs. Sorin stood with the passenger door held open for her.

Decebel stared at the empty space that had been Jennifer. He closed his eyes and took in a deep breath through his nose, relishing her scent. Shaking his head, he opened his eyes.

"Jennifer," he whispered her name reverently to the empty plane. "I most definitely don't see you as a sister, and I don't think I could stay out of your way even if I wanted."

Chapter 4

Jen sat in the garden behind the mansion, still wearing the parka she had put on hours ago. It was late and cold, but she didn't want to be inside just yet. She didn't feel like answering the questions she knew her two best friends would undoubtedly bombard her with. She lifted her head up to the clear sky, marveling at the thousands of stars that lit up the darkness.

A twig snapped on the ground to her left. Jen turned in the direction of the sound to see Alina coming towards her, wrapped in a heavy coat, carrying two coffee mugs. She couldn't help but smile at Alina as she took the offered mug. Jen felt the heat from the steam rise and caress her face as she drew the cup to her lips.

"So, tweedle dee and tweedle dumb sent you, I see." Jen indicated to the hot chocolate she was thoroughly thankful for.

Alina let out a small laugh as she sat down on the bench next to Jen. "Guilty as charged, I'm afraid."

Jen shrugged her shoulders, accepting that there was no way her two friends would leave her alone. She was glad it was Alina who had come. Something about her was so peaceful and comforting.

"Jen, are you unhappy here?" Alina asked gently.

"No," Jen said quickly. "No, Alina. Your home is wonderful and you and Vasile have made us all feel so welcome."

"Then why do you want to leave so badly?"

Jen looked slyly at Alina from the corner of her eye as she took another sip. She swallowed slowly, savoring the warmth that traveled through her. "No offense, Alina, but I know that you know about the fur ball." Alina laughed at Jen's insistent digs at Decebel.

"Okay, guilty. Yet again." Alina smiled, then it faded slowly as she placed her hand on Jen's arm. "Give it time, Jen. If it's meant to be then it will be." Jen started to interrupt but Alina continued before she could. "I know you think that because you aren't having any of the mating signs it's hopeless, but we've never been around someone with werewolf blood as diluted as yours. There is no telling the repercussions, so be patient, little one. He'll come around."

Jen slowly nodded, even though inside she still had serious doubts.

"I guess I need to go see Jacque and Sally and do a little damage control." Jen grimaced.

"That would probably be wise," Alina told her as they stood and walked back to the mansion together.

Jen opened the door to Sally's room to find her two best friends sitting on the floor, going over the homework their tutor had assigned them. Neither of them stopped to acknowledge her and she could admit she deserved the snub.

"So, I guess I need to apologize for being a complete ass," Jen told them, remorse written across her face.

Sally looked up at her slowly. Her eyes were drawn together in a glare that would stop a grown man. "Look, Jacque. The prodigal wolf returns. Isn't that sweet of her."

Jen winced at Sally's words, which were laced in sarcasm and dripping with vehemence.

Jacque gave Jen a passing glance as if she were nothing more than a gnat. "Huh, so it is." And she went back to her homework.

Crap, Jen thought. She was going to have to grovel. How she hated groveling. "I really am sorry. I know that you guys were worried and that you're mad at me for being selfish."

Sally sat up abruptly. "Worried, yes. Mad, no. Hurt, definitely. Jen, you won't talk to us about what's going on. You've been sulking around here for the past two months. You won't talk about the wolf blood thing, you won't talk about Decebel, and then you throw the hissy fit of the century and start packing your stuff, spouting off how you can't do it anymore. We are sitting in the dark twiddling our freaking thumbs." Sally's voice had slowly gotten louder as her rant continued. "I change my mind, we are mad. Hurt, mad and worried."

Jacque stared at Sally like she had grown a third eyeball while Jen was looking for a hole to crawl into.

"I'm sorry, Sally. I don't know what else to say, but truly I'm sorry. I've just been so, crap, I don't know. Frustrated, scared, lonely-"

"Lonely?" Jacque interrupted, obviously hurt.

"Not because you guys haven't been there," Jen added quickly. "I can't describe it. Okay," Jen stopped and sat down by her two best friends, "you want me to talk, here goes. When Decebel left after your ceremony, I felt like a hole had been cut inside of me. I don't know how to describe it other than utter loneliness. I've been so stinking frustrated because I don't ever get depressed over a guy. I mean, hello, I'm Jen. I don't *need* a guy." She ran her hands through her long blonde hair in agitation. "But there I was, pining after a werewolf and I don't know why. I don't understand why he just left like he didn't give a damn." Jen wiped the tears that were now staining her face. "And bloody hell, I'm sick of crying."

Jacque sat up and took Jen in her arms; Sally wrapped hers around them both. The three girls sat there silently while Jen tried to get her scattered emotions under some sort of control.

Finally, Sally broke the silence. "Well, you're forgiven. Just quit being so stubborn and talk to us, okay?"

Jen nodded as she wiped the last of her tears away. "Talk, got it. I'm all over it, boss," she teased.

"So, you going to spill what happened today? You know, with you and…" Sally hinted.

"Between me and White Fang? Well, I will admit that when I saw Decebel I was shocked. As in 'what the hell do you mean a woman sat on a toilet so long that she became attached to it' shocked."

"Oh, snap. I forgot about that. That was wicked." Jacque cringed.

"Hey. Lucy, Ethel, focus," Sally snapped.

"Oh, right." Jen shook her head. "So shocked, because he was the last wolf I expected to see. To top it off, he was sweet. Which only ticked me off…" Jen trailed off, remembering how Decebel had momentarily gone to another place while looking into her eyes.

"What?" Sally asked.

"It's probably nothing, but there was one point when he was looking at me and he sort of zoned out. I had to say his name several times before he snapped out of it. Then I felt him pull back, if that makes sense. I mean emotionally. It was like he put a wall up between us."

"Hmm, sounds like it's time for me to investigate," Jacque said.

"Oh, by all means. We know your sleuthing skills are legendary." Jen rolled her eyes.

"Hey, I'm just honing my skills," Jacque said indignantly.

"Whatever you say, Sherlock," Jen teased.

"Alright, so spill the rest. What else did he say?" Sally asked eagerly.

Jen proceeded to tell them, at their insistence, word for word what was said between her and Decebel. And true to form, Jacque and Sally spent the remainder of the night dissecting the conversation. Jen swore they had it down to an art form.

Chapter 5

Decebel lay on his bed, staring aimlessly at the ceiling. He couldn't sleep. Every time he closed his eyes he saw her face. Jennifer. Her scent was burned into his brain, and the hurt he had caused was etched in his memory. Her face had been clouded with it on the plane. For the first time in his long life he was truly unsure about the path he was to take.

The feelings that were stirring inside him towards Jennifer were foreign to him. The only thing he could compare it to was what he had felt for Cosmina, his younger sister. She had been the brightest light in his life. Sweet, kind, and gentle. There wasn't a day that went by that he didn't feel the hole inside caused by her death. Somehow, when he was with Jennifer he didn't feel so empty, so alone.

He kept waiting for the mating signs to happen, to hear her thoughts, for his markings to change. At the same time he feared the changes. If the mating signs appeared he would have no choice. He would have to claim Jennifer, and that scared him more than anything had since the day he watched his sister die in his arms.

He thought back to that gruesome day, how helpless he had felt. Cosmina was being courted by two wolves, one of which was her true mate. After several months of more or less passive pursuit, they challenged one another. Cosmina had to be present at the challenge per pack law. Decebel had begged her not to go but she wasn't a rule breaker. Cosmina always did what was expected of her. The wolves fought and the victor took pity on the other wolf and let him live. The losing wolf had gone feral at the idea of not having Cosmina and attacked her before anyone could stop him.

A true mate would never be able to lay a hand on his mate – it went against everything inside them. Their wolf would sooner die than lift a hand against his mate. The wolf had decided that if he couldn't have Cosmina then no one could. Decebel had reached the wolf a moment too late – Cosmina's throat had been ripped and the blood poured out of her in a flood.

Cosmina's true mate had been consumed with so much rage he became dangerous to the pack, and because it was Decebel's sister he choose to be the one to kill him. It wasn't uncommon to have to kill a true mate that hadn't been bonded yet. Decebel couldn't imagine wanting to live without his mate bonded or not.

The rage that consumed Decebel had given him more than enough strength to kill the guilty wolf and he had torn him limb from limb. As he held his sister and watched the light fade from her eyes, she spoke her final words.

"When the time comes, brother, don't fight destiny. Let it happen even if it doesn't happen the way you think it should." And then she was gone.

Cosmina had always had the ability to know things, future things. Nobody understood it and the pack had long ago accepted it.

Now as Decebel laid on his bed, his emotions a turbulent storm inside him, he had to wonder if she had been talking about Jennifer.

He grabbed his phone off the nightstand to check the time. One a.m. He groaned. Tomorrow – or today, rather – was going to be miserable if he didn't get any sleep. As pack Beta it was his job to train the younger wolves. Even in the twenty first century it was necessary for the wolves to know how to defend themselves, in human and wolf form.

After the training he was due to attend a conference call with Vasile. Some of the surrounding packs had called and asked to speak with Vasile, but didn't specify what it was about. When Decebel had asked if he had any inkling of the topic, Vasile nodded solemnly and told him that whatever it was he didn't think it was a good thing. Although packs tried to keep peace between themselves, there were times it was easier said than done. Werewolves were extremely territorial and it didn't take much for them to get in a pissing contest – no pun intended.

With a frustrated sigh he grabbed the ear buds to his iPhone and put them in, then turned on Jason Walker's "Down." He normally listened to classic rock, but he needed something soothing to calm him tonight, something to help him focus. He closed his eyes and listened as the words of the song poured over him. As he listened, he felt like it was written just for him. With every word Jennifer's face became clearer in his mind. Her infectious smile, her eyes twinkling with mischief, the quick wit that could cut a person in half – or make them feel like the most important person in her world.

Pictures ran through his mind of his time in the States when she was in the wreck, the fear that had ripped through him when he had seen her still form on the ground. He remembered feeling so out of control as the doctors tried to treat Jen when his wolf didn't want anyone near her. He let out a low growl as his mind wandered to her little stunt with the human male, Matt. Decebel clearly remembered the name Jennifer had whispered in his ear. He still hadn't talked with her about that night, about what had happened with this Matt character. He grinned slowly to himself as he finally began to drift off. He planned on talking with her very soon about Matt, and Decebel had a feeling she wasn't going to be too pleased about it.

That just made his smile bigger.

"Jen, wake up." Sally pulled the covers off her sleeping friend, allowing the cold air to flow over her. "If you don't get up, I'm getting some water and we'll relive some of those fond memories from the hospital."

"I really think you need help, Sally," Jen mumbled. "Throwing water in my face, throwing my suitcase out of the window, and you think I'm disturbed? It's time for the wicked witch to look in the mirror and ask who's the fairest of them all."

Jen sat up and tried to rub the sleep from her eyes. "What time is it?" she groaned.

"It's nine a.m. and we are supposed to meet with the tutor in thirty minutes. Get moving. We all know how long it takes you to become a person in the morning. I swear you're as bad as Jacque," Sally admonished as she grabbed Jen's hand and pulled her off the bed, pushing her in the direction of the bathroom.

"Bloody hell, Sally. I'm up," Jen whined. As she closed the bathroom door, Sally heard her mumble, "Note to self, lock bedroom door at night to keep perky morning people out."

Jen stood in front of the bathroom mirror, a towel wrapped around her, and combed the tangles from her wet hair. She wasn't going to lie to herself and say she wasn't nervous about today – she was beyond nervous knowing he was here. Decebel, the werewolf she couldn't seem to let go of, no matter what her mind was telling her. Her heart was giving her mind the finger.

Jen jumped at the sound of Sally banging on the bathroom door.

"Okay, sleeping beauty, let's go. You're not going to a beauty contest."

Jen snatched the door open. "Try a different Disney character Thelma, 'cause in order for me to be Sleeping Beauty I would have to be asleep." Jen's words came out a little louder than she intended, but Sally didn't seem to be phased by it.

"Okay, Jen. Talk. What's up?" Sally narrowed her eyes. Her best friend was wound tighter than a roll of fishing twine.

Jen stepped out of the bathroom and headed towards the closet. She grabbed a pair of underwear and a bra from the dresser and began sifting through clothes. Finally settling on a pair of low rise Levi's and a warm fleece pullover, she stepped out of the closet and took a deep breath. "I'm nervous. Decebel's back, as in he's here in the mansion, which means the chances of me seeing him are much greater than when he was gone."

Sally stepped up to her friend and wrapped her arms around her for a quick hug. "He's really gotten to you." It wasn't a question. Sally had never seen steady, confident Jen in such turmoil.

"I need to do something, Sally. I don't know what but I can't stand this. I've never wanted a guy I couldn't have. As conceited as that sounds, truth is truth."

Sally's finger was tapping her lips as she closed her eyes in thought.

"Um, what's cooking in that sadistic brain of yours?" Jen asked nervously.

Sally's eyes snapped open. "I was just thinking that maybe if you met someone else then you could get past your furry problem."

"My furry problem? Really? You make it sound like I have abnormal leg hair growth or something." Jen rolled her eyes.

"Look." Sally stopped Jen before she could walk out of the room. "Let's just give it a go. You, me, and Jacque – tonight. We'll get Sorin to take us somewhere where there are going to be guys. Then you can do your thing."

"My thing?" Jen asked, raising her eyebrows.

"Yeah. You know, your thing. The hottie hunting thing."

Jen laughed. "Man, it sounded like such a good idea at the time."

Sally groaned. "Oh, come on, Jen."

Jen interrupted her before Sally could continue. "Don't. Don't do that whiny voice."

"Then say you will go tonight," Sally challenged. "Or are you chicken?"

"You really like living on the edge, don't you, Thelma?"

"Hey, I'm just calling it how I see it." Sally shrugged.

Jen growled as she threw her head back. Sally knew she couldn't stand to be called a chicken. Jennifer Adams was many things, but a chicken was not one of them.

"Fine, I'll go." She paused, thinking about Sally's idea. "I think a night out is just what the doctor ordered."

"Excellent." Sally grinned, rubbing her hands together in suppressed glee.

"Man, you scare me sometimes, Sal. Truly, you do." Jen grabbed Sally's hand and began walking towards the bedroom door. "Let's do this."

"If that tutor tries to cram anything else into my head, I swear it's going to explode," Jacque whined.

"I feel ya. This three hours a day is kicking my super fine butt." Jen groaned as she slid into a seat in the dining room. "I mean, I get that she has to get seven hours of school into three, but seriously."

"I know, right?" Sally agreed as she laid her head on the table after taking a seat across from Jen.

Jacque sat at the head of the long table and leaned back against the chair.

"How are you, Luna?" She heard Fane's voice in her mind and felt his fingers run across her cheek. It made her shiver involuntarily.

"Oh, ya know, aside from my brain feeling like it's going to become mush and ooze out of my ears, I'm great." She heard him chuckle which made her grin like an idiot.

"I see you've been working on that constipated-looking face when you talk to Cujo," Jen teased.

Jacque just rolled her eyes at her friend.

"The girls are wanting to go out tonight. That okay with you?" she asked Fane.

"Sure, what time? My father has a conference call that was supposed to take place this afternoon, but has been pushed back to later this evening."

"That's fine. We were going to get Sorin to take us. They kind of want it to just be the girls."

That really made Fane laugh. *"I'm sure Sorin will be so happy to know that you all consider him one of the girls."*

Jacque laughed out loud, causing Sally and Jen to roll their eyes at her. "Sorry," she mumbled.

"So you cool with that, wolf-man?"

"I guess as long as Sorin is with you then I can deal with it. I love you, Jacquelyn."

"Funny that. I was just thinking the same thing about you." Jacque felt Fane's lips against hers. She was still getting used to being able to feel him even though he wasn't with her.

"Got the green light for tonight." Jacque grinned

Jen looked at Sally, then back at Jacque. "Did you smoke something this morning and not share?"

Jacque rolled her eyes. "Do you really think I have to smoke something to get happy when I wake up next to Fane every morning?"

"Okay, point to you," Jen said, waving Jacque off.

"Operation 'forget bossy werewolf guy' has been green-lighted?" Sally asked.

Jen covered her face and groaned at Sally's words. "Did you seriously just say that? Operation forget bossy werewolf guy? Really, Sally?"

Sally nodded in all seriousness.

"Well, if you're going to call our night out an operation – and you know how I love ops – at least get it right. It's operation 'forget freaking fine, brooding, bossy werewolf guy'," Jen supplied.

"Good call." Sally bumped fists with Jen, glad to see her friend was regaining her snarky sense of humor.

"Okay, girls. I think we need to head out and begin phase one of operation triple F, double B, WG." Jacque tried to say it with a straight face but as soon as she realized that B and G rhymed in her little abbreviation she lost the battle. Jen and Sally were laughing along with her as they all headed up the stairs.

"What exactly is phase one?" Jen raised her eyebrows at Jacque.

"Phase one, my dear, is find your inner hoochie mama."

"Ahh, I get it." Sally nodded. "It's all about embracing your inner skank."

Jen shook her head. "I think the air is thinner here because you two are clearly not getting enough oxygen to the brain."

"Oh, come on. Give us a break. Out of all of us, you've got inner skank-embracing down to an art form," Sally told her.

"True, very true, Sally. I am expert on all things skank." Jen was laughing as hard as Jacque and Sally when Decebel came around the corner.

The three girls froze while Decebel continued forward until he stood in front of Jen.

For a brief moment they simply stared at one another. The intensity that flowed between them was strong and nearly suffocating.

"I put your clothes and your suitcase in your room," Decebel told her.

Jen took a step back, surprised at his words. Decebel had seen the clothes in her suitcase, and by clothes she meant her womanly garments. She knew her face must be bright red because Decebel's eyes were glowing as she looked back at him. Before she could respond he leaned down and whispered in her ear.

"Please don't allow your friends to throw your clothes out the window. I had to make sure the wolves who found your things gave up all of the souvenirs they took – souvenirs that would cause your beautiful face to turn ten shades of red." She felt his breath on her neck, and he inhaled deeply before walking away.

Jacque had once told her that when a werewolf pulled that little stunt, he was taking in a person's scent. She shivered at the thought and couldn't help turning to watch Decebel walk away.

Jen finally noticed her two friends, who were staring at her with mouths open wide.

"Did you two hear that?" she asked.

Both girls shook their heads, still unable to speak, still stuck in their state of shock at Decebel's behavior.

"Bloody hell, you two. Don't just stand there. Get in my room so I can give you the 411." Jen pushed her two best friends towards her bedroom door, all the while trying to figure out what had just taken place in the hall.

Once in the room Jen shut the door and leaned back against it. Head pressed back, she closed her eyes and slowed her breathing. Blasted wolf was going to give her a heart attack. Frustration rippled through her. Why him? Why did her heart have to pick the one guy she would never be able to have?

"What did he whisper in your ear, Jen?" Jacque questioned.

Jen shook her head, trying to clear it. "He told me to not let my friends throw my clothes out of the window," she paused and looked pointedly at Sally, who had the good sense to look sheepish, "because he had to get my clothes back – which he called souvenirs – from the wolves who apparently found them." She chuckled to herself, knowing she was once again the color of a beet. "And from the tone in his voice, said souvenirs must've been my womanly garments."

Jacque laughed. "Did you just call your bras and panties 'womanly garments'?"

"That is classic." Sally laughed along.

"Could you two Pollyannas focus, please?" Jen admonished.

"Sorry," Jacque said, trying to pull herself together. "No, really. I'm good. Please continue."

Jen rolled her eyes. "Then he did that whole sniffing thing that you said Fane does to you."

Jacque's head snapped up. "He scented you?" The alarm in her voice caused some unease to rear its ugly head in Jen.

"Um, yeah. That a problem?"

"It's just awfully possessive – and very intimate. If Fane saw another wolf scent me he would tear into him."

Jen pondered on this only briefly before she decided it was time to move on. "Let's forget it all. I don't even want to get into the fact that Decebel has seen -"

"Your undergarments," Sally snorted as she interrupted Jen.

"Oh, shut up, Thelma," Jen snapped as she headed towards the closet in search of the night's outfit. *Okay*, she thought to herself, *need to draw on my inner skank*. She laughed as she started flipping through her clothes. Sally and Jacque joined her in the large closet and began their own searches.

"Ooo, how 'bout this?" Sally asked as she held up a short, distressed denim mini skirt and halter top.

"Um, Sally, we are in Romania in the winter time. Ring any bells?" Jacque asked.

"Oh, right. Cold. Got it," she said as she hung the outfit back up.

Jen pulled out a pair of low rise Lucky jeans. She and Jacque shared a love of the brand. Next she grabbed a deep plumb colored sweater with a plunging neckline. It had a fitted cut for a snug fit.

"I like." Jacque nodded in approval.

Jacque and Sally each borrowed shirts of Jen's. Sally chose a deep red sweater with wide arms that hung elegantly off her shoulders. Jacque picked her color of choice, a hunter green sweater dress that she planned to wear with dark grey leggings and boots. With their choices made, they headed off to their prospective bathrooms to change.

"Okay, meet back here in twenty for phase two," Sally advised.

"Dare I ask what phase two is?" Jen asked apprehensively.

"It's been too long since we've been out if you have to ask," Sally told her. "Hair and makeup, Jennifer. We have to take all this natural beauty up in here and make it shine."

"Riiiiight, shine. I'm on it, boss," Jen teased.

Chapter 6

"Come on! Really, Skender? That's all you got to give these pups?" Decebel growled as he watched the wolves he was training spar.

Decebel knew that his frustration wasn't really coming from the wolves' inadequacies but from a certain mouthy blonde who had her claws in him so deep he could feel the blood running down his back. The sad thing about the whole situation – he liked it. *Yeah*, he thought, *there is definitely something wrong with me.*

Skender growled at his Beta.

"Save it for the fight, Skender. You wouldn't be growling at me if you didn't know I was right." Decebel stepped into the sparring circle that was painted onto the gym floor. "Take a break for a minute," he told him, then turned to the young wolf known as Stelian.

Decebel grinned wolfishly. "Ready for a real challenge?"

Before the pup could respond, the Beta attacked.

Decebel taught mixed martial arts to all of the wolves, even the females. It was imperative they all know how to defend themselves in case another pack ever attacked. Granted, it had been over a century since the last pack battle, but Decebel was a firm believer in "better safe than sorry".

He delivered a series of strikes and kicks practiced in Muay Thai. It was a form of kickboxing, and the predominant mixed martial art he taught along with Judo – ground fighting.

Stelian tried to counter Decebel's moves, but no matter what he did he couldn't keep the strikes from hitting their target. After only five minutes Decebel took Stelian to the ground.

Decebel didn't bother holding the pup down. He jumped to his feet and stepped back, indicating the sparring was done.

Decebel checked his watch and saw that he had only twenty minutes until he had to be in the meeting with Vasile and the other Alphas.

"That will be all for today," he told the younger wolf. "You did a good job."

Decebel grabbed his towel off the floor and headed back to his room to take a quick shower. As he walked, his mind wandered back to where it always seemed to – Jennifer.

He remembered walking through the wing of the mansion that housed the unmated males and catching her scent. Decebel could admit now that maybe he had slightly overreacted when he tore into the room and found two males rifling through her suit case. So maybe he didn't have to throw Dragos through a wall. And, yeah, he could've kept from tossing Dorian right on top of Dragos. But in that moment his wolf had taken over, and all he could think was that her scent was around unmated males, that they were touching her things – things only he should know about. Decebel had glossed over that little tidbit, about why on earth he thought he had a right to know about her underwear.

He'd felt that if he didn't get her things and her scent from their room he was going to kill someone, no doubt about it. One of those pups would have died that night. Thankfully, they had been somewhat intelligent and immediately submitted. When Decebel questioned them about how they had gotten Jennifer's things they had told him about how a suitcase had fallen out of a window from the mansion. Being stupid twenty somethings, they saw women's lingerie and just had to check it out…. Stupid young wolves.

Decebel had somewhat calmed down before he returned the suitcase to Jennifer's room, but he hadn't really been prepared to run into her. He had to say, though, that seeing her alone – or without other males around her, rather – calmed his wolf down immensely. It was something else he didn't want to examine. After all, why should she calm his wolf? There were no mating signs.

The Beta let out a low growl as he entered his room and headed for the shower. He had to stop thinking about her, it was only ticking him off. He called the twenty-something's stupid, but at the moment he made them look like geniuses.

Decebel walked into Vasile's office. A large screen had been set up for the video conference with the other pack Alphas. Vasile was sitting at his desk and Fane and Skender were sitting directly in front of the screen.

"Fane, what time did Sorin say he would be returning with the girls?" Vasile asked his son.

Decebel watched curiously as Fane's head snapped up. "He didn't," he ground out.

"Well, where did they say they were going to?" Vasile continued, very obviously ignoring Fane's irritation.

"They didn't say."

Decebel smelled the lie Fane had just spoken and that was enough to tell him something was going on.

"Excuse me, Alpha, but when you say Sorin and the girls, do you mean -"

Vasile cut him off before he could finish. "Jen, Jacque, and Sally, of course."

Decebel felt his wolf perking up and had he been in wolf form his hackles would have risen. "You say they went to a club?"

"Yes. Sorin said they came to him and begged him to take them out for a girls' night. Something about getting Jen and Sally hooked up with – I think they used the words 'hot Romanian mojo', or some nonsense." Vasile rolled his eyes. "You know how those three talk. It's like a foreign language all on its own."

Decebel had stopped listening after the words "hooked up," and before he realized what he was doing he was headed for the exit.

"Decebel, stop." Vasile's voice dripped with authority and Decebel had no choice but to freeze. His Alpha had given an order and used his power. Decebel could not disobey.

"Alpha, you have to know those three are going to get themselves into some sort of trouble. They are like magnets for mayhem," Decebel tried to reason with his Alpha. He felt Vasile's power ease up and he was able to turn and face the other wolves. He made eye contact with Fane and growled. "You knew this was their plan and still you let your mate go?"

Fane chuckled. "Wait until you have a mate, brother, then tell me how you *let* her do things or don't *let* her do things, and while you're sharing I'll laugh as you are pulling her shoe out of your ass."

Decebel was not amused, and even though he understood that being mates was a partnership there had to be times when, as her protector, you had to put your foot down.

"Sorin will watch the girls and keep them safe. I have complete confidence in him," Vasile placated. "If after the conference with the Alphas you still feel the need to go corral them then you have my blessing, and my sympathy."

Decebel relented and took a seat in one of the chairs next to the couch. Just as he sat down the screen lit up and there were four men each in their own little square looking back at them. Decebel was quite surprised to see Dillon Jacobs, Jacque's father, among them.

"Did you know he would be in on this?" Decebel whispered to Fane.

Fane shook his head. "I'm as clueless as you."

Vasile walked from around his desk and stood behind the couch. He was Alpha and he would not sit in the presence of another Alpha, even if over a computer screen.

"Dillon, how are you doing?" Vasile asked Jacque's father.

"I'm doing well, Vasile. Thank you for asking." Dillon looked at Fane. "Fane, how are you and your new mate?"

"We are doing very good," Fane told him. Neither Fane, Vasile, or Dillon mentioned that Fane's new mate was Dillon's daughter. If the other Alphas did not know, it wasn't something they could potentially use against Dillon's or Vasile's pack. Though it was a sad way to live, packs could be very volatile between one another. Wolves were cunning and always looking for a way to have the upper hand.

"I would like to introduce the members of my pack that are present," Vasile told the Alphas.

Pointing to each wolf as he spoke, he announced, "This is Decebel, my Beta." Decebel gave a single nod in acknowledgment of the other Alphas. Not disrespectful, but neither was he conceding their dominance over him. Truth be known, Decebel could be Alpha of his own pack – he was more than dominant enough. But events in his life and his loyalty to Vasile had shaped his choices, leading him to where he was now.

"This is Fane, my son and heir," Vasile continued. "And this is Skender. He is among my top four wolves."

When Vasile finished his introductions then each man on the screen introduced himself. There was Dragomir from Hungary, Thad from Serbia, Victor from Bulgaria, and Dillon from the United States.

Introductions complete, Vasile and his wolves waited for one of the four Alphas to explain why they had called a conference.

"I realize it is not common practice for us to meet this way, Vasile, but the other Alphas and I are concerned about the continuation of our species," Dragomir explained. "You see, it has been over a decade since any of my wolves have found a mate. It has been half a decade since any children have been born. We are becoming a dying species."

For a moment, no one spoke. Then Vasile took a step forward, arms crossed, and looked at each Alpha briefly before he spoke. "You have obviously come up with some sort of plan if you have called this meeting. What is this plan to help our species survive?"

This time it was Thad who spoke up. "After discussing it with Dragomir I decided to do some digging into our pack archives and see if there was any documentation that might help." Thad's words began to pick up speed as he shared what he had discovered.

"There were many practices done by older packs that have simply faded from knowledge. One such practice was called The Gathering," Thad picked up what looked like very old parchment and began to read, "I am Damon, Alpha of the Bulgaria pack. This is the account of the four packs, Hungary, Serbia, Romania, and my own, Bulgaria, all of which have agreed to a truce. The Alphas of these four packs have met this night and decided to implement a new tradition. It shall be written into our pack records as a tradition to be followed every four years. The decree is as follows: All pure blooded, unmated pack members of age must attend The Gathering. The Alpha, four dominant mated pairs, and his mate shall accompany these pack members. The unmated females may bring ladies to help prepare themselves for The Gathering. The Gathering shall take place in the Transylvania Alps on an estate that has been purchased by three pack Alphas as a gift to our species to use for this event. The purpose of The Gathering is to help bring unmated wolves from other packs together and hopefully find true mates among them. It is in our nature to be territorial and uncooperative with other packs, but if we do not set aside these habits and put the greater good of the species first, we will one day cease to exist. This world will go on as if Grey werewolves had never been. If an Alpha and his unmated pack members are invited to join in The Gathering and they refuse, it will be treated as an act against the species and that Alpha shall be subject to a challenge. If he is defeated, his pack members will be split among the other packs. We must be vigilant if we are to survive. We must recognize that the very things that often make us strong and keep us safe have the potential to annihilate our kind."

When Thad finished reading, each of the wolves could only stare, dumbfounded. Of the many things this meeting could have been about, this had not even registered on their list of possibilities. Vasile himself had never heard of such a decree in his long life. He could appreciate the fact that it was definitely a way for the unmated to find their other half, but it was also a risk to put that many unmated males together. For that reason alone he understood the importance of having dominate mated couples there.

"Are you telling us that you want to implement this decree now, in this day and age?" Vasile asked incredulously, but continued before another could answer. "Gentlemen, we do not live in a time where females are told what to do. We live in the twenty first century with liberated women."

"Vasile, we know this concept is foreign and somewhat outdated, but we are not human." It was now Victor, the Alpha of Bulgaria, who spoke up. "We may live in their world but we do not, cannot live like them. We are a species created for pack, for family. Our males, especially the dominants, do not have the luxury like human males to date whomever they want for as long as they want. They need the light and peace a true mate will bring them. They need the darkness that resides inside their wolf to be kept at bay by this true mate. What better way to help our own than to bring them together?"

"I suppose if we present it in such a way that it is seen as in the best interest of our species, maybe the unmated will accept it and see it in a positive light," Vasile conceded, knowing that if these Alphas had set their minds to do this then there was little he could do to stop it without bringing a war to his door.

Vasile noticed that Dillon had not spoken up. "Dillon, what have you to say regarding this manner?"

"I was approached by Thad, and although in the past it was harder to include packs that were so far away, modern travel has obviously fixed that. The Alphas thought it would be good for an

American pack to come and bring new blood, so to speak. I think the idea has merit and is worth exploring."

Before Vasile could respond, Thad spoke again. "We thought, if you would concede, that because your son found his mate in the United States that it would be pertinent of us to include an American pack. Since you knew Dillon Jacobs he was the first we thought of."

"Are there no secrets in this world anymore? " Decebel muttered. Thus far, however, he didn't have any real objections to the idea. The person that he would not want going wasn't full blood, so he didn't have to worry about that. *Thank the moon*, he thought.

"We have also decided, as Fane's mate is not full blooded, that it would perhaps be wise to include half blooded and dormant in The Gathering. Obviously they are potential true mates."

And there's the other shoe, Decebel thought.

Now he had a problem with it. If this was their decree, then Jennifer would be required to go. Since she was under Vasile's care, and had wolf blood – essentially making her pack – she most definitely had to attend this Gathering.

This day just keeps getting better and better, Decebel thought as he ran his hands though his hair, clenching his jaw. First he found his mangy pack mates going through Jennifer's things, then he found out Jennifer was at a club doing goodness knows what with some mutt – or worse, a human. A low growl rumbled in his chest at the thought. Now Jennifer would be required to be around other unmated males. Decebel was well aware of the fact that his whole day, good and bad, revolved around a mouthy, perverted, bossy blonde, and someone save him, because at her side was the only place he wanted to be at the moment. Vasile's words finally brought him back to the here and now.

"Since you have obviously taken it upon yourselves to plan this without consulting me first," Vasile words were laced with power – even the Alphas on the screen could feel it and averted their eyes from the Romanian Alpha, "have you also set a date for The Gathering?"

"We meant no disrespect, Vasile," Dragomir told him. "You were in the U.S., busy with your own issues and we did not want to burden you with this until you were back with your pack."

Vasile gave a simple nod in acknowledgment of his words, but continued to stare them down while he waited for an answer.

"The date is set for one month from today," Thad answered. "It is to be held in the traditional location of the Transylvania Alps and the large estate mentioned in the decree has been updated and enlarged over the years. It is now being prepared for our arrival."

"I will concede you this," he began and the others let out a breath."But," Vasile continued, his voice calm and controlled, "if ever again you make such decree without my knowledge, without my input and without my okay, I will remind you why I am Alpha to the largest pack in the world. I respect you all as Alphas and I expect the same from each of you."

"As you have said, so shall it be." Each Alpha spoke in their own language, acknowledging Vasile's dominance.

"I will be in touch as the time draws near," Vasile told them just before he turned the screen off, effectively ending the conversation. He turned to Decebel. "Get Dillon on the phone."

Decebel nodded as he pulled out his cell and dialed Dillon Jacobs' number. He handed Vasile the phone as soon as he heard the other wolf's "hello".

"Dillon, its Vasile. When will you be arriving?"

"I thought I would come a couple days before to check out security. When are you planning on telling the girls?" Dillon asked.

"The sooner the better," Vasile responded. "Those three are nearly as hot headed as a full blooded Romanian she-wolf."

Dillon chuckled.

"I talk to you soon," Vasile told him and ended the call.

Vasile rubbed his face as he finally relented and sat down in one of the empty chairs.

"Do they really expect Jennifer to go to this *gathering*?" Decebel spat the word as if it were some disgusting bug.

"I don't have a choice, Decebel." Vasile glared at his Beta. "Whether you and your wolf have accepted it or not, she is pack. No matter the amount of blood in her, she has Canis lupis in her veins and that makes her subject to our laws. Deal with it however you need to. Growl, throw a fit, allow your wolf to hunt, accept your attraction to her – do whatever it is you must, but get over it. Are we clear?"

"Crystal," Decebel growled, but submitted by baring his neck.

"Skender," Vasile addressed the wolf who had been sitting quietly and observing as was his custom. "I need a list of all the unmated pack members."

"I'll have it for you within the hour," he answered as he stood up and headed out of Vasile's office.

"Decebel, arrange for a pack meeting tomorrow evening. We will meet in the largest media room at 8 p.m."

"Done." Decebel nodded.

Suddenly, Fane stopped pacing. He closed his eyes as if concentrating.

"What do you see, son?" Vasile asked.

Fane was catching glimpses from his mate's mind, though she was trying to block him. She still hadn't learned that now that they were mated it would take undivided concentration to block him. The little vixen and her two friends were causing quite a stir in one of the local bars. He saw Jen in her mind. She was on the bar...dancing. Fane grinned.

"What are you grinning about?" Decebel growled, knowing he wasn't going to like the answer.

"I think it's time we break up their girls' night out before Jen falls off the bar," Fane told him, and though he tried he couldn't hide the teasing laughter in his eyes as he watched his words penetrate Decebel's mind.

"She's in a bar?"

"Oh, she'll do you one better than that, Beta." Fane chuckled. "She's *on* a bar, as in dancing on a bar. The patrons are quite taken with her."

Decebel was out of his seat and ripping the door to Vasile's office open before Fane finished his sentence.

"Did you have to taunt him?" Vasile scolded.

Fane shrugged. "Seeing the steely, calm Beta all riled is too much to pass up, Alpha."

Vasile tried to hide his smile as he shook his head at his only son. "Fine. But hurry up and go with him or he'll tear the damn bar apart. I don't have the time or energy to deal with that mess."

"As you say." Fane winked at his father as he followed after Decebel.

"Luna, I'm giving you fair warning. Your little night out has been found out by the object of your taunting. Do you think it wise, my love, to bait a dominant male?"

Fane could feel her surprise at hearing his voice in her mind. He smiled; he loved surprising her. It was a nice change of pace as he was usually the one being surprised.

"Crap. Is he on his way here?" Fane heard the anxiety in her voice.

"Hell is on his heels, love."

"You are enjoying this entirely too much, White Fang."

"Aw. Now, Jacquelyn, that is no way to speak to your mate." Fane laughed.

"Just remember, wolf-man, I will follow through with my threat to have that dog house built for you. Now how long?"

"You wound me with your words, Luna."

"Fane, I'm not playing with you. How long till the brooding fur ball arrives?"

Fane did not bother to tell Jacquelyn that he and Decebel had been driving while they'd been conversing. The bar was only five minutes from the mansion. He grinned to himself as he and Decebel climbed out of the Hummer. Decebel had parked directly behind Sorin's vehicle, effectively blocking any chance for escape.

As Fane pulled open the door to the bar, he took in the scene and nearly lost his composure.

"You're looking stunning, Luna, although your assets are accentuated a little too much for my liking." Fane watched as Jacquelyn's eyes, big as saucers, met his across the bar. He grinned wickedly. Raising his eyebrows, he whispered in her mind, *"Gotchya."*

Chapter 7

As Sorin pulled into the parking lot of the small bar, all he could think was that Decebel and possibly Fane were going to skin him alive once they found out he'd let the three harpies talk him into taking them out. There weren't any clubs for the girls to go to, so they had helpfully suggested a bar.

Yeah, Sorin thought. *I walked right into that one.*

"This is going to be great." Jacque grinned as she opened the door and got out of the Hummer.

"I'm pretty sure I'll have a more positive attitude once I've been introduced to this wonderful friend called vodka I hear so much about in this country," Jen grumbled.

"Absolutely no drinking," Sorin announced.

All three girls stopped mid-stride and looked at Sorin, at each other, and then broke into laughter.

Sorin growled, which only caused them to laugh more. *This was a bad idea*, Sorin thought to himself as he pulled the door to the bar open. The dark interior was lit up briefly by the street light and sounds from inside filled the night as the girls walked in with Sorin bringing up the rear.

All three girls stopped and allowed their eyes to adjust to the darkness. Then Jen took the lead and headed directly for the bar. Sorin picked up his pace and met her there at the same time.

"Hey, Costin," Sorin addressed the bartender who was also a member of the pack. " Nu alcool pentru art.hot. trei musketeers. (No alcohol for the three musketeers)"

Jen turned to Sorin. She raised an eyebrow and grinned wickedly. Sorin swallowed, not liking the look in the she-wolf's – no matter how dormant she was – eyes.

Jen looked back at Costin and smiled warmly. "Hey, Costin. I've seen you around the mansion but I don't think we've been formally introduced. I'm Jen, and these are my two best friends, Jacque and Sally." The girls smiled and waved at him.

Costin winked at them, causing them to blush. That wink was all the encouragement Jen needed. She leaned closer over the bar and batted her eyes at the young wolf. "So, we've been wanting a night out to, ya know, relax. Surely you can help a girl out?"

Costin smiled widely, then looked at Sorin who was dutifully trying to stare the wolf into submission. Much to Jen's amusement Costin winked at Sorin.

"I don't think one small drink will hurt anything, Sorin."

"We are eighteen, after all," Jen helped.

Sally raised her hand, "Well I'm no- "

Jen slapped her hand down before she could finish. "Sally's older and hates being lumped in with us younger women," she covered while glaring at Sally, daring her to contradict her.

Sally looked at Jacque, who simply shrugged her shoulders.

Jen turned back to Costin, again smiling. " Unul deget mic a bea apoi atunci, dragoste? (One little drink then, love?)" she asked in nearly flawless Romanian.

Sorin was shocked into silence, as were Sally and Jacque. Costin recovered the quickest and poured three shots of vodka. He turned and looked at Sorin.

"Tu ai luat al tău chipeș plin, frate. (You have your hands full, brother.)," Costin told him with a grin.

As each of the girls picked up a shot glass they clinked them with each other's.

"Here's to hot Romanian wolves." Jen winked at the bartender, then downed the drink. All three girls coughed as the vodka burned their throats.

Costin chuckled. "It gets easier with each glass," he told her as he poured them all another.

Sorin growled in frustration. "Bloody hell, you better give me one of those. When Fane and Decebel skin me I want to be sedated a little."

Costin chuckled again. "It'll be okay, old man. They just want to have a little fun, and they're safe. Everyone here knows that she, " he nodded in Jacque's direction, "is the Prince's mate. No one will mess with them."

"It's not anyone messing with *them* that I'm worried about, Costin."

Costin watched as Jen hooked her iPhone up to the speakers of his stereo on the side of the bar. She cranked up the volume. As the music poured out she began to dance around the room. He watched as her body swayed in perfect rhythm with the beat, all those in the room mesmerized by the blonde beauty.

Costin looked back at Sorin. "You're going to need another one of these," he told him as he poured another shot. Then he poured himself one as all three girls began dancing around the room, picking different men to dance with.

Sorin watched the girls closely. Although Costin was correct in that all the bar patrons knew who these girls were and none would dare try anything, he was still going to catch hell.

An hour and a half later Sorin watched in absolute horror as Jen danced on the bar to some song about aliens.

Sally laughed and clapped. "That's her theme song," she shouted over the noise.

"What?" Jacque shouted back.

"Remember how I told you about her getting drunk with that nurse in the hospital so that I could come see you in the ICU?" Sally asked.

"Yeah, what's up with that? Was that really necessary?"

"Okay, I will admit it wasn't our best plan, but that's not the point." Sally waved her off. "What I'm trying to explain is that after Jen's little escapade, I found her in the shower of the hospital room, singing at the top of her little inebriated lungs this Katy Perry song, only she replaced most of the words with werewolf terms. It was freaking hilarious. The best part?" She paused, eyebrows raised. "Decebel heard her!"

"Shut up!" Jacque slapped her friend on the arm.

"Didn't I tell you that part?" Sally asked.

"Um, no. I think I would remember that. I remember you telling me she walked out of the bathroom naked and you had to give Decebel a heads up."

"Oh, man. Now that was priceless. I don't know what he was saying but he was freaking out." Sally's words wound down as she let out a small sigh. "Man, good times."

Both girls watched as Jen got her groove on. Guys all around the bar cheered her on. No one touched her, especially with Sorin glaring daggers. Costin would hand Jen a shot glass every now and then, but she was so gone at that point that she didn't even realize he was just giving her Sprite.

Sally's head jerked up when she heard Jacque swear.

"What? What's wrong?" Sally asked, concerned as she watched panic fill Jacque's eyes.

"He's on his way."

Jacque and Sally both turned to look at Jen who was now cat crawling across the bar, her perilously low cut top threatening to give up all its secrets.

Jacque's head snapped around as she felt her mate's power fill the room, and just behind him was a very large, very pissed off Decebel. Jacque looked back at Jen. *Crap*, she thought. He walked in just as one of the drunk patrons was got brave enough to stick a five dollar bill in the back pocket of her jeans. To his credit, he did it so carefully that his hand never made contact with her body. *Pretty impressive*, Jacque thought. She was abruptly pulled from her thoughts when the loud room was suddenly plunged into silence. Well, except for one drunk, singing Jennifer Adams. At this point she had busted out into "It Girl" by Jason Derulo.

"Oh, brother. Here we go," Sally muttered under her breath.

"You can be my it girl, baby you're the sh- " Decebel stepped directly in front of Jen, effectively pushing the other males out of the way and cutting her off before she could continue.

Jen looked around, realizing for the first time that the music had stopped. She looked back at Decebel, then over at her two friends. A big grin spread across her face when she saw Sally and Jacque.

"Heeeeeyyy!" She waved like she hadn't seen them all night. Decebel grabbed her hand.

"Jennifer, it's time to go. Now." Decebel waited for her to start climbing off the bar. When she just stared at him, he let out a low growl.

"Jennifer, don't push me right now. Let's go."

"I'm not ready to go," she said simply as she twisted her wrist out of his grasp. "Besides, Cos here has another drink for me don't ya, îndrăgostit băiat (lover boy)?" Jen giggled as Costin's eyes got big. He stepped away from the bar when Decebel's glowing eyes fell on him.

Costin held his hands up. "Beta, I've been giving her Sprite for a while now," he tried to reason.

Decebel growled but turned back to Sally and Jacque. "When in the bloody hell did she learn Romanian?"

Sally and Jacque shrugged.

"She was doing that whole Romanian thing when we first got here. Your guess is as good as ours," Sally told him.

"*She* is standing," Jen started as she hopped off the bar, stumbling into a werewolf who had the unfortunate fate of standing too close to the drunk girl, "right here." She stumbled again. "I mean, here. She, I, am standing right here."

Decebel pulled her away from the wolf she had stumbled into. "Yeah, we can all see how well you are standing right there."

Jen's head snapped up at his words.

"Ouch," Jacque muttered.

"Hmm, not a good choice," Sally whispered.

Fane growled at his mate and her friend. "Would you two quit pushing him?" He spoke just as softly as they had.

Jen pushing away from Decebel brought the attention back to them.

"What is that supposed to mean, you, you, mean -" Jen growled low as she struggled to think through the fog of alcohol. "Stupid wolf," she finished.

Decebel took a step closer to her. "Stupid wolf? Really, babe, that all you got?"

Jen glared at him, the frustration of the past two months building up in her alcohol-induced thoughts.

"Oh dear, we are in trouble," Jacque murmured under her breath.

"Ooo, nice Harry Potter reference. I like," Sally whispered back with a grin and a fist bump.

Jen looked away from Decebel. Her eyes scanned the area around her until they fell on what they searched for. She smiled sweetly as she gingerly stepped around Decebel, who watched her with wary eyes. Jen reached across the bar and snagged the soda gun next to Costin, who was trying really hard to look invisible.

"Jennifer," Decebel warned.

"Oh, Decy, what are you worried about? Could it be that you're scared that a little ol' dormant me could kick your bossy, grumpy, growly, fine ass?" She pointed the nozzle at him.

"This is not gonna end well." Sally cringed.

Jacque nodded her head in mute agreement.

"Jennifer," Decebel growled her name as he tried to grab the soda gun from her hand. "Don't embarrass yourself. Let's just call it a night."

Jen was trying to figure out where the trigger was, but slowly, dangerously looked up at his words. "Embarrass myself? Are you kidding me?" She threw the soda gun on the bar and turned to her two best friends. "I'm out. You two coming?"

Without waiting, Jen headed for the exit. Despite the alcohol in her system she was fuming, and truth be told, the alcohol was probably not helping contain her temper.

She could feel Decebel's eyes on her as she walked away from him and knew the confrontation wasn't over. No, he definitely had more to say to her, but he wasn't the only one that had words to turn loose. She smiled to herself. *If Decebel wants to dance*, she thought, *then I'll dance. We'll just see if he knows the steps and can keep up.*

Once out in the parking lot Jen turned back towards the door, arms folded across her chest, ready for battle.

Decebel came storming out of the bar with Sorin, Jacque, Sally, and Fane trailing behind him. He walked right up to her, their bodies only a breath apart.

"What the hell were you thinking? Dancing on a bar, drinking with a bunch of men?" As if he suddenly remembered his part in it, Decebel turned on Sorin, who took an automatic step back. "And what were you thinking bringing them here?"

"They wanted a night out. Nothing happened, Decebel. Everyone knows who they are and to whom they belong," Sorin tried to pacify the fuming wolf.

"Would you get a freaking grip, man?" Jen ground out. "It's not like I was stripping or letting any of those fur balls touch me, so I don't know what your problem is."

"My problem? " Decebel glared daggers at Jen. "My problem is you are seventeen."

"Eighteen," Jen, Sally, and Jacque all said at the same time.

Decebel looked at the other two girls, who both suddenly became very interested in the gravel on the ground.

"Whatever," Decebel continued. "You're too damn young to be in a bar drinking, throwing yourself around like -"

Jen slammed her hand into his chest, cutting his words off. "You had better think really hard about what's about to come out of your mouth, flea bag, because you can't un-say it and I won't forget it," she warned him.

Decebel's lips pressed together, his eyes narrowing. "Let's just go. We can finish this conversation later." Decebel proceeded to take Jen's arm to lead her towards the vehicle he and Fane had arrived in. She jerked her arm away and followed Sally and Jacque to Sorin's Hummer.

She turned towards Decebel, continuing to walk backwards. "You have to earn the privilege of my company. And just a tip – being an over baring, egotistical, doom and gloom, party crashing butt head isn't exactly the way to get her in your ride. So there's your creative insult Dec, stick that in your pipe and smoke it!" With that she turned back and continued on to the vehicle, climbing in without another backward glance.

When Decebel took a step in her direction, Fane grabbed his arm to stop him. "Just let it go, Dec. You both need to calm down. You can talk to her once you get to the house."

Decebel didn't comment but continued to glare at the car Jen had just climbed into, which was now driving away.

"The NERVE!" Jen yelled in frustration as she climbed out of the Hummer with Sally and Jacque right behind her. "He completely ruined my buzz."

Sally rolled her eyes. "Well, by all means, skin the pelt off the wolf for daring to mess with your buzz."

Jen flipped Sally off. "That's not the point. The point is that he thinks, for some reason, that he has the right to tell me what to do."

The girls headed up the stairs towards Jen's room.

Once behind her door, she threw herself on her bed and stared up at the ceiling.

"Are you okay?" Jacque asked with true concern in her voice.

"I'm just confused and all this vodka sloshing around in my brain is not helping matters."

"The vodka will do it every time," Sally put in. "Messes with the brain waves and whatnot."

Jacque looked at Sally."What the crap are you talking about?"

Sally shrugged. "I'm just saying."

Jen laughed. "That's my line, Thelma."

"My bad, Louise. I was just going with the moment," Sally joked.

Jacque sat down on the bed next to Jen. "I really think you need to talk to him. Be blunt. I mean, we both know you struggle with being blunt but you could give it a go."

Sally and Jen laughed at Jacque's sarcasm.

"I just don't know where it's going to get us," Jen said in exasperation.

"By the way..." Sally looked at Jen, crossing her arms across her chest. "When and where did you learn to speak Romanian exactly?"

"Yeah," Jacque added indignantly.

Jen laughed. "I got on the internet and picked out a few phrases that I knew, if I used at the right time, would get under Decebel's skin." Jen continued to grin. "Worked like a charm. Did y'all see his face?"

"What did you say?"

"When I spoke to Costin the first time – by the way, did y'all notice how drool worthy he is? Okay, not the point. Anyways, I said 'one little drink then, love?'"

Sally and Jacque both laughed.

"The second time I spoke to Costin," Jen continued, "I called him lover boy."

"Huh, no wonder Decebel blew a gasket," Sally voiced.

"So did you learn anymore?"

"Oh yeah, but I'm saving them. It's got to be just the right moment and when he least expects it," Jen explained.

Jacque leaned her head down to her hands and rubbed her face, chuckling."I swear, Jen, I can't decide if you're a genius or a psycho."

"I admit it's a fine line," Jen said matter of factly, "and I'll be the first to confess that on any given day my toe grazes one side or the other."

All three laughed just as there was a knock at her door. They froze, looking at each other, then watched as the door opened.

"Are you freaking kidding me?" Jen muttered under her breath. "Knock, wait, be invited in – it's really a simple concept. But does the pissy werewolf get it? Noooo, of course not. That would be too damn polite."

Decebel stepped in. His eyes landed on Jen and his large body seemed to cause the room to shrink. Jacque stood and started to walk away from the bed. Jen grabbed her hand, pleading with her eyes for Jacque to stay. Jacque shook her head and pulled her hand free.

"Talk to him," she mouthed to Jen.

As Sally and Jacque headed out of her room, Jen muttered under her breath, "Traitors."

Jen heard the click of the door as it closed, an ominous sound that caused goosebumps to cover her arms. She continued to lie back on her bed, but after several minutes of silence she finally sat up.

Jen looked at the wolf standing across her room. He had propped himself up against the wall, arms folded across his chest. *The classic Decebel pose*, she thought to herself with a mental chuckle.

Neither spoke as they both continued to stare at one another. Jen met his gaze head on but eventually allowed her eyes to wander. She would never get tired of looking at him. His dark hair was cut short on the sides, and longer on top, sweeping gently across his forehead. His warm amber eyes she swore could stare a hole in a person. He had a straight, tapered nose and full lips. His face was chiseled and smooth, as if carved from stone. He was handsome – very handsome.

She wasn't sure how tall he was but he matched Fane in height and Jen remembered Jacque saying Fane was 6'4". His broad shoulders filled out the snug, white t-shirt he wore. His skin tone was a warm golden tan, a color that would take Jen weeks of laying out in the sun to achieve. He had a narrow waist and long, powerful looking legs.

Decebel cleared his throat, causing Jen's head to snap back up to his face. He looked smug, which only served to tick Jen off more.

"What do you want, Decebel?" she asked, and was pleased that her voice sounded so steady when she felt anything but.

Decebel continued to stare at Jennifer, emotions swirling inside him that he couldn't seem to get a grasp on.

"I -" he started, but seemed to be confused about what to say. "You can't go around dancing on bars and downing vodka like it's water."

Jen stood up, arms stiff by her side. "Says who? You? Well, here's a news flash: you aren't my dad, you aren't my brother, and YOU AREN'T MY KEEPER." Jen's voice got louder as her anger flared.

"I'M YOUR M- " Decebel roared, pushing himself from the wall. But he caught himself before he finished his sentence, nearly biting his tongue in the process. His breathing had increased, he was shocked at the words that nearly flew from his lips.

He didn't understand where it had come from but it felt true, right. These thoughts sped through his mind in a matter of seconds. He continued to glare at her and spoke again, no longer yelling, but his words were firm. They were law. "I'm your Beta, and as such, you do take orders from me and you will follow them." Decebel cocked his head to the side, suddenly remembering something. "And where in the world did you learn Romanian?"

Jen grinned at that. "The internet is a wonderful place to learn new things, Beta. It would be a great place for you to learn a thing or two."

Decebel took a step towards her. "I have a feeling I'm quite a bit ahead of you in the education department of most areas." His eyes sparkled wickedly.

"Oh, my furry little friend, you would be surprised at what I know," Jen said, matching his suggestive tone word for word, syllable for syllable.

Decebel narrowed his eyes at her. "What is that supposed to mean?"

Jen shrugged as she turned her back on him, having learned from their lessons on pack etiquette it was a huge slap in the face to a dominant wolf. She heard Decebel growl and take a step towards her. *My Beta, my ass*, she thought as she continued to ignore the wolf stalking her.

She could feel his nearness and knew that if she took one step back she would bump against his body. A delicious thought, but she cut that off abruptly as she reminded herself that he was on her shit list at the moment, and he possibly had found himself a permanent reservation on it.

"Whether you believe it or not," Decebel's mouth was close enough to her ear that she felt the warm air from his breath cross her skin and it caused a shiver, "it's for your safety that I set such rules."

"You aren't my Alpha. Vasile knew where we were going and he had no problem with it." Jen's voice was low but no less potent than his.

"That may be, but once your behavior puts your safety in jeopardy I have every right to order it to cease immediately."

Jen could feel her blood begin to heat, her face flushed. "My behavior?" she gritted through her clenched teeth. "I'm not a kid, Decebel. I don't need your orders."

"You are a member of this pack. You will follow orders whether you like it or not, for the safety of the pack as well as yourself. You need to get used to it, Jennifer." Decebel placed his hands on her shoulders and gently turned her around. Placing two fingers under her chin, he raised her face to look up at him.

Decebel clenched his jaw and briefly closed his eyes as he saw the unshed tears in her eyes.

"I didn't mean to hurt you, Jennifer."

"Don't flatter yourself, Beta. I'm not tearing up 'cause I'm hurt. I'm pissed." Jennifer didn't take her eyes from Decebel's as she fumed, "You could really use a lesson in people skills. Add those to your puppy classes and learning to knock and not barge in, and that should keep you busy enough that you won't have time to worry about my extracurricular activities."

Decebel's lips turned up in a slight grin and once more his eyes twinkled wickedly. Jen did not like the thought that was obviously skimming his brain.

"Since you are so hell bent on me learning manners, perhaps you should be my teacher." Decebel took a step back and continued to watch her with a mischievous grin.

Jen couldn't help her own small smile in response to him. So sue her, he was adorable when he smiled like that. "In your dreams, Beta."

"Perhaps," he said softly. As he turned to leave, Jen heard him say under his breath, "Goodness knows I can't get other dreams about you out of my head."

Jen flushed at his words but thought surely she had heard him wrong. He turned back to her before he pulled the door closed. "I hope you enjoyed your little escapade tonight, Jennifer, because on future occurrences I will accompany you." His words were unbending. "In fact, if you leave the mansion for any reason I will be your escort." Decebel winked at her, shutting the door just before a hairbrush flew across the room and smashed against it loudly. Jen's loud words followed the noise.

"The only place you'll be escorting me is to the vet so you can have the foot I'm going to shove up your behind removed!"

Chapter 8

"I love you too mom," Jacque spoke into her cell phone as she snuggled into Fane's embrace. "Things are good here. The tutor keeps us busy and we are learning all sorts of things."

"How is Jen doing?" Lilly asked her.

"She's okay, just a little confused about things. It will all come out in the wash."

Lilly chuckled, "My forever optimist," Jacque could hear her mother's smile through the phone.

"I'll let you go, I just wanted to let you know I'm thinking about you and miss you so much," Lilly choked back tears.

"I miss you too. I'm happy, I want you to know that," Jacque reassured her.

"I know, and that's what I want for you. Be happy, live a wonderful life with Fane."

"Will you come see me soon?" Jacque asked hopefully.

"We'll see about this summer maybe."

"Okay, love you."

"Love you too Jacque, very much. Bye," Jacque hit the end button on her phone and closed her eyes briefly. She loved talking to her mom but sometimes it made her heart feel so heavy.

"I love you Jacquelyn. I know it was a lot to ask you to come here," Fane told her gently.

" I don't regret coming Fane," Jacque turned to look into his eyes, "I want to be with you. I just miss her, and that's okay."

He kissed her forehead gently and breathed her scent deep into his lungs.

"What do you think is going on with Decebel?"

Fane was quiet for a moment. "I don't really understand it, but he treats Jen as if she's his mate. All the signs are there. I think he's probably worse because he doesn't understand it either."

Jacque thought about that. She felt bad for both Jen and Decebel. She knew that Jen was head over heels for the wolf, and couldn't imagine what it would be like to love Fane but not be able to be with him. Jacque prayed for both their sakes' that whatever it was that was going on would work itself out quickly.

"Are you okay, love?" Fane asked her gently.

Jacque turned so she could look into Fane's eyes. "I just hate seeing Jen hurt. And Decebel, for that matter," she told him honestly.

"You're a good friend, Luna, but this is something that they are going to have to work out on their own."

"If they don't kill each other first," Jacque added, only half joking.

Fane chuckled. "There is that possibility. And its chances have actually greatly increased."

Jacque watched his eyes as they clouded over in thought.

"Hey, wolf-man." She traced his lips with the tip of her finger, drawing his attention. "What is it? What's going on?"

Fane leaned down and kissed her gently before he answered.

"In the meeting I attended with the other Alphas, we learned they have decided it's in the best interest of our species that we bring back an old tradition," he explained.

Jacque pushed herself up into a sitting position, turning so she could see Fane's face clearly. "Why am I getting 'this sucks' vibes from you, babe?"

"Well, love, essentially because although it could be beneficial, in light of the situation between Jen and Decebel it is more likely to be detrimental…to one of them. I'm taking bets on Decebel since Jen seems to have quite the mean streak."

Jacque grinned briefly at that.

"So what's this tradition?" she asked.

"Over a century ago several packs used to have an event called The Gathering,"

"Ooo, sounds very Stephen King-ish," Jacque interrupted.

Fane smiled at his mate and her never ending commentary.

"The Gathering was brought about for unmated pack members to come and meet in hopes of finding their true mate. It was written into pack law that if a pack was invited the Alpha could not decline or it would be considered an act against the species."

"Bloody hell," Jacque muttered, staring off into nothing as she thought about how this would affect her best friend.

"Does Jen have to go even though she isn't full blooded?"

"Unfortunately, the four Alphas involved have decided that since my mate isn't full blooded it proves that any person with any wolf blood in their genetics must attend because they are possible true mates." Fane took a deep breath and let it out before he continued. "The good news is my parents have to go, and you and Sally can go and act as Jen's help. Naturally, where you go I go, so I will attend as well. There will also be some other mated pack members that will help with security."

"Security?" Jacque asked, confused.

"It's not really the best idea to put a bunch of unmated males together, particularly when there will be unmated females up for grabs," Fane explained.

"Ahh, that's a valid point. So why are they thinking this is a good idea?"

"They feel it's worth the risk since so many Canis lupis aren't finding their mates." Fane wrapped his hand around Jacquelyn's wrist and tugged her to him, pulling her into the curve of his body. She laid her head on his chest as she continued to think about this new development. Fane continued, "The mated pairs will help keep the unmated in line. There will be a pack meeting tomorrow night,"

"What exactly did you mean by Sally and I being Jen's help?" Jacque interrupted.

"Well, a century ago they called them ladies in waiting. They were basically there to help prepare the unmated female for the event by helping her dress, fixing her hair. That was when clothes for women were a little more elaborate. But the Alphas figure it would help the unmated females be at ease if they had a few friends with them."

"So you're telling me that, essentially, we are going to be Jen's servants?" Jen asked dubiously.

"For lack of a better term," Fane agreed reluctantly.

"For the sake of my sanity and future friendship with that nympho, do not tell her that. Can you imagine how she would take that and run a stinking marathon with it?"

Fane chuckled. "We will be delicate on how we broach the subject."

"Of course, she may be too preoccupied with the whole unmated males checking her out thing to really care about having a servant,"

Jacque added. "Man, if Decebel wasn't in the picture she would be in her idea of heaven – a bunch of hot werewolves checking her out."

"Love, you forget I'm the only wolf you are supposed to refer to as hot," Fane teased.

Jacque snuggled closer. "It goes without saying, wolf-man, you are the hottest of them all."

Fane growled. "Prove it," he challenged.

Jacque leaned back to look into his eyes and saw the desire that filled them.

"Now?" she asked, surprised by the abrupt change in subject.

"We can't solve Jen and Decebel's problem tonight, love, nor can we change whether or not The Gathering will take place. What we can do is love one another. What I plan to do is forget about all others but you, Luna. For the rest of the night you will forget all others but me."

Jacque smiled slyly at her mate. "Bossy much?" she teased.

"I want you," he said simply, not attempting to gloss over his demand.

"And so you shall have me," Jacque whispered as she clicked the bedside lamp off, leaving only the moon to light their room.

"So, for clarification purposes..." Jen sat in the media room on one of the overstuffed couches the following morning. Jacque sat on the floor, leaning against a chair that Sally occupied. Vasile and Alina sat opposite Jen on another couch while Sorin and Decebel both stood on either side of the room, propped against the wall. "Because I have a teeny, tiny amount of werewolf blood in me I have to go to what essentially amounts to a mating dance and let other unmated wolves sniff me?"

Sally snorted with laughter. "Sorry, got a visual."

"Nice." Jacque high fived her.

Jen glared at her two best friends. "If you two are done with your little moment could we please focus on this upcoming disaster?"

"Sorry, Jen. Don't mind us. By all means, continue freaking out." Sally waved Jen on.

"Thank you," Jen said matter of factly. "Okay." She looked back at Alina and Vasile. "So have I covered the basics?"

"It's really not as uncivilized as you are picturing it, Jen," Alina told her gently. "It's like a social gathering. They will divide you into groups, as there are quite a large number of people. In the evenings everyone will gather in the great hall for dinner and dancing. But during the day you will be told where you are to be. A group of unmated females will be meeting in various locations on the estate with unmated males. There will be Alphas and mated pairs present at all times. You will never be alone with an unmated male unless you find your true mate. From Jacque and what you have been learning about the pack in tutoring, you know that there are distinct signs when you find your true mate."

Jen couldn't help her gaze drifting over to where Decebel stood. When their eyes met, Jen felt chills run over her body at the intensity of his stare. Alina's voice drew her attention back.

"You will receive an itinerary once we arrive."

"Tonight at the pack meeting," Vasile continued for Alina, "you will meet some other unmated females who will be attending as well. I think you, Jacque, and Sally should spend some time with them and get to know them. We want you to feel safe, Jen. No one will force you to do anything, and if you happen to meet your mate don't panic, okay?"

"Alpha," Jen smiled ruefully, "when have you ever known me to panic around yummy werewolves?"

A growl resonated through the room.

"Oh, stick a cork in it, B," Jen snarled at Decebel.

Vasile cocked his head to the side as he looked at Jen. "B?"

"Yeah. Ya know, for Beta. Although, I like it because I could also be calling him the technical term for a female dog and he wouldn't know it. So really, calling him B totally works to my advantage," Jen explained in all seriousness.

Everyone turned when a quick burst of laughter came from the right side of the room. When Sorin saw everyone turn their eyes on him, he quickly began coughing. Holding up his hands, he finally composed himself. "Pardon me, Alpha. I seemed to have swallowed wrong."

"You have to be careful while swallowing smart ass comments, Sorin," Jen teased. "They tend to have a choking effect."

Sorin winked at Jen, who refused to look at the ominous wolf in the room currently staring a hole in her head.

Jen looked back to Vasile. "Okay, so the moral of the story is find a mate, don't panic, and try to avoid any male pissing contests…literally." Jen winked at Decebel as she said this and he lifted his lip in a snarl.

"That sounds about right," Vasile agreed. "I think today you should just go about the rest of your day as usual. Try not to worry about The Gathering."

Jen snorted. "Yeah, I'll get right on that."

Thad, the Alpha of the Serbia pack, held a cell phone to his ear as he listened to his contact.

"There is to be a pack meeting tonight announcing The Gathering," the voice on the other end told him.

"Will the three Americans be in attendance?" Thad asked.

"Yes."

"I expect you to befriend them, earn their trust." Thad paused. "I'm still working out the details of the plan, but as soon as I have figured it out I will be in contact. Remember, don't contact me. I will be in touch with you."

"Yes, Alpha." Then his contact disconnected the call.

Thad sat down in his office chair, looking out over the mountains of his territory. All he had to do was be patient and let his quarry come to him. The Gathering was a month away, he had plenty of time to finalize the plan. *Once everything is said and done, I will have taken down the most powerful Alpha in a century.*

Decebel knocked on the door to the pack infirmary. Remembering Jennifer's words, he grinned and waited for Dr. Steele to invite him. *Wouldn't Jennifer be proud of me?* he thought.

"Come on in," he heard Cynthia Steele yell through the door.

Decebel turned the knob and pushed the door open, sticking his head in before walking through. "Is this a bad time, Cynthia?"

"Decebel, hey." Cynthia took her glasses off and set down the book she had been studying. "No, not at all." She waved him in.

Decebel closed the door behind him and stepped into the area that was used to treat their pack. The room consisted of several large hospital beds along one wall and across from those, two surgery areas that were separated by partitions. Cynthia had a desk immediately to the right of the door with several file cabinets behind her. There was also a lab area set up with various machines, microscopes, and sharp looking objects that Decebel preferred to stay away from.

Part of Cynthia's punishment for her part in the kidnapping of Jacque was serving the Romanian pack as the on-site physician. Vasile, at Jacque's pleading, had spared Cynthia physical punishment, but Vasile had stripped Cynthia of her career. She would practice medicine for the pack and in turn the pack would provide her with lodging, food, the essentials – but until Vasile decided she would not be paid and her freedom was very limited.

"What can I do for you?" she asked him.

Decebel took a chair on the opposite side of her desk. Once seated he looked straight at Cynthia, who quickly averted her gaze. "I need to know what you know about dormant wolves."

"I don't know that much," she told him.

"Then I need you to find out about them. Find out if there is any documentation of their mating tendencies and the occurrences that have gone along with them." Decebel leaned forward, elbows on his knees, hands clasped in front of him.

"What's going on, Decebel?" Cynthia asked, her brow furrowed in question.

He let out a frustrated breath. "I thought I would have time to deal with whatever it is that's going on between Jennifer and I, but now with this gathering..."

"Oh, yeah. Vasile told me about that," she said, nodding her head. "He wants me to go in case there are injuries during the inevitable fights between the unmated males."

Decebel nodded. "We'll be lucky if there aren't any casualties, to be honest."

"So, this thing between you and Jen..." she prompted.

"I don't know what it is. There are no mating signs other than the urging of my wolf and how I react in her presence," Decebel explained. The frustration he had been feeling was evident in the way his body tensed as he talked. "I can't hear her thoughts, my markings haven't changed – yet the idea of another male near her makes me crazy. She's all I think about. Her scent has become a part of me, and I have a ridiculous urge to make sure she has my scent on her."

Cynthia watched him as he spoke, observing the way his eyes began to glow as he talked about Jen. There was something going on, that was for certain.

"Everything you're describing indicates you have found your true mate," Cynthia told him. "I'll look into the pack archives and see if there is any documentation on dormant wolves. She may be your mate and it may take something major to create the bond, just like it took something traumatic to bring out the wolf genetics in her. Or she may just not be your mate."

Decebel growled, not liking the doctor even suggesting that Jennifer didn't belong to him. *Yeah, I'm in trouble.* This gathering was going to prove to be the ultimate test in self control for him and his wolf.

Decebel stood. "Thank you. I really appreciate your help." Before he reached the door, he turned and added, "And your discretion."

Cynthia was completely surprised the dominant wolf had come to her. That alone proved that Jen was really getting under his skin. She turned to her laptop and pulled up the database for the history of packs the world over. Amongst the thousands of files surely there was something documented on a dormant. She began searching through files – opening, skimming, and closing, over and over. *Yeah,* she thought, *this is going to be fun.*

Chapter 9

Jen and Sally walked together to a large meeting room. The pack was meeting in five minutes for the announcement of The Gathering.

They had essentially done nothing all day. It was Saturday – so no lessons. Jen had been forced to endure Sally's endless reassurances that she wouldn't leave her side at the event they'd deemed Mate Fest 2010. They had also opted not to venture out after Jen told them about Decebel's declaration to always be with her when she left the mansion.

Sally had asked, "And how did you respond?"

"I told him the only place I would go with him was to the vet," Jen said innocently.

"We all know that there was more to your comment than that, Virginia. So go on, share the rest of what I'm sure was a most enlightening statement for Decebel," Jacque prodded.

"Fine. I added that he would be going to the vet to have my foot pulled from his ass. I didn't see his face but I'm sure he felt, as you said, enlightened."

Sally had been taking a sip of water at that exact moment and spewed it everywhere.

"I'm interested to meet these other unmated females," Jen told Sally. "I'm hoping they're cool. Ya know what I mean?"

"If in 'cool' you mean non-psycho, jealous, female dogs – then yes, I know what you mean," Sally retorted.

"Man, Sal. I have seriously rubbed off on your once sweet, innocent disposition." Jen chuckled. "And by design, Sally dearest, they are female dogs, they can't help it."

Sally looked at Jen out of the corner of her eye. "You really crack yourself up. And by the way, maybe the real Sally is finally surfacing after years of repression."

"Yeah, you just keep telling yourself that, Sigmund. While you're at it why don't you explain to us the theory of conditioning," Jen teased her best friend.

"I'm just saying."

"Once again you prove that I have clearly influenced you." Jen's eyebrows rose as she glanced at Sally. "I'm not saying that's a bad thing. I mean, truthfully, most people would seriously benefit from a personality adjustment compliments of Jen Adams."

Sally snorted. "Does it get heavy?"

"Does what get heavy?"

"That big head you lug around 24/7, 365." Sally patted Jen on the back. "It just seems like maybe your neck or back would begin to hurt at some point."

"Wow, Sally. I'm impressed you aren't just going for a psychology degree! Right now you seem to be running for mayor of 'I think I'm funny' town."

Sally laughed at Jen but quickly stopped as they walked into the meeting room. Chairs lined the walls and were also lined up in rows in the middle of the room. The room wasn't full yet but it was quickly becoming so as people filed past them.

"Guess we should snag some chairs," Jen muttered as she walked into the room, heading for the far right corner.

"Why are we sitting way back here?"

"This way we can see the whole room and do some recon."

"Great, here we go with the black op lingo. Were you a Navy SEAL or some special forces officer in a past life?" Sally asked.

"It's a gift. It comes so naturally that you think I've had formal training." Jen winked.

"Yeah, that's exactly what I was thinking. And, by the way, Hogwarts accepted you and is awaiting your arrival."

"Ha ha, good one," Jen said dryly. "You have my vote – you'll be mayor in no time."

Sally rolled her eyes as they both continued to watch people enter and sit in the large room.

"Ooo, ooo!" Sally smacked Jen's leg as she spotted Jacque and Fane. "There's Simba and Nala."

"Nice," Jen laughed, then hollered to get their attention. "Hey, princess! Over here."

Jacque spotted them and pulled Fane in their direction.

"Hey, why are you guys sitting way back here?" Jacque asked.

"Here we go," Sally murmured.

"We're doing recon," Jen explained.

"Recooooon, riiiiight," Jacque repeated, one eyebrow raised dubiously.

"Oh, shut up and sit down."

Fane chuckled and sat down next to Sally, pulling Jacque onto his lap. Jacque looked back at him and smiled.

"This way we are sure to have enough chairs for everyone," he explained with a grin.

"Oh, right. We definitely want to make sure there are plenty of seats." Jacque smirked.

"Well, as long as we are being so conscientious," Jen cut in. "Sally, why don't you go climb up in Sorin's lap and I'll," she pointed as a guy walked past her, "grab that hottie and pull up a lap as well."

Jen felt a hand rest at the nape of her neck as a voice spoke softly next to her ear. "If you need a lap to sit on, ţinere de meu inimă (holder of my heart), mine will be the only available to you."

She watched as Decebel sat in the chair next to her and felt her stomach drop as he winked at her.

"I better stay in this chair. It has a tendency to walk off if left on its own." Jen hated how breathless her voice sounded and was mentally kicking herself for letting him see how he affected her. By the smug look that slid across his face he was indeed well aware of it. *Damn werewolf*, she thought to herself.

Sally looked over at Jacque and grinned, obviously loving the play between Decebel and Jen.

Jacque leaned over and whispered in Sally's ear, "I give it two days before he lays one on her."

"You're being generous. I say less than twenty four hours."

"Is that a bet?" Jacque asked, eyebrows raised.

"Better believe it," Sally answered. Her lips eased into a crooked smile.

Jen leaned around Sally and glared at her two best friends. "What are you two betting on?"

"Good grief. What, does she have eagle ears or something?"

"No, you dork. Your whisper is just you talking in normal volume but making your voice raspy. Really, you sound more like a chick who's been smoking for thirty years." Jen shrugged. "I'm just throwing that out there. You can take it and apply it at your leisure."

Fane was chuckling at Jen's words when Jacque elbowed him, causing him to cough.

"You don't get to laugh, wolf-man." Jacque turned back to Jen. "Thank you for that observation, Sherlock."

"Always glad to help a friend in need, Watson." Jen grinned at Jacque's irritated look.

Sally rolled her eyes. "Will there ever be a time that I don't have to send you two to opposite corners?"

"When hell freezes."

"And the people there finally get that glass of ice water they've been waiting on," Jen added.

Jacque reached around Sally, her fist balled. "I like that one."

Jen bumped Jacque's fist and winked. "I know, right? I came up with that one just now."

"Ooo, pretty and quick witted."

"What can I say, wolf princess? I'm the total package."

Decebel looked over at Fane. "A face tu fiecare a lua ce ei say?(Do you ever get what they say?)"

Fane smiled at his Beta. "Nu mai incerce sa, (No longer try)."

"Good call." Decebel nodded.

Jen looked over at Decebel, her eyes narrowing. "No talking in foreign tongue when around the Americans."

Decebel leaned towards her, the gleam in his eyes causing Jen to tremble. "But Jennifer, I thought you spoke Romanian." He looked around at Sally and Jacque. "Weren't you two under the impression that she spoke Romanian?"

Jacque and Sally nodded despite the daggers Jen was staring their way.

"That was thoroughly impressed upon us, wouldn't you say, Sally?" Jacque turned to look at her.

"Wait. Uh yeah, I distinctly remember a bar...vodka...and I'm almost positive Jen speaking in Romanian to the hot bartender." Sally was grinning from ear to ear as Jen's face grew red.

"I hope you two aren't attached to your undergarments because I just got the sudden urge to have a bonfire," Jen growled out.

"Note to self: hide underwear."

"Or you could just solve that problem by not wearing any." Jacque heard Fane's voice through their bond. Her jaw dropped open and her face turned bright red as she turned to look at her mate.

Jen looked at Sally. "Looks like Fane had a suggestion about the princess' undergarments. If I had my guess, I'd say he told her I couldn't burn them if she didn't own any."

If Jacque could've turned any redder she would have. "How? What..." Jacque stuttered as she looked at her blonde friend, trying to figure out how she knew what Fane had been thinking.

"It's a gift, Watson. But really what it boils down to is when it comes to chicks and underwear, guys will always say they don't mix."

Decebel coughed as he choked on his laughter while Fane had buried his face in Jacque's back, his shoulders shaking. Jacque and Sally both looked at their friend with open mouths.

"Another tidbit you might be interested in is when it comes to chicks and open mouths, guys -" Decebel leaned over and covered Jen's mouth with his hand and warned her with a glare to swallow her words.

"Thanks, Dec. That's usually my job," Sally told him. "But I was in such shock that I couldn't get my limbs to move."

Decebel inclined his head. "Is that why you always seem to stand so close to her?"

"It's of utmost importance that whoever is within her reach be ready at any and all moments to intercept what might come from that wicked tongue."

Jen was frantically trying to talk around Decebel's hand at Sally's comment. Decebel was quickly learning how Jennifer's brain worked, and could only imagine what she wanted to voice in regards to Sally's wicked tongue comment. He leaned forward to whisper in her ear. "I'm going to uncover your mouth. It would be wise of you to just let the wicked tongue comment slide."

Jen glared at him from the corner of her eye, and after a tense moment finally nodded once in submission. Decebel slowly uncovered her mouth, ready if need be to slap it right back over her lips.

The room began to get quiet and they all directed their attention to the front of the room. As Vasile welcomed everyone for coming and began to explain about the meeting he had with the other

Alphas, Jen leaned over to Decebel. "You owe me. Sally walked right into it with that whole wicked tongue thing."

Decebel chuckled and whispered back, "For some reason, ţinere de meu inimă (one who holds my heart), I have a feeling there will be plenty of opportunities for you to embarrass your friends for questionable comments they innocently walk into."

Jen shrugged. "True enough, but you still owe me. And what are you calling me when you speak Romanian? You've said the same phrase to me twice now."

Decebel patted her leg, causing all sorts of tingling sensations. "Dar tu romaneste, Micul meu lup. (but you speak Romanian, my little wolf)"

"I know what lup is and I am not a wolf. Whatever else you said I'm sure is a load of crap as well."

"My sweet Jennifer." It was his turn to lean in close. He drew in a deep breath, taking in her scent. His eyes closed as a new smell hit his nose. It was subtle, but it was most definitely there. "I didn't notice it before but I assure you, your scent says you are most definitely wolf." *My wolf*, he heard his own wolf growl, but he kept those words to himself.

Decebel leaned back in his chair. He couldn't focus on what Vasile was saying, not after catching this new scent on Jennifer. He tried really hard to hide his surprise, but he was almost positive this new scent was the mate scent. There were several things that identified a female as a true mate to a male: the ability to hear each other's thoughts, the markings on the male changing, new markings appearing on the female – ones that matched the male's like a puzzle piece – and a scent that only the true mate would recognize.

The first two had definitely not happened between Jennifer and Decebel, but the scent, *her* scent had changed. It was very, very subtle and it was taking everything in him not to pull her into his lap and bury his nose in her neck. *Yeah*, he thought, *that wouldn't freak her out.* Decebel shook his head and tried to set aside this new development so he could listen to his Alpha.

"The Gathering is to take place in a month," Vasile was saying as Decebel tried to catch up. "I want every unmated female to choose one or two mated females from the pairs I have chosen to attend to act as their companions. These females will help the unmated prepare for the evening dances and should she meet her true mate they will also stand as witnesses."

"Do we have to go, Alpha?" Jen heard a pouty voice on the far left side of the room and craned her neck to see who had spoken. Vasile motioned for the wolf to stand and Jen watched as a petite girl rose from her chair. Her hair was cut short in a pixie style. She had big, expressive brown eyes and a small mouth. Her olive skin tone only added to her exotic look.

Vasile's eyes softened and he smiled gently. "Unfortunately, Crina, this is out of my hands. We have been invited and if I refuse it would be considered an act against our species."

The she-wolf named Crina huffed and sat down. "Well, that's a bitch." The room vibrated with low chuckles at her words.

Jen grinned and turned to Sally and Jacque, who were grinning as well. "I like her," she told them.

Decebel overheard Jen's words and looked at her. "I don't think you and Crina should hang out, Jennifer."

Jen cocked her head to the side, her lips pursed. A wave of jealousy rushed over her. "She an old flame, Decebel?"

Decebel sat up straight, clearly caught off guard by the question. "No," he answered flatly.

Jen's eyes narrowed dangerously. "A current flame?" She didn't even recognize her voice as she growled at the thought of Decebel with another woman.

Decebel watched as Jennifer bristled while waiting for his answer. Then it dawned on him – she was jealous. He couldn't stop the chuckle that slipped past his lips. He saw her body tense and realized that laughing wasn't the smartest move he could have made.

"Jealous, Jennifer?"

"Of course not," she spat at him. "I just think with as much as you flirt with me, if you are *involved*," the word came out like it was repugnant to her, "then you need to take your flea-infested self elsewhere."

"And if I'm not involved? What then?" he asked softly, almost a challenge as he looked into her eyes.

Jen stopped breathing at the heat in his look. She was mesmerized as she watched his eyes begin to glow. Amber met her blue ones and she felt herself being drawn closer to him.

"Jennifer," Decebel whispered her name. "What if I'm not involved?"

His hand on her leg finally brought her out of her trance. She took a gulp of air as she realized she was getting light headed from lack of oxygen. She shook her head and looked at Decebel in shock. "*Bloody Hell!*"

She abruptly stood as the whole room turned to look at her. Jen didn't know what had just happened but she knew she had to get as far from Decebel as she could right at that moment. She couldn't think clearly when he was around, and she sure as hell couldn't think when he looked at her like that, and said her name in that voice, and touched her… *Crap*, she thought. *I'm so screwed.*

Decebel stood to follow her but Sally grabbed his arm. She didn't even flinch when he snarled at the one who would keep him from following Jennifer.

"Sit. Down," Sally said firmly to the furious Beta.

The room was deathly quiet when the door slammed shut behind Jen. All eyes were on the group in the corner. Decebel eased back into his chair and met the stares of the other wolves. One by one they submitted to their Beta and looked away.

"As I was saying," Vasile continued. "All unmated members will attend The Gathering. The mated pairs who will attend have already been informed."

"What about the dormant American?" a male wolf in the middle of the room asked.

Decebel snarled. "She is not your concern."

"Decebel!" Vasile growled.

Decebel bared his neck at his Alpha in submission. "My apologies, Alpha."

Vasile looked back at the other wolf. "The answer to your question, Stelian, is that any and all with wolf blood of any amount are required to attend. Jen is a dormant, but she is a member of this pack. An unmated member," he amended. Decebel growled at the words. "And as such, she will participate just like any pack member." Vasile nodded for the wolf to be seated.

The meeting continued on for another hour with questions and frustrations being voiced. Through the entire process Vasile was patient and answered each question, but was unbending and firm. He made it very clear that his pack would attend and that any males who found themselves in an altercation would be dealt with harshly. The room broke into laughter when he said that he wanted it clear that this was not an opportunity to hook up and scratch an itch.

"We are there to seek out true mates. Do not disrespect someone else's mate by putting your hands, mouth, or any other part near what does not belong to you just because you are attracted to them. I will not punish any wolf who challenges another male because he was stupid enough to touch another's mate, even if she hadn't been mated at the time. Do I make myself clear?"

"As you say, so shall it be," the room said in unison.

Jacque grinned at Sally. "Jen would have been all over that. 'Any other part near what does not belong to you'," she repeated Vasile's words. "She's going to be ticked off that she missed an opportunity to embarrass Decebel."

"Totally," Sally agreed.

Fane lightly slapped her thigh. *"Luna, behave."*

"Make me," she challenged as she leaned back, causing him to growl low in his chest.

Vasile finally dismissed the meeting. As Jacque stood, Fane whispered in her ear, "I suppose your challenge will have to wait since you want to find out what caused Jen to leave so abruptly?"

Jacque smiled at her mate, but before she could answer Sally spoke. "I know why she stormed out of here."

Decebel's and Jacque's heads both whipped around. "You do?" they both asked at the same time.

Fane raised an eyebrow at Sally's words.

Sally in turn eyeballed Decebel. "Jen never really learned how to use an inside voice. So, Decebel, why don't you share how she asked you if you were involved with Crina, and how you never really gave her an answer but instead taunted her, and then nearly made her hyperventilate with desire."

Decebel's head cocked to the side, his eyebrows drawn together. "How -"

"I would say it's a gift, but really I'm just nosy as hell. And *damn*, boy, the look you were giving her nearly had *me* in a puddle."

"Shut up!" Jacque squealed. "Are you telling me Jen stormed out of here because he got her all hot and bothered?"

Sally was grinning from ear to ear. Decebel looked like he would be perfectly happy if the universe would just swallow him whole.

"She was angry when she left," Decebel defended.

"Yeah, angry because she's got it bad for you, Sherlock," Sally told him, rolling her eyes.

"Really? She likes me?"

Jacque laughed at Decebel's cocky smile.

"Um, if you aren't her mate that's not a good thing, Casanova," Jacque reminded him.

Sally nodded in agreement, scrutinizing Decebel. "Let's just hope that she finds her mate at Mate Fest so she can get over you."

Decebel took a step towards Sally. Fane stepped around Jacque and laid a hand on Decebel's chest, stopping him. "Easy, Beta."

Decebel closed his eyes taking slow breaths, leashing his wolf. Then Sally's words worked past the jealous fog. "Mate Fest?" he questioned.

Sally grinned. "Jen deemed it."

"Naturally," Decebel muttered with a slight smile.

Chapter 10

Decebel made his way to Cynthia's office after the pack meeting. He needed to share this new development about Jennifer's scent changing and see what the good doctor had to say about it.

The door to the infirmary was already open when he arrived. He walked in to find Alina and Vasile sitting across from Cynthia's desk.

"Decebel." Vasile inclined his head.

"I'm sorry, Alpha, I didn't mean to interrupt. I can come back," Decebel told him, backing out of the room.

"Actually, I would like to talk with you about what happened in the meeting."

Decebel cringed mentally, remembering how he had snarled at Stelian for daring to worry about Jennifer's fate.

"Of course." He stepped back into the room and grabbed an extra chair. He brought it over and sat next to Vasile's.

Vasile stared at his Beta for several moments before he spoke. "Is she your mate?" he finally asked.

Decebel let out an audible sigh. "I don't know, Vasile," he answered in a rare show of vulnerability, shown by using his Alpha's first name. It let Vasile know that Decebel needed his friend's guidance just as much as his Alpha's.

Vasile nodded. "Explain."

"I don't hear her thoughts, my markings are the same. She hasn't mentioned that she has any marks on her body. That said, my wolf has claimed her." Decebel ran his hands through his hair, the frustration evident in his tense jaw as he continued to speak. "I've been battling him for the first time in over a century. No matter how much I remind myself that there aren't mating signs, my wolf doesn't care. He has claimed her and he wants her."

"So other than how you feel about her, there is no evidence that she could be your true mate?" Alina asked him gently.

"Well, actually..." Decebel looked over to Cynthia, who had been silently listening to the conversation. "While I was sitting next to her in the meeting I caught her scent." He paused.

Cynthia perked up. "And?" she asked.

"It's changed," Decebel told her. "It's very faint but I swear I could smell the mating scent on her."

"What did she smell like?" Vasile asked carefully. Decebel knew Vasile only asked because he would have another wolf scent Jennifer to see if what he smelled matched what Decebel did, but he still bristled. Asking another wolf what his mate's scent was to him was like asking a human man to pass around his wife's lingerie. In other words, it was extremely personal.

"Before, she always smelled like warm vanilla." Decebel thought back to the meeting, when he had breathed it in so deep. "But today there was a hint of cinnamon. It was just barely there, but it was intoxicating." Decebel's words softened as he thought about Jennifer's scent, remembering how it had stirred his wolf.

"Interesting," Cynthia murmured. "How long have you been back?"

"A couple of days. Why?" he questioned.

"Since you've been back, when you're around Jen would you say the encounters are intense?" she asked, ignoring his question.

Decebel chuckled. "You could say that. Again I ask, why?"

"Before you came in I was discussing with Vasile and Alina what I had found just before the pack meeting. I came across a documented case of a dormant wolf being mated to a full Canis lupis." Cynthia glanced down at some papers then back at Decebel. "It's actually journal of an Alpha from over a century ago."

"That's good, right?" Decebel asked apprehensively.

"Well," Cynthia paused, "it's good because now we have something to sort of...gauge the progression of a mating between a dormant and full. But it has the potential to be dangerous."

"Dangerous?" Decebel interrupted, not liking the idea of something causing harm to Jennifer. "How can this information possibly be dangerous?"

"Let me explain to you what was documented and then I will go into how it applies to to you and Jen," Cynthia began.

"I'm listening," Decebel told her as he sat up straighter in his chair. His wolf perked up, which really threw him for a loop since his wolf usually kept quiet unless on the hunt or in battle.

Cynthia gathered together the documents she had printed off and began to read.

"I met my true mate today. Not for the first time, but it was the first time the bond had appeared. I had always been strangely intrigued by her, but let it go as curiosity because of her mysterious air. I was caught completely off guard when I heard her thoughts for the first time. She was in danger, serious danger. I heard her cry out for help – in my mind. I started running, without regard to where I was or what I was doing. All that my wolf could think was that we had to get to her, had to save her. I ran for what seemed like forever and finally I broke into a clearing. There, tied to a post, my mate stood.

"Tears streamed down her face, making the bruises that marred her cheeks shine. I felt the blood in my veins begin to heat. My heart sped up and my eyes, I know, were glowing as rage poured into me, fueled by my wolf's need to protect our mate. Her clothes were torn, disheveled rags. Her hair was covered in dirt as if she had been dragged on the ground. She made no sound out loud as her tears continued to flow, but her mind was a turbulent storm of fear, anger, betrayal. She turned and looked straight at me. My breath caught as glowing azure eyes locked onto his. It was instinct to reach out to her mind."I'm here, Rachel," I reassured her. "All will be well." Her eyes widened, the only indication that she'd heard and recognized me. Then they closed. Tears clear as diamonds and numerous as raindrops from a summer storm covered her fear-filled face once again.

The crackle and flash of orange flame finally shook me from my shock and I realized there were men and women all around. Several were lighting wood and hay they had stacked under her, my mate. They were going to burn her alive. Any control I had snapped, the pull of the horror I was witnessing being the final tug. I lost it. For the first time in 200 years I lost control of my wolf. My phase was instantaneous. I lunged forward, taking down any who dared to block my path. I made no distinction between male or female. As far as my wolf was concerned they were all guilty and would suffer the wrath of an Alpha. Screams filled the air as one by one I destroyed those who hadn't run in fear, but instead in their stupidity thought they had a chance against me.

"I got to her just before the fire reached her bare feet. Mercifully she passed out just as I phased back to my human form. I untied her as quickly as I could, pulling her away from the flames that seemed to come alive, reaching with arms, seeking out their prey. I carried her, never looking back. I took her to the pack village, to my home, which would now be hers."

Cynthia stopped there and looked up from the papers. "I'm going to skip ahead to after she awakens and they begin to interact. He describes his feelings towards her and I think that might be helpful for you. Then I'll read what he believes kept him from recognizing his mate and what it took to pull her dormant wolf to the forefront."

Decebel nodded, his only acknowledgment of her words as his brain processed what she had already read.

"Rachel isn't shocked that I'm a Canis lupis. I couldn't believe she knew all this time. Her family has been adamant about passing down their history from generation to generation. I met her over a year ago. She is the daughter of a gypsy healer, Melinda, who comes to the village to help with minor illnesses. I knew that her mother's family had served the pack as healers for generations, but what I didn't know was that Rachel's great grandmother had a brief affair with a pack member. As a result, a little girl had been conceived. Rachel is a fourth generation dormant Canis lupis, which is virtually unheard of and certainly never mated.

"Rachel has been with me a week now. She has been surprisingly accepting of our circumstances. I think it's because she has been around the pack and, unbeknownst to me, had known about true mates and the pull. I find the more time I spend with her the more I crave her. We haven't completed the Blood Rites. I haven't even kissed her, although I find myself needing to touch her, a brush against her as I walk by, a brief hand on her back, a light caress on her face as she sleeps. She needs my touch, I feel it in her though she tries to block her thoughts from me. When I do catch bits of them I am amazed at the insight she has into why it took so long for the

mating signs to happen between us. I've finally decided to talk with her about it. I feel if I don't resolve this and claim her soon no one will be safe.

"*I asked Rachel about her thoughts on our mating. I thought I would have to coax it from her, but she was surprisingly forthright. She said she had spoken with her mother about it and the experience her mother had as a healer is what helped her devise her theory, one that seems to be playing out as I write this.*

"*Melinda believes that because the wolf blood is so diluted in Rachel that something had to happen to trigger that animal part of her, something intense. She said it's like what little amount of wolf lives in her was buried so deep that only something happening that required the help of her wolf caused it to come forth. Rachel had been in trouble when the bond connected us. I asked her what had happened that people she knew would do such a horrible thing to her. Rachel told me that even though she is a dormant, one trait appeared once she became a woman. Her eyes had begun to glow. Anytime she was scared, or angry, or even excited her eyes would shift from blue to glowing azure.*

"*Rachel's best friend had seen it happen and promised to tell no one. She broke her promise. She told her mother that she thought Rachel might be a witch. That was all it took. Cry witch and the righteous will emerge shouting their indignation and pointing their damning fingers.*

"*The villagers had taken her from her home while her mother was away and sentenced her to death. To death, with no proof. That was when I found her. Her dormant wolf had known they needed help and had pushed forward to cry out to their mate. Melinda is convinced that had Rachel and I not known each other or had contact for the past year – in other words, had her mate been a stranger to her – she would not have been able to reach out to him, to me.*

"*Melinda also asked if I noticed the bond growing stronger now that Rachel and I are together all the time. I explained to her how I was feeling and how the emotions and needs are growing stronger. For an unbonded Alpha, that is dangerous. She told me to be honest with Rachel about my feelings, the bond, the Blood Rites, all of it.*

"Rachel and I completed the Blood Rites last night, and completed our mating. It was the final link from my wolf to hers, dormant or no. This morning the mating marks appeared on her back. They're beautiful. My marks have changed as well. She teased me and told me they were very manly.

"Despite Rachel's dormant Canis lupis blood, I don't think our bond is weaker than other full-blooded mated pairs. From talking with my other mated males, Rachel and I experience the same intense feelings as they do, when apart...and together."

Cynthia finished reading and the room was silent. Decebel looked straight ahead, thinking of all the possibilities, outcomes, and yes, even the dangers that came with this information.

"What became of Rachel and her mate?" Decebel's voice broke the silence tight with frustration.

"From what I continued to read, it is believed that her mate died in a werewolf battle. Of course that would mean that Rachel died. But there is not documentation of her death. So in reality no one knows what became of them."

Vasile was the first to break the tense silence. "Do you see why Cynthia feels this is a dangerous situation?"

Decebel didn't respond at first. Finally, he gathered himself. "My options?" He looked directly at Cynthia.

Cynthia took a deep breath and leaned back in her chair. "Create some intense reaction from Jen or leave it alone."

"Neither of those is acceptable," Decebel growled.

Cynthia actually laughed. "Leave it to a dominant wolf to expect someone to pull a solution out of their -"

"Cynthia," Vasile cautioned, his eyes narrowing.

"I beg your pardon, Alpha," she submitted. "What I meant to say was, acceptable or not it is what it is."

"What are your reservations about pursuing her?" Alina asked him.

Decebel looked at Vasile. "I don't want a mate."

Cynthia's eyebrows drew together. "What?"

Alina continued to hold Decebel's stare, and as an Alpha in her own right, she would not back down. Decebel eventually relented out of respect, not a lack of dominance. He let out the breath he'd been holding.

"I had a sister, a long time ago. I failed to protect her. I decided then I did not ever want someone else relying on me for their safety."

"But Vasile and I rely on you every day. The other wolves, the ones you train, the unmated females all rely on you to protect them. How is having a mate any different?" Alina questioned.

"I have backup when it comes to all those you just named. You know as well as I do, Alina, that when it comes to your protection Vasile is the end all. If you are left unprotected, if your protection fails, Vasile will be the one responsible. That's part of being mated, bonded. Vasile alone considers himself responsible for your safety. I don't want that responsibility again."

"You are willing to spend your entire existence spiraling further into darkness because you are afraid of failure?" Cynthia asked, unable to hide her disbelief. "You would pass up something that others consider precious and an honor? Not only that, but you would doom her to live with only half her soul. Really? That's what you are willing to sacrifice?"

Decebel was growling at Cynthia when she finished.

"You don't understand. You aren't a male of this species; you aren't an Alpha. Have you any idea what's like to watch the one you loved and were bound to protect die in your arms because you didn't get there fast enough? DO YOU?" Decebel snarled.

"Decebel." Vasile didn't raise his voice, but his words were full of power.

Decebel backed down but his body shook with anger at Cynthia's words, knowing they were the truth.

"This is what I would have of you, Beta." Vasile faced Decebel, making it a formal command. Anything less wouldn't get Decebel's cooperation. "You will be part of Jen's security. If you don't want to pursue this possibility, fine. I suggest that you wait and see if she finds her true mate at The Gathering. If she does not, then you will take part in seeing if she's your mate through the methods this document has shed light on. You will not leave Jen to the fate of being only a shell of what she should be. Do you understand?"

Decebel growled but nodded his head. He finished formally, "As you say, so shall it be."

Decebel turned to leave, but Vasile spoke up before he could make it out the door. "Decebel, you are choosing this. If you so much as breathe on another wolf at The Gathering because of Jen, you will suffer the consequences."

"Understood," Decebel acknowledged. He walked out of the room, leaving with not only more questions but complete and utter confusion.

Decebel knew that the moment he saw another wolf put his hands on Jennifer he would not be able to control his wolf, yet he had stupidly agreed to guard her. He was doing the very thing he wanted to avoid. He was her protection. Damn his Alpha and his meddling.

Jen paced her room like a caged animal. She couldn't believe what a fool she had made of herself, but at the moment all she had been able to think about was getting away from a certain wolf.

She was so screwed. How had she gotten to this point? She'd been telling herself over and over that he wasn't an option. She might as well have had a license plate made as many times as she had repeated it to her heart. Yeah, well her heart was doing its own thing because it didn't give a royal, flipping, fat pig that Decebel was supposed to be off limits. Something in her reached out to him. Every time he was near her she just wanted to rub up against him and curl up in his lap. *Can we say coming unhinged, boys and girls,* Jen thought.

Back and forth she paced. "Okay," she said to the empty room, "Mate Fest 2010 is the answer. I have to really, really try to find my mate." Once again her heart piped in its two cents   while Jen was telling it not to waste its money. *Decebel is our mate,* it told her. "Nope, not happening. I'm not listening to you. La la la la la la." Jen plugged her fingers in her ears and closed her eyes. It was at this point that Sally walked in.

"Who are you not listening to, exactly?" Sally asked, looking around the room.

Jen swung around, dropping her hands quickly. "Hey, Sal. What's up?" she asked, reaching for calm but falling five thousand feet short.

"Yeah. Well, about that..." Sally folded her arms and raised a hand to tap her chin with a finger. "What's up? Hmm. See, you jumping up like you were sitting on a fire cracker and then bolting out of the meeting like said fire cracker was trying to bite your butt…yeah, that's pretty much what's up."

Jen cringed at the picture Sally painted. "Okay, so it wasn't my best moment," she muttered.

"Ya think?" Sally asked, her eyebrows rising.

"You don't know what it was like..." Jen's voice was reaching that high-pitched point when she would normally have thrown something at someone else using it. "Sitting there next to his furry hotness, his eyes doing that smoldering thing, his voice deep and soft, his hand being all handy. I mean seriously, Sally, it was either jump and run for the hills or crawl up in his lap panting like some desperate wench."

Sally laughed. "Did you just say desperate wench?"

"Shut up, Sally."

Sally held her hands up in surrender. "Hey, don't shoot the one pointing out your dumb metaphors."

Jen rolled her eyes at her best friend as she plopped down on the floor, leaning her back against the bed.

"So, what's the -" Sally started to ask but was interrupted when the door to the room flew open.

"I'm here!" Like a turbulent wind, Jacque came rushing in. "I'm here," she panted. "What's the plan?" Her head snapped back and forth between Jen and Sally.

Jen nodded her head in Jacque's direction. "What the bloody hell is wrong with her?" she asked Sally.

"I'm beginning to think it's the s-e-x," Sally spelled, covering the side of her face so Jacque couldn't see but speaking in a loud whisper. "All the lack of oxygen from the panting, heavy breathing, and what not is killing her brain cells."

Jen busted out laughing, "That would be even funnier if my brain wasn't trying to fill in the what not."

"Could we please refrain from talking about my sex life," Jacque ground out.

"No, there will be no refraining because then you would want me to talk about the attraction I'm trying to ignore to the wolf who is still not an option even though neither one of us can seem to stay the hell away from the other." Jen took a deep breath and barreled on. "If we cease talking about your sex life then you two hyenas will expect me to tell you how when I'm near him I feel like electricity is running over my skin. You would want me to explain how my heart speeds up and my breathing becomes erratic every time he whispers in my ear. You would force me – against my will, mind you – to describe to you the many times I have daydreamed hearing his voice in my mind, seeing marks cover my skin, seeing his marks change. So, hell to the no. Request denied. Do not pass go, do not collect two hundred dollars. In summary, we cannot stop talking about your sex life."

Sally was standing with her jaw dropped open and Jacque was staring at Jen like she had sprouted wings from her butt.

"Well, okay then," Sally finally spoke. "I think talking about Jacque's sex life has really shed some light on things. Don't you, Jacque?"

"Some light? Crap, my sex life has illuminated a whole stinking football stadium."

"Who knew?" Jen shrugged innocently.

"What's the plan, Jen?" Sally asked soberly, "We all know you have one, so spill."

Jen stood up and started pacing again. "I've got to find my mate, I've got to stay away from B, and I've got to pull it together." She blew a breath out, ruffling her bangs.

"Okay, operation MAP starts now." Jacque grinned.

"Operation MAP?" Jen asked dubiously.

"Um, wolf-princess, would you please elaborate on the title?" Sally prodded.

"M, mate, A, avoid, P, pull," Jacque explained.

"Ooo, MAP. Like we're *map*ping out her future. I like." Sally winked at Jacque.

"I know, right? It fits, like we're making a map out of this mess," Jacque added.

Jen smiled and nodded her head enthusiastically, "Oh, I've got one," she said, joining in. "It's like you're making a map to lead your crazy asses out of my room."

"Hey," Sally said indignantly.

"Hey, if the shoe fits, Sally. I'm just saying, if it fits all you can do is wear it to the best of your ability. Let me tell you, you are doing some wicked justice."

Jacque laughed and Sally's head snapped around as she glared at her.

"You have to admit that was pretty funny."

Sally thought for a minute and then grinned. "Yeah. I guess she deserves props, but I'm still calling it operation MAP."

"Fine, crap. Let's get this op in the works," Jen relented.

"Yes!" Jacque and Sally said at the same time, giving high fives.

Jen shook her head at her two best friends. *Loyal, yes. Giving, for sure. Crazy as loons? Without a doubt,* she thought as she grinned while Sally and Jacque both talked at the same time, gradually getting louder as they talked over one another. Jen decided to try and make the most of them as they came. She had a feeling they were going to get few and far between once at The Gathering.

Chapter 11

Jen, Sally, and Jacque spent the next four weeks learning about different packs that were going to be present at The Gathering. They learned the names of the Alphas and their mates, if they had one. They learned about the different pack traditions and practices. Jen found it interesting that though there were some things that were universal in the Canis lupis world, packs were very individualized.

It was now two days before they left for the Transylvanian Alps and they, along with three other unmated females and eight unmated males, were in the large gathering room of the mansion to learn to dance.

"I don't need lessons on dancing," Jen muttered under her breath as she stood with Sally and Jacque against the back wall.

"I think Vasile wants the dancing to be PG rated," Jacque teased.

Jen faked indignation. "Excuse me, but my clothes stay on."

"Mostly," Sally mumbled, erupting a laugh out of Jacque.

"Oh, COME ON! That was one time!" Jen groaned. "I swear, lose your clothes at a party one time and they never let you live it down."

"Ooo, now this sounds right up my alley." Crina, the wolf who had spoken up at the pack meeting, came bouncing up with another girl. "Hey, we haven't formally met. I'm Crina and this brute is Mariana." Both girls gave friendly smiles.

Although Mariana wasn't really a brute, she was very tall. Standing next to the pixie Crina, she did qualify as classification brute.

"Hi, Crina. I'm Jen. These two yahoos are my best friends, Sally and Jacque."

Both girls bared their necks briefly at Jacque. It had been explained during one of their lessons that, although Jacque held no real power right now, the pack would show her respect for her place with signs of submission, such as baring their necks.

Jacque gave a single nod in acknowledgment of their submission.

"So, you ready for Mate Fest 2010?" Jen asked them.

Crina smiled. "Mate Fest?"

"It seemed so much more twenty first century than The Gathering."

Crina nudged Mariana. "I told you they would be cool, didn't I?"

Mariana smiled. "Yeah, boss. You told me." She looked at Jen conspiratorially. "She said anyone who could get Decebel all in a tizzy the way you do has to be cool."

Jen didn't just laugh at that, she cackled. "He makes it too easy."

Crina smiled with her and added, "Just so you know, I don't know what is between you two, but neither I nor Mariana have designs on him."

Jen sobered and looked at both girls. It hadn't dawned on her until that moment that there might be others in the pack who had an interest in Decebel. Before she could stop herself, she let out a low growl. Jen watched Mariana's and Crina's eyes get big and heard Sally's intake of breath, but before she could turn, a strong arm came around her waist and pulled her away.

"What the -" she started, but was cut short when a woman in the far corner hollered:

"Grab a partner!"

Jen was turned abruptly and found herself face to face with Decebel.

"Hello, Jennifer." He grinned unrepentantly.

"Decebel, so nice to see you. It's been what, three weeks since you've graced me with your presence?"

"Ahh, yes. About that – please forgive me for my absence. I've been working out your security detail."

"My what?" Jen asked cautiously.

Decebel took Jennifer's left hand and placed it on his shoulder, took her right hand in his left, then wrapped his free arm around her waist, drawing her close.

"Your security detail," he told her again, now much closer to her ear. "Vasile has placed me in charge of your security while at The Gathering, so I have been back and forth between here and Transylvania working out the kinks."

Jen made an "oh" motion with her mouth but said nothing else. She was actually in a small state of shock after not seeing Decebel for days on end. To suddenly have him here in front of her, this close, was a bit overwhelming. Although there was no way in Hades she would ever 'fess up to it.

They danced in silence for several moments before Jen blurted, "You're a really good dancer."

Decebel chuckled. "You didn't think that something that walked on four legs would be able to waltz?"

Jennifer grinned at him. Decebel could almost see the thoughts form in her mind.

"Actually, when in your four legged form, waltzing would be rather similar to you in your two legged form. Only, you wouldn't need a partner because you'd already have plenty of legs." Jen couldn't help the giggles that bubbled out at her own little joke. Decebel growled at her, but it was only half-hearted.

Their banter was cut off by another shout. "Switch!"

"Beta, may I cut in?" Costin, the wolf from the bar, stood next to a now frozen Jen and Decebel.

Decebel abruptly let go of Jennifer. "Of course." He nodded to the other wolf and walked off without a backward glance.

Jen watched as Decebel walked away and then looked at Costin.

"What crawled up his knickers?" she wondered out loud as she once again assumed the dancing stance.

"Aw, he's just a little sore that I stepped in. He doesn't share his things well."

Jen glared at Costin. "I am not one of his things," she ground out.

Costin chuckled but covered it quickly with a cough. "Of course you're not."

The rest of the lesson was spent switching partners periodically. All the while, Decebel kept his eyes glued on Jen and whomever she happened to be dancing with.

"So, how do you feel about this whole Gathering thing?" Crina asked Jen.

After the dancing lesson ended, the five girls had all gone in search of hot chocolate and were now gathered around the dining room table.

"Honestly," Jen paused as she took a sip of her hot chocolate, "I'm kind of looking forward to it. It's something to take my mind off of other, I would like to say unsavory things, but mother of pearl if he isn't the most savory fur ball this side of anywhere."

"Girl has got it bad," Jacque told Crina and Mariana.

"Decebel is hot, no doubt," Crina agreed.

Jen's head snapped around and a growl came from somewhere inside her.

Crina held her hands up in surrender. "Whoa, I'm not infringing on your wolf." She bared her neck to Jen and something inside her settled. It was freaking weird.

Jen shook her head, attempting to clear out the haze that filled her mind.

"Sorry about that. I don't know what that was but it was, man, I don't know what."

Mariana spoke for the first time. "It was you claiming what's yours."

"But there are no mating signs."

"Here we go," Sally threw in.

Jacque nodded in agreement. "Once you get her wound up it's like watching the energizer bunny. Y'all better get comfortable."

"What if they just haven't appeared yet because you are a dormant?" Mariana offered.

Jen propped her elbows on the table and then put her face in her hands. "I've thought of that. But seriously, it's been several months since we met and in those several months I was in a major car crash and burned, found out I had werewolf blood, moved to a new country, oh and turned eighteen. You would think that something in there would trigger, well, something."

"But it did," Mariana told her. "It triggered interest on both your parts, didn't it?"

Jen thought about her words.

"When did you really start to notice Decebel?" Crina asked.

"After I woke up from the coma. He came into my room to check on me. Which was bizarre, to say the least. I remember thinking 'wow, that is yummy'."

Sally laughed. "She practically had to wear a bib around him she drooled so much."

"Sally, how's that election coming for mayor?"

Jacque looked puzzled. "What?"

Sally shook her head. "Don't mind her. She's lacking in brain cells lately because they've been fried by hormonal overload."

Jen rolled her eyes and made a "W" sign with her fingers while mouthing, "whatever".

Mariana looked at her watch. "Well, it's getting late so I guess we should head out. Look for us at Mate Fest and we'll hang out. Us wallflowers need to stick together."

Jen smiled. "Sounds like a plan. It was really nice to meet both of you."

Sally and Jacque piped in their agreement and said goodbye as the two other females left the dining room.

"I guess we should call it a night," Jacque said, downing the last of her hot chocolate. "One day left before we head into the testosterone-coated hills of Transylvania."

All three girls rinsed their cups and headed to their rooms.

Jen had just reached her door when she felt it. Someone was watching her. There was no doubt in her mind who it was. She turned to see Decebel standing at the other end of the hall, staring at her. Neither moved for several minutes. Then he started walking towards her.

Jen didn't know whether to go into her room, run, or stand frozen and quite possibly pass out from lack of oxygen. His long strides ate up the distance between them quicker than she would have thought possible and suddenly, he was there – less than a foot away from her.

She couldn't speak. All she could do was stare into those amazing amber eyes.

Decebel closed his eyes and took a deep breath. Once again he detected that small bite of cinnamon in her scent.

"Jennifer," he whispered.

"Uh-huh," was all Jen could manage.

Decebel's right hand came up and pushed her long blond hair back away from her face and neck. He leaned forward and placed his nose against her neck, just below her ear, and took another deep breath. Jen seriously thought she was going to pass out. *This cannot be happening.* She wanted to pinch herself to make sure she was really awake. When Decebel pulled back, she saw that his amber eyes were now glowing.

"I don't know what's going on between us, ținere de meu inimă," Decebel told her, his voice husky. "I will tell you it scares me."

"Scares *you*? How can anything scare *you*?"

Decebel chuckled as he gently cupped her face, his thumb tenderly caressing her jaw line. "There is much you don't know about me, Jennifer, much about my past that has shaped who I am today." He paused as he watched her. "I can't stay away from you, and now our blasted Alpha has made me your protector."

"And you don't want to be my protector," Jen interrupted with a whisper.

Decebel heard the insecurity in her tone, but admired her for not looking away from him when she voiced it. "The problem isn't that I don't want to be your protector, it's that I want to be more."

"Oh," Jen breathed out.

"I don't know how I'm going to get through this, this..." Decebel searched for the words.

"Mate Fest?" Jen offered, which brought a heart stopping grin from Decebel. She nearly swooned. *You have got to get a grip,* she told herself. *Jennifer Adams does not swoon. Drool, definitely. Stare without shame, for sure. But swooning is forbidden.* She decided her inner dialogue was really beginning to get out of control.

"Yes, this Mate Fest. I don't know how I'm going to get through it without killing another wolf."

"Is there anything I can do to help?"

"Don't touch another male. Don't let another male touch you." Decebel's lips were tight as he spoke, betraying the carefully conveyed control.

"Okay, no touching. Got it."

Once again they stared at one another in silence. Gradually Decebel began to lean into her and Jen realized he was going to kiss her. It was also then that she realized how desperately she wanted, craved that kiss. Her eyes drifted closed as she waited, and waited. *What the - ?,* she thought as she opened her eyes.

He hadn't moved any closer.

"Are you going to kiss me?" Jen asked boldly.

Decebel grinned, but it left as quickly as it had come. "I can't."

She frowned. "You can't, or you won't?"

"It's not that simple, Jennifer." Decebel started to pull back but Jen grabbed his hand and pulled it back to her face. She held it next to her cheek and let his heat seep into her. She had never felt anything better than his touch in her life.

"It is that simple. You either do or you don't. It's a choice, Decebel. *Your* choice. So don't tell me you can't. Unless your lips are super glued to some object, they are up for grabs. So what gives?"

"I think you need to speak with Dr. Steele, then you will understand what's at stake from something as innocent as a kiss."

He watched as that all too-familiar wicked gleam filled Jennifer's eyes. "Who says it has to be innocent?"

Decebel did step back this time and she let him go.

"Get some sleep, Jennifer. I'll see you tomorrow," he told her gently. After a small smile at her, he left.

"Okay, see you on the flip side."

Jen entered her bedroom after watching Decebel walk away until she couldn't see him any longer.

"See you on the flip side, Jen? Really?" she asked herself out loud. "Do you want someone to ask you to write an expert account on how to be effectively lame? Because let me tell you, blondie, you are all over it." *Pathetic*, she thought, *I'm a groupie and I'm talking to myself.* "Ughh."

She quickly went through her routine of getting ready for bed, the whole time remembering the feel of Decebel's flesh on hers, his breath on her neck. There was no way she was going to survive this with her heart intact. She knew that when this was all said and done, she would come out an empty shell if she didn't come out with Decebel by her side.

The real question she found herself facing after her little encounter with the fur ball in the hall was, how do you go about looking for a mate when you would rather be trying to convince the one you want to pursue what was slapping him steadily in the face?

"Yeah, good luck with that," Jen told herself.

"So I guess I'll see you in a couple of days?" Jacque asked her dad through her cell phone.

"Yes. And I'm bringing Tanya. She really wants to meet you. You okay with that?"

"Yeah, it's cool. It was bound to happen one day, right? There's no time like the present," Jacque told him, her voice coming out unnaturally high. She felt herself settle as Fane wrapped his arms around her from behind and placed a gentle kiss on her neck.

"Thank you, Jacque. I know it's a lot to ask. So I'll see you soon, then." He disconnected the call.

Jacque set her cell phone down on the bedside table.

"Well, this ought to be fun. It's going to be a cozy little meet and greet," she told Fane, frowning.

"It will be okay, Jacquelyn, it's a large estate. If you and Tanya don't get on there will be plenty of places for you to slink off to."

Jacque pulled out of his arms and turned on him abruptly. "Slink? I do not slink, wolf-man."

Fane smiled and winked. "I knew that would do it."

Jacque growled and tackled him to the bed. "So you think if you prick my pride I will be less likely to evade the confrontation I so badly want to avoid?"

Fane nodded. "That about sums it up."

"How well you know me already, pesky flea ball."

"Again with the fleas." He growled and tickled her. Jacque squealed, unsuccessfully trying to fight him off. He finally relented and pulled her close.

"All will be well, Luna," he whispered.

"I know," she agreed, "but there's always a variable that isn't accounted for, ready to throw things off kilter. Then all is no longer well."

"Ahh, love. Where did such pessimism come from?"

"I guess Jen's worry is rubbing off on me. I just wish she and Decebel would fish or cut bait."

"Fish or cut bait? I'm not familiar with this," Fane told her, his brow furrowed.

"It means get on with it or move on. It's so obvious they are meant to be together,"

"He can't claim her without mating signs. She has to participate in The Gathering," Fane warned her.

"Then there will be a blood bath," Jacque told him somberly. "Because the first man brave enough to lay a finger on Jen is going to see firsthand what happens when another touches a mate. Signs or no, Decebel's wolf has claimed Jen. And Jen's wolf, what little there may be, has claimed Dec. Not to mention her heart."

Both fell silent as they thought about the consequences that were sure to come. But like a speeding train without brakes, nothing short of a miracle could stop them.

Chapter 12

"Do you think it was wise of you to make Decebel her protector?" Alina asked her mate.

Vasile continued to stare at the road as he drove towards the site of The Gathering.

He knew it was a gamble placing Jen in Decebel's care. "I don't know," he admitted. "I guess I'm trying to force him into action. Maybe if he sees others pursuing her he will get over this fear and make a move. Or I could just be setting up some poor wolf's demise."

Alina watched him carefully while he spoke, noticing the faint lines that ran along his skin. Even after two centuries her mate was still unbelievably handsome, but it seemed the stress of life was catching up with him.

"Sometimes dominant wolves have to be pushed over the edge when they won't jump on their own. Why do you think that is?" Alina's tone was teasing.

Vasile's lips lifted slightly. "Even us dominants have to have one flaw, Luna, otherwise it wouldn't be fair."

Alina laughed and shook her head at her mate's forever cockiness.

"I spy something green," Sally announced.

"Trees," Crina hollered, while Mariana called out, "Grass,"

"Nope," Sally answered.

"What's the point of this game again?" Crina asked.

"Mindless entertainment," Jen announced. "It's what Americans are known for."

Fane and Decebel laughed at Jen's words.

Vasile had devised the riding assignments, and so Jen, Jacque, and Sally had been paired with Crina and Mariana as well as Decebel and Fane. *One big, happy family,* Jen thought as she looked around the cab of the Hummer. She was really glad that Crina and Mariana had turned out to be cool. It would have sucked big time had they turned out to be ninnies.

"Anymore guesses?" Sally asked.

"I think we've had enough of I Spy, Sal," Jacque told her.

Sally's face fell briefly, but perked up when she said, "Okay, how about -"

Before she could finish, Jen cut her off. "How about we discuss the plans for when we arrive at this little 'meet your baby daddy' festival."

The entire vehicle erupted in laughter at Jen's slang. Jen blushed ferociously when Dec gave her a heart-stopping grin.

"How do you all keep from peeing on yourselves when she's around?" Crina asked, wiping the tears that had welled up in her eyes.

"No doubt, it's tough," Jacque told her. "And sometimes it's wise to bring a change of clothes if you're going to be around her for any extended period of time."

After the laughing and bantering finally died down, Fane addressed Jen's earlier question.

"I think tonight there is a large gathering with all the packs to lay out the ground rules and purpose behind The Gathering," Fane explained. "There will be lots of mated pairs all around and Alphas to keep the males in check."

"I feel like I should wear a raincoat or something," Jen only halfway joked.

Crina laughed. "I take it you're afraid someone's going to hike a leg?"

Jen grinned. "I knew from the moment I heard you take on Vasile I would like you."

Decebel rolled his eyes. "Great, now we're really outnumbered."

"Don't you forget it, bucko." Jen tossed a crumpled piece of paper but he caught it before it hit him.

"You do like to push your luck don't you, Jennifer?" he asked her.

"Push it, or just give it a great big shove. Whatever gets the job done." She winked at him and then slid down into her seat. "I'm going to try and catch some Zs before we get there. I have a feeling I'm going to need my wits about me."

"That could be a problem, Jen. You have to have -" Sally started.

"Not another word, Sally." Jen's words were followed by snickers from the other girls, and then the vehicle fell silent.

Thad watched as his wolves set up the meeting room with chairs and tables for the packs. The American pack had already arrived and was getting settled into their rooms. The others were due to arrive any moment.

Thad's eyes followed the movement around the room but his mind was elsewhere. He couldn't help but wonder if he would finally find his true mate among those who were coming to The Gathering. Two centuries was too long to be without a mate. Especially when the other Alphas were all mated. He wasn't a weak Alpha by any means, but it was a fact that a mated Alpha was a stronger Alpha. So regardless of his own strength, until he was mated he would not stand a chance against another.

Thad was pulled from his thoughts when the double doors to the large room opened. He watched as Vasile and his mate entered. Behind them he saw his Beta and Fane, the Grey Wolf Prince. The sheer size of them blocked any view of those who might be behind them. Thad was sure that was a tactical move on Vasile's part. His females would be well protected. *That could be a problem, but not insurmountable,* he thought.

"Daaaaang," Jacque whispered as the double doors opened and they walked into a large room. "Would you look at this place!"

"I feel like Beauty in Beauty and the Beast," Sally whispered to Jen. "You know, when she walks into the grand ballroom for the first time?"

"Well, you got one thing right, Sal," Jen murmured as she too took in her surroundings, "we are not short on beasts."

Jen tilted her head back at Jacque's prompting and her own mouth dropped open at seeing the height of the ceiling. That wasn't the only thing that had their mouths hitting the freshly waxed floor. Painted on the ceiling was a forest covered in shimmering snow. Somehow the artist had achieved a nearly three dimensional effect, and by looking at it you felt as if you were falling into the painting. Among the hills and trees there were wolves. Some were running, others lying quietly.

The theme was quite obvious once you picked up on it, Jen realized. There wasn't a single wolf alone. Each one was paired with another. And as she looked harder she could see that every pair was touching. The wolves running side by side were painted so that their tails intertwined as they ran, the ones sitting together had one tucked in close to the other, and those lying down had one wolf literally curled around the other, protecting, sheltering. It was beautiful, and the meaning was clear: wolves weren't meant to be alone. They were created for a mate.

Jen pulled her eyes from the compelling painting when she felt a tug on her sleeve. She turned just as Mariana was waving them all to follow.

"This handsome gentleman offered to show us to our rooms," Mariana told them. Jen looked back and saw that Vasile was talking to some other guy who looked to be in charge of something. They probably weren't needed. She looked at Jacque and nodded in the direction Mariana was headed.

"I'm in. You?"

"Lead the way," Jacque answered.

Jen didn't know if she should say something to Decebel, but she figured, He's got wolf hearing, surely he'll hear us leaving. Not only that, but there was no way Fane would not keep tabs on his little she-wolf. So she shrugged her shoulders and followed the rest out of the large room. With her back turned she didn't notice Decebel nod to Costin, a silent order to keep an eye on the girls until he could leave without appearing disrespectful.

"Vasile." Thad raised his voice to be heard across the room as he made his way over to the Romanian Alpha. "So glad that you could come."

"I want our species to thrive just as you do, Thad. Our pack appreciates you inviting and giving our single pack members a chance to possibly meet their true mates."

Decebel felt his skin begin to prickle as Jennifer got farther and farther away from him. He was very close to simply ignoring protocol and going after her, but that would make Vasile look bad in the eyes of other wolves and he wouldn't do that to his Alpha. He just kept reminding himself that Costin would keep an eye on her and not let other wolves near her. Still, his wolf was restless. *This is going to be a long week*, Decebel thought.

"What time should I have my pack down for the gathering tonight?" Vasile asked Thad.

"We are to begin at six, so you probably want to have them down a little before to get seated. I will have two of my wolves show you to your rooms." Thad looked around Vasile at where the girls had been standing only moments before. "It looks like the dominant males have already made themselves known to your females." He chuckled.

Decebel growled, but before he could get much sound out Fane elbowed him hard in the side. Decebel coughed. He cut his eyes at Fane, who had the gall to wink. His red headed mate was rubbing off on him already.

After Thad and Vasile finished talking, Vasile turned to the pack members who had stayed with him. "Follow those two gentlemen, they will take us to our rooms." Vasile indicated two wolves standing directly in front of a large staircase in the entryway.

As they climbed the stairs, Vasile positioned himself in between Fane and Decebel. "I want you two and Sorin to go and make sure the girls stay out of trouble until tonight."

"As you say," Fane and Decebel spoke at the same time.

When they reached the top of the staircase, Decebel's head snapped to the right. There was loud laughter coming down the hall.

He nudged Fane. "My bet is we'll find trouble down that way." He indicated the direction the giggles were coming from.

"Are we going to survive this week?" Fane asked Decebel wearily.

"What's this *we* crap? You're mated, you can go hole up with your woman. I, on the other hand, get to be smack in the middle of the *festivities*," Decebel said the word as if it were a disease.

Fane laughed and patted Decebel on the back. "However I can help, Beta, I will. But I don't envy you when it comes to being responsible for Jen."

"No doubt. She's a handful."

"You wouldn't have her any other way, would you?"

"Not on my life," Decebel admitted shamelessly.

Just as they reached the door from which all the noise was coming, they heard – for the first time – male laughter. Decebel snarled as he grabbed the doorknob and threw the door open. Fane was right behind him, immediately searching the room for Jacque. He wasn't as angry as Decebel because he'd been able to feel Jacquelyn, and knew there was no danger.

Of course, danger isn't entirely what Decebel is worried about, Fane thought.

Jen nearly rolled off the bed as she laughed. The two guys who had lead them to their rooms were hilarious, though it wasn't completely them. They didn't understand a lot of American sayings and when they repeated them or tried to use American slang, it came out really funny.

"So are you liking Romania?" the wolf called Damion asked her.

"Well, it's cold," Jen started, "but it's alright. We got to go out to one of the dives and dance. Costin over there," Jen pointed to Costin who was standing in a corner with his arms folded across his chest, looking way to close to being mini-me Decebel, "hooked us up with drinks. He even let me dance on the bar."

"Forgive me, but what is a dive? And how do you hook a drink?"

Jen, Sally, and Jacque couldn't help the laughter that bubbled up at his innocent question.

"Sorry, Damion. We aren't laughing at you," Sally explained when he began to look even more confused. "It's just we don't really think about how our words must sound to someone who doesn't use the same slang."

Damion waved her off, obviously not offended.

"So a dive is like a bar or club, you know, somewhere to hang out. When I said hooked up I mean like helped us out, or provided us with something."

Damion grinned and looked at his pack mate Adrian. "I think I like this term 'hook up'. What do you think?"

Adrian nodded. "So would it be correct for me to say I want hooked up you?"

That did it – even Costin's stoic façade fell apart. The entire room erupted into laughter. This time Jen did fall off the bed and landed next to Damion, who helped steady her just as the door flew open.

Jen looked up and the first word that came to her mind flew right out of her mouth, "Shit!" She slapped her hands over her mouth, which only made her lose her balance more and she fell forward, *across* Damion's lap. *So not good.*

The room suddenly plunged into deathly silence.

Decebel's eyes landed on Damion and then at Jen as she struggled to right herself from Damion's lap.

His eyes began to glow and, for the first time in a long time, his wolf won.

Jen watched in complete horror as several things happened at once. Decebel lunged for Damion as Fane, Costin, and Sorin, who had appeared out of nowhere, all lunged for Decebel. Jen felt herself be pulled back and she tumbled onto her butt.

"We haven't been here thirty minutes," Jacque said, sitting down next to her.

Sally pulled up some carpet on Jen's other side. "Wow, that's impressive."

Crina and Mariana, who had been sitting close to Costin, came over. "I guess I know where I need to be if I want free entertainment," Crina teased.

"Yyyep," Jen said with a pop on the "p." "Just call me prime time, because if this kind of crap follows me all week, my ratings are bound to soar."

Jacque snorted. "Lucy, esplain this mess." she used her best Ricky Ricardo voice.

"Ahh, Ricky, I just wanted to surprise you." Jen tossed back.

Sally laughed with them. Then the collective group of five cringed as Decebel got one good punch across Damion's face before the other males finally pulled him back.

Dang, he's strong, Jen thought.

Finally Decebel collected himself and shook the others off. "I'm fine," he said, holding his arms up in surrender.

Damion wiped the blood from his lip, his eyes now glowing an eerie green.

Sorin stood in between the wolves, his hands held out between them as if to hold them off.

Decebel growled when Damion continued to meet his eyes. Damion finally relented and dropped his eyes.

Jen muttered, "Good grief."

"Charlie Brown," Sally finished.

Decebel's eyes fell on Jen, which made her squirm, only she didn't know why because she hadn't done anything wrong. Jen continued to meet his stare and the longer she held it the angrier she got. Finally she stood up, causing Jacque and Sally to scramble to their feet, not wanting to be the only ones on the floor. Fane walked over to Jacque and took her hand.

"We need to go," he told her gently.

"Do you think it wise to leave just now?" Jacque asked through their bond.

"Most definitely," Fane answered as he tugged her towards the door.

When no one else made to follow Fane and Jacque, Decebel growled, "Everyone out!"

Suddenly everyone was in motion. Jen grinned to herself as she began to head to the door with everyone else. She heard Crina chuckle behind her, obviously having caught on to what she was trying to do.

"JENNIFER." Decebel's voice wrapped around her, pulling her to a halt.

Damn Beta, she thought.

"Good try," Crina whispered as she squeezed past Jen.

"Scream real loud if you need to be rescued," Mariana told her, then winked. "We'll send someone."

"Yeah, thanks for that, wolf-girl."

The door clicked shut, leaving Jen alone with one very large, very angry wolf.

She turned around slowly and made her way towards the window, almost casually.

"So, how are you liking the weather?" she asked as if he hadn't just nearly torn a man in half.

"What part of 'don't touch another male' didn't make it through that thick skull, Jennifer?" Decebel's voice was deep and low.

Oh, hell no, Jen thought. *He did not just imply what I think he did*. She whipped around and pinned him with ice blue eyes. "You know what, Decebel? I think this whole thing," she motioned between them, "is a conflict of interest. Yeah, the more I think about it the more I think it's detrimental to *your* health for you to be on my security detail."

"A conflict of interest?" he repeated sarcastically.

"Exactly. Your interest in me has caused your good sense to become conflicted, or impaired, actually. Wait, I'll do you one better than that – your good sense has kissed your ass goodbye on its way out the door, waving and smiling with well wishes."

Decebel stood dumbfounded at the anger in her voice. *Why is she angry?* he wondered. He was the one who had found her in another wolf's lap. Oh, that was not a good thing for him to dwell on. He felt his canines trying to lengthen and took a deep breath, pulling his wolf back.

"All I know is we are apart for five minutes and you're cuddled up next to some pup."

"Cu-cud- cuddled," Jen was so angry that she couldn't even get her words out. "If you would open your freaky glowing eyes and quit jumping to conclusions, you would have seen that I wasn't cuddled in his lap. I fell off the bed and landed next to him. You barging in surprised me and I lost my balance, that's when I ended up in his lap."

"He's interested in you," Decebel bit out.

"Of course he's interested in me, flea bag. There is all kinds of interest to be had up in here." Jen couldn't help but goad him on, it was just too stinking easy. She could almost see steam rising from his head at her words.

"You aren't helping, you know."

"You didn't ask for my help, B. You barged in here thinking the worst of me and then acted like a barbarian. *Then* you accused me of purposely throwing myself at some guy I don't even bloody know." Jen was to the point that she just really wanted Decebel out of her room. Her emotions were raw. She had been having fun, laughing and, sure, flirting a little. But much to her chagrin, no matter how hot Damion and Adrian were – who, by the way, were mega hot – she wasn't interested. *Then Decebel has to come in and be all, well, all Decebel.*

"Look, we need to take five, okay? Go get a Kit Kat and give me a break."

Decebel cocked his head to the side, obviously not understanding her reference.

She shook her head. "Never mind, just leave. Is that clearer for you?"

"You want me to go?" Decebel took a step back, obviously caught off guard by her statement.

Yeah, well, that's what you get for being something that rhymes with stick, Jen thought angrily. "Can you not get that through your thick skull?" She threw his words back in his face.

Decebel felt like she had slapped him, and realized how his words must have made her feel.

"Jennifer..." He took a step towards her, his voice much gentler.

Jen held her hand up to hold him off. "Save it. I'm not ready to hear how you didn't mean to hurt me and blah blah, boo hoo. Okay? I just want to chill out before this thing tonight."

Jen walked to the door, pulled it open, and waited.

Decebel stood there for a moment, still completely shocked that she was kicking him out. Finally he shook his head and made to leave. As he walked through the door he heard her mutter, "It'd be nice if you could try not to pee around my door." Then she slammed it shut. Decebel heard the lock click in place.

Jen leaned her back against the door and slid to the floor. She drew her knees up and looked around the room. It was very elegantly done in candlelight and sage. It had a calming effect – well, when there wasn't a raging werewolf standing in the middle of it.

She closed her eyes as she leaned her head back. "Well, this has started out splendidly. Fall in one little lap and all goes to hell in a hand basket" she said to no one.

Jen jumped when there was a knock at her door. She rolled her eyes and growled, "Go away, fur ball. I told you I'm done."

"Jen, it's Cynthia. I think we need to talk."

Jen's eyes popped open and she stood up. "I think you read my mind."

Chapter 13

Thad answered the knock on his suite door and wasn't surprised to see his contact on the other side.

"You have news for me?"

"Can I please come in? I'd rather not be seen in the hall."

Thad stepped back so she could enter.

"I've decided that if someone spots us I will simply lead them to believe there might be a bond going on between us. That will explain any rendezvous." She shut the door behind her. "Now, Jen is under Decebel's protection and it's serious. Jen claims there are no mating signs but Decebel acts as if she is his mate."

"Well, you will just have to make sure to earn the Americans trust. That way when you finally lead them to their demise no one will be suspicious of them being with you. Does your sidekick suspect anything?"

"No."

"Good," Thad walked over to the wet bar and poured himself a drink. He didn't offer one to his guest. "I have a plan to get Vasile alone. I can't take the chance of Fane or Alina being there. I'm thinking that once the girls are out of the picture and Fane's mate is dead, I will give the appearance of wanting to help Vasile, gain more of his trust. Then it should be easy enough to take him out. It would make things easier if Jen and Decebel were bonded – take out one, the other falls. Got to love how the fates worked that one out."

Thad took a sip of his drink and, with a nod, dismissed the contact. "You know what I want you to do. Don't disappoint me."

"Yes, Alpha," she answered and turned to go.

Thad dialed his Beta as soon as the door closed. "Damion, report."

"Decebel's mated, no doubt. No male would react that strongly unless it was family or a mate."

"Hmm. Well, he might be easy enough to deal with. If Jen is suddenly missing, Decebel would probably remove himself from the equation," Thad thought out loud.

"What would you like me to do, Alpha?"

"Unfortunately you are going to, as the American's say, take one for the team. Continue to pursue Jen. Let's shake Vasile's Beta up a bit and keep him distracted."

"As you say," Damion responded and ended the call.

Thad checked his watch for the time and saw that it was getting close to the first gathering. He still needed to shower and dress.

"Planning the downfall of a pack is more time consuming than one might think." He chuckled to himself as he headed for the shower.

Fane ran his hand down Jacquelyn's back as she lay on her stomach on their bed.

"What's on your mind, love?" he asked her gently.

Jacquelyn let out a loud huff. "I just can't believe the way Decebel lost it back there."

Fane laid down on his side next to her and propped himself up on one arm. He continued to rub her back, unable to keep from touching her at any opportunity. If anyone had told him being mated would be so indescribable, he would have said they were exaggerating, but truth be told Jacquelyn amazed him. Every day he felt more and more blessed at having her in his life.

"I don't see how he can deny anymore that she is his mate," Fane admitted. "A male would only respond that strongly to his mate being touched by another."

"I don't get it," Jacquelyn told him as she turned to look at him. "Why do y'all freak? It was an accident that she even landed in the dude's lap. Are wolves that insecure?"

Fane chuckled. "You forget, Luna, we are not human. I know it is hard to truly grasp but an animal lives in us, is a part of who and what we are. That part of us will always respond in its own nature. Natural wolves are very territorial. I think because we add our human emotions it just amplifies our wolf's traits. I wouldn't call it insecurity when we respond to another male touching our mate, more an issue of protection. You've seen the depths to which I will go to protect you."

"Very familiar, yes," she agreed with a grin.

"Well, for me it just makes sense that it's better to avoid the possibility of something happening to you. You can effectively do that by avoiding situations that open doors to those possibilities. If a male doesn't touch you, he doesn't have the opportunity to harm you."

Jacquelyn laughed at him. "I think that's a little overboard, wolf-man."

"You may, but that's why I'm Alpha."

Jacque's eyes widened. "Did you seriously just say that?" She sat up abruptly and pushed at his chest, putting him flat on his back. Jacque leaned over him. "Take it back," she growled, but still there was a hint of humor dancing in her emerald eyes.

"But I *am* Alpha," Fane told her, his brow drawn together.

"Maybe, but you implied that because of that you get to boss me around."

Fane ran the back of his fingers across her cheek. Jacque closed her eyes at the feel of his skin against hers. "As Alpha, I do get to give you orders,"

"Is that so?" she challenged, her eyes still closed, savoring the closeness between them.

"That's so." Fane switched to the more intimate way of communicating between them. *"And right now I'm ordering you to kiss your mate."*

Jacque's eyes popped open and, grinning wickedly, started to get up. Fane quickly wrapped an arm around her waist, drawing her down to his chest. "Where are you going?"

"You told me to kiss my mate," she answered. "I have to go find him, cuz my mate wouldn't be such a bossy butt."

"Bossy butt?" Fane laughed.

Jacque poked his chest. "Don't laugh at me or I'll bite you."

Fane drew her closer and leaned up to whisper in her ear. "Promise?"

"Geez, Jen's influence reaches further than I realized."

Fane stared into her eyes, a silent challenge, daring her to do as he ordered. She moved closer and leaned down as if to kiss him, but nipped him instead and tried to squirm away before he could retaliate. But his werewolf reflexes were faster. He flipped her on her back and quickly pressed his lips to hers. When he pulled back, Jacque was grinning.

"What?" His eyes narrowed.

"*You* kissed *me,* oh great Alpha." Jacque laughed. "I win."

Fane groaned. "Why do I have this sense of dread that this is a foreshadowing of our very long life to come?"

"And you will love every minute of it."

Fane stood and pulled her up as well. "I will more than love it, Luna," he agreed impenitently. "Now, we must get ready and then go gather up Sally and Jen."

"Sounds like a plan, Stan," Jacque chimed.

"Who is this Stan?"

Jacque laughed. "We have really got to work on your lingo."

"Work away, my love."

"So, let me see if I'm catching what you're throwing." Jen sat up a little straighter as she faced Cynthia and tried to wrap her brain around what the good doctor was telling her. "According to this Alpha from way back, in order for the mating signs to become apparent there has to be some sort of catalyst?"

"Pretty much," Cynthia answered.

"Huh, who knew?" Jen's eyebrows rose as she considered her options.

"The problem is, and I don't know if he has talked with you about it, but Decebel is reluctant to push it."

"Well, if by talk you mean cornered me in the hall and tactfully told me he couldn't kiss me because, and I quote, 'it's not that simple, Jen,' then sure, he talked to me." Jen rolled her eyes at the memory of Decebel's words.

"What is it with men and their inability to commit?" Cynthia wondered out loud.

"I don't know that it's their inability to commit so much as they're just scared witless."

"Witless?" Cynthia smiled.

"Yeah, I'm trying to clean up my potty mouth."

"How's that going for you?" Cynthia teased.

"It's painful, but necessary." Jen winked at her. "Well, I don't really know what I can do about the B-man. I'm not saying I don't want to look into it because there is obviously something there – it's practically beating us both over the head. At the same time I can't make him do anything. Freaking stubborn flea infested punk."

Cynthia stood up from where she had been perched on Jen's bed. "You better get ready for tonight. All your bags have already been put in your closet, and the pack paid for some extra nice clothes for you to wear as well."

"How'd they know my size?"

"That's what nosy friends are for, Jen." Cynthia grinned as she headed for the door. "My advice to you, dormant – when a dominant won't do the necessary thing because other things in his life have made him leery, it may be necessary to force his hand."

Jen cocked her head to the side. "That has potential for disaster written all over it, doc." Jen smiled. "I like it!"

Cynthia laughed as she pulled the door closed behind her.

Jen headed for the closet and she started humming. She realized as she stepped into the closet that she was humming Katy Perry's "ET". She shook her head, trying to dislodge the song. "Yaaaa, no, don't need to go there." And even alone she blushed at the memory of the pictures Sally had showed her from that utterly embarrassing morning. Thankfully Decebel had yet to bring it up, and Jen definitely would not be opening that particular can of *"what the hell was I thinking."*

She started flipping through the clothes that had been hung by whoever had drawn that particular straw. She had to smile. Jacque and Sally had definitely had their grubby little paws all up in this little endeavor. It was apparent that they were dressing her to either make Decebel pant like the wolf he was, or to drive him insane with jealousy. This was going to be fun indeed…probably the understatement of the century as far as Jen was concerned. She grabbed an outfit and headed towards the bathroom. This time she was humming Natasha Bedingfield's "Strip Me".

"I'm so messed up in the head." Jen laughed out loud.

Dillon Jacobs stood with his pack on the far left side of the large gathering room. He had yet to talk with Jacque because he wanted to let her get settled in. Then word had gotten around that Decebel had attacked Thad's Beta, so he had gone and talked with Vasile, who assured him things were most certainly out of control. Not the answer Dillon had been hoping for, but Vasile said it was a necessary evil. Dillon responded by saying the Americans were rubbing their pension for drama off on his pack. Vasile had simply laughed him off.

Dillon had decided that he better warn his wolves to be on alert for any retaliation from Thad's pack. His next warning had been for the unmated males of his pack, and had gone something like, "And for goodness' sakes, stay the hell away from Jennifer Adams. She's the blonde flirty one. If she heads your way, I had better see you running for the hills like your life depends on it. Because, frankly, it does." Of course, his more dominant wolves had seen this as a challenge and asked why, if Decebel and Jen weren't mated, did they not get to see if she was a potential mate for one of them? Dillon had calmly but firmly explained that Decebel was, in his own right, strong enough and dominant enough to be an Alpha of his own pack. Out of loyalty to Vasile he served him. In other words, he would wipe the floor with their hides if he felt challenged. Dillon did not come all the way to Romania to witness a bloodbath, and he certainly hadn't brought his mate to put her in harm's way.

Back in the present, Dillon felt arms slip around him from behind, bringing a smile to his face. He turned to look into his mate's eyes.

"How you hanging in there, Alpha mine?" Tanya asked him.

"I'm just ready for this week to be done. Preferably without loss of limbs or life."

Tanya smiled. "Such an optimist. Is Jacque just the same?"

"Sickeningly so." Dillon chuckled. "She really is a positive person. You're going to like her."

Tanya sighed. "The pertinent question is, will she like me?"

"Mate, what's not to like?"

Tanya laughed at her mate's teasing, thankful that he was beginning to loosen up a bit. She suddenly stiffened in his arms and Dillon turned his head to see what had caught her attention. The Romanian Pack had arrived and Jacque had just spotted them. He watched as she smiled and waved. He read her lips as she mouthed, "I'll come visit shortly." Dillon nodded and turned back to his mate.

"She said she will be over shortly, so you have a small reprieve to fret and worry some more, my love." Dillon grunted when Tanya retaliated by poking him in his ribs.

He saw the three other Alphas who had been involved with organizing The Gathering and decided it was time to take their seats.

He indicated towards the table that had been assigned to them. "Shall we?"

"Don't suppose we can bail out now?" Tanya asked, only half joking.

"Nope, I'm afraid we have dug our graves and now must get coffins measured for us."

"There you go again, ever the optimist." Tanya took the seat he pulled out for her and watched as the rest of their pack followed suit, ready to hear what the night's activities would be.

Chapter 14

Victor, Alpha of the Bulgaria pack, stood at the front of the room. Raising his voice so everyone could hear, he announced, "If everyone would please take their seats so we can get started. The quicker we get the business over with the sooner we eat."

A group of males at a table to his left all beat on the table and gave loud whoops at the mention of food.

Victor motioned for them to quiet down and waited a few more moments to allow everyone to get seated.

Jen went to reach for her chair at the table that had a sign in the center with elegant script that said *Romanian Grey Wolves Pack*. Before she could pull it, another hand reached past her and quickly slid the chair out.

"Allow me."

Jen turned abruptly, caught off guard by Damion's sudden appearance.

"I'm sorry, Jen. I did not mean to start you."

Jen couldn't help the grin. "You mean startle me."

"Oh. Um, yes. Startle you," Damion repeated. He backed up just a step and, without shame, looked her up and down.

Well, Jen thought, *let's not be shy then*. She knew what he saw. The black top she picked out was off the shoulder on one side, so one arm and half her back was left completely bare. It was encrusted with crystal rhinestones, which began at the top and continued on down, growing sparser as they went. The other arm was sleeved and came to her hand at a point and had a loophole for her middle finger to slip in. Her hair was up in a twist, beset by crystal rhinestone dangly earrings. She wore her, and her best friends', signature low-rise Lucky Brand jeans and there was a hint of flesh revealed when she moved. Black, high heel boots completed her ensemble.

"You look stunning," he told her as he took her by the hand and lifted it to turn her in a circle. "Let me get the whole effect."

Jen couldn't stop the blush that she knew was rising clear from her bare shoulder to the tips of her ears. When she was facing him again Damion grinned, and it was one of those easygoing grins that you can't help but smile back at. So she did.

Then, as if just remembering what he was doing, he motioned to her chair,. "Please, have a seat. I just wanted to come by and make sure you were okay after this afternoon's -" he paused, and Jen beat him to it.

"Disaster?" she offered.

"Exactly. Your Beta was very upset."

Jen snorted. "Understatement. I'm fine. No matter his temper, B would never hurt me."

"B?"

"Yeah. It's not for what you might think, although I am tempted at times. B for Beta," Jen told him with a wink.

Damion grinned and pushed her chair in as she sat down. He leaned over her shoulder, too close for her comfort. "Save me a dance tonight, won't you?"

Jen was so tense at his nearness that she finally just nodded to get him to move back. He straightened up and walked away just as Decebel arrived.

"What did *he* want?" he asked Jen, then looked at her for the first time. His eyes glowed immediately. *Score one for the little man*, Jen thought. Decebel recovered quickly. "What are you wearing?"

"Let's deal with both of these absurd questions one at a time, fur ball, because they each deserve equal amounts of grief. First, Damion asked me to marry him and have his babies. Lots and lots of babies," Jen told him with a completely straight face.

Sally nearly choked on the gum she'd been chewing and Costin, who was standing next to Decebel, began to cough.

Decebel growled.

"I'm considering it," Jen addressed Sally. "I mean, what do you think, Sal? It's not like I've had any other offers and who knows if I will ever find my true mate. Gosh, if I can even have a true mate, that is."

Sally was trying desperately to keep a straight face. "Well, you don't want to rush these things, Jen. After all, you are only eighteen."

Jen tapped her chin as if to really think about it. "That is true. But if I hook up with Damion now, just think of all the little flea catchers we could make together. Think about how some would have my blonde hair and his – OWWWW!" Jen yelled.

Her head snapped around to look at who had pinched her. To her utter surprise it was Alina, and there was a gleam in her eyes Jen had never seen.

"Jen, tone it down just a little, okay?" Jen knew this was her Luna speaking, not Fane's mother. It was her first glimpse at Alina really putting her foot down.

Jen nodded and turned to look at Decebel. The smug look on his face erased all chance of toning it down. "And second, I'm wearing what was hung in my closet. Which was bought and paid for by this pack, and I look awesome. So unless the words that are fixing to come out of your mouth are, *Jen, you look awesome,* or *Daaang girl, you are hot* – I would even accept, *I like your shirt, Jen* – unless it's along those lines, I strongly suggest you just keep that muzzle of yours closed."

She turned back towards the table, looking anywhere but at Decebel, who had taken a seat next to her. She could feel the anger pulsing from him; it was nearly tangible. She wondered if anyone else was picking up his vibes as strongly. *Whatever*, she thought, *I'm done dealing with him for today*. Jen decided right then that she was going to have fun tonight, and that was that.

Jen maneuvered to look at the front of the room along with everyone else, when a tall, lean man began to speak.

"On behalf of the other Alphas who helped arrange this historic meeting, I want to say thank you to everyone for coming. My name is Victor. I am Alpha to the Bulgaria Pack. My mate is Adrianna." He indicated a tall slender woman who stood briefly from her seat and gave a small wave.

"As your Alphas have told you, the purpose of this Gathering is to allow unmated Canis lupis the opportunity to meet others whom they otherwise might have never met. Let's face it, the odds are stacked against us when it comes to finding our true mates. Some have been looking for centuries, to no avail. It is our sincerest hope that many of you will indeed find your true mates among those here." Victor paused as another man walked up to the front. "I want to introduce you to Thad. He is the Alpha to the Serbia Pack, and the mastermind behind The Gathering."

Thad thanked Victor and turned to address the room.

"We understand that we took a risk in bringing so many unmated males and putting them in such a confined area with females. Rest assured we have taken measures to protect everyone and those who do fight will request a proper challenge. The challenges made will not be to the death, but to submission. We did not come here to lose pack members. Make no mistake, there will be severe consequences for those who do not control themselves and their wolf." Thad looked over to Victor's mate and motioned for her to join him. "Now I will turn it over to our event coordinator, Adrianna."

The tall she-wolf made her way to the front and Jen noticed how graceful she was as she walked, so feminine. She was very pretty with long, dark chocolate hair, thin lips, and big brown eyes.

Jen realized she was able to see Adrianna way too well for the distance at which she was sitting. *This is getting weirder and weirder*, she thought. *Going to have to have another chat with Cynthia.*

"Tonight will be one of three nights that we meet as a complete group. On the other nights, each pack will have its own meal in a designated location. If you are so blessed and meet your true mate and want to have a dinner alone, you may request one via the drop box at the entrance to this room. Simply write your request, the time you wish to eat, and where. It will be arranged.

Now, your Alphas have each been given an itinerary with your specific schedule on it. Please follow the schedule. We have arranged it so that every female and male will have a chance to meet in one of the group settings. If this seems a little too planned for you, I will tell you there is a method to our madness. You see, an idle, unmated male werewolf is a potential problem. So we have attempted to avoid the problem altogether by ensuring there is something for you all to do at all times. If you are not having a group activity then you will be with your pack.

Tonight's festivities are simple – we will dine together as one big family. Then the room will be cleared for dancing and mingling.

Those are all the announcements for now, so without further adieu, dinner is served." As she announced dinner, women and men carrying trays of food were suddenly bustling about the room, setting down dishes and drinks on tables.

Jen looked over at Sally. "I'm having serious Hogwarts deja vu."

"I'm so with you."

The room settled down into quiet murmurs as people began filling their plates with food. As Jen reached for the salad bowl at the same time Decebel did, their hands touched. Jen jerked hers away so fast that she dropped the bowl. Thanks to werewolf reflexes, Decebel caught it before it spilled all over the table. Jen never even looked his direction. She was angry. So angry, in fact, that she didn't understand why she was sitting next to him.

She looked at Sally and waited until she caught her eye. Then she motioned between them with a small hand movement. Sally knew Jen very well and understood instantly what she wanted.

Sally nodded "okay," because she also knew that Jen was a major hothead. She might do something she would regret if she continued to sit next to Decebel while obviously angry with him.

Jen stood up and grabbed her plate. Decebel started to say something, but Alina once again stepped in. She placed a hand on Decebel, drawing his attention, and simply shook her head. Decebel growled but let Jen pass without engaging her.

Sally stood as well and walked around, swapping chairs with Jen.

"So, how does everyone like their rooms?" Jacque asked, trying to smooth over the tense moment.

"Our room's great. Isn't it, Mariana?" Crina piped in.

Mariana nodded and swallowed the bite she had just taken before she answered, "Oh, definitely great."

"Excellent," Jacque said awkwardly.

The rest of the meal was carried out in near silence with only minute amounts of small talk here and there. When the plates were cleared from the tables they were all directed to stand on the edges of the room while most of the tables were folded up and removed with most of the chairs.

Jacque grabbed Fane's hand and looked at Jen and Sally. "I've got to run over and say hi to Dillon and meet his mate."

"You want us to come?" Jen asked.

Jacque shook her head. "No, I got this." This was something she needed to do on her own…well, on her own with Fane.

She found them in the same corner they had occupied earlier, standing and watching just as the Romanian pack had been.

"Hey, Jacque." Dillon's face brightened as he pulled her into an awkward hug.

"Hi, um, Dad," Jacque fumbled.

Jacque's hand tightened on Fane's as Dillon pulled his mate over to his side.

"Easy, love. You don't have to be besties," Fane soothed through their bond.

"Did you just say besties?" she asked incredulously.

"Luna, I'm surrounded by three teenage girls. What do you really expect?"

"Huh, guess I shouldn't be surprised." She shrugged inwardly.

Fane chuckled.

Jacque brought her attention back to her father and his mate when Dillon introduced Tanya.

"Jacque, this is Tanya Jacobs, my mate and Luna of our pack."

Jacque smiled with what she hoped was a friendly smile. "It's nice to meet you, Tanya."

Tanya's smile was warm and genuine. "Dillon has told me a lot about you,"

"Don't believe everything, it's not nearly as bad as it sounds," Jacque joked.

They all laughed, albeit a bit nervously.

"Well, it looks like they're going to have some dancing so we won't keep you, but I hope that we can get to know one another," Tanya told her.

"That sounds nice," Jacque said truthfully. "I'm sure we can have lunch or something."

"Great," Tanya responded with another warm smile.

Jacque and Fane headed back to where their pack waited.

"Well, that wasn't as bad as you thought, was it?" Fane asked as he wrapped an arm around her waist and pulled her close.

"She was nicer than I expected," she admitted.

"You want me there when you have lunch with her?"

Jacque grinned up at him. "Always my protector."

Fane's face grew serious. "Always, love."

Once the room had been arranged so that there was room to dance, they watched as a new table was rolled in with stereo equipment on it.

"We're fixing to jam." Crina smiled.

"What exactly do you think they are going to let us jam to?" Sally asked.

Jen caught Costin's eye and waved him over. She wasn't taking chances with the music. "Hey, see if they will let you provide the music," she told him.

"I didn't bring any music, Jen."

Jen held up her iPhone, shaking it from side to side. "Gotcha covered, my furry friend."

Costin winced at the nickname, but smiled as he took her phone. "I'll hook us up." They both laughed at him using the slang she had taught them earlier that day, when all hell broke loose. *Who knew teaching slang to foreign werewolves could be detrimental to your health?* Jen shrugged to herself.

"So, ladies." Jen turned towards the group of girls spreading her arms wide, and in one of those amazing moments when things line up perfectly, she said, "Let's dance," just as the music started pounding through the subs. Jen grinned. "Yeah, I'm that good."

Sally and Crina were the first to step up. Crina took off onto the open floor, arms in the air, body moving to the beat as Jason Derulo's voice blasted through the speakers. Sally squealed, "I love this song!" and headed to the dance floor, swinging her hips. Jen gave a short nod to Jacque, who kissed Fane and then headed towards her.

"Mariana." Jen motioned. "Come on, chick, we're going to bring the house down."

Mariana laughed. "Alright, you're on."

All three girls headed to where Sally and Crina were dancing and more guys and girls joined in.

They all danced and laughed and danced some more. Jen couldn't remember when she'd had so much fun. Costin turned out to be an amazing dancer and was nearly always in the middle of the bunch, breaking it down.

The next song came on and Jen froze. Sally and Jacque's heads snapped around as Katy Perry's voice filled the room – to be specific, Katy Perry's "ET" filled the room. Jen's two best friends looked at her as they, too, stopped moving. Everyone else was still swaying with the beat like a sea tossing with the wind. Jen watched as Sally and Jacque's eyes got wider and wider.

"Damn," Jen muttered under her breath just as strong arms came around her and she felt warm breath against her neck.

"I believe this is our song," Decebel purred in her ear. Jen swore at any moment she was going to be a puddle on the floor and Jacque would have to sop her up with some Bounty paper towels. Why she thought specifically of Bounty paper towels, she had no idea. She was trying really hard to focus on anything but Decebel's warmth against her. To her complete mortification he began to move…with the beat. Sally and Jacque's jaws dropped.

Jen mouthed, "Save me," to her two best friends, but evil traitors that they were, they both started dancing and completely ignored her plea. *Oh, those two heifers are going down,* she promised herself.

After a few moments, Jen decided she could either look goofy standing stiff while Decebel danced or she could throw caution to the wind and bring it.

Mind made up, Jen turned in his arms and began to sway with the music. She smiled to herself; she always liked throwing caution to the wind. She raised her arms in the air as she swayed and moved. Decebel had his hands on her hips, moving with her, and being the gentleman that he was, he left room between their bodies. Which, Jen kept telling herself, she was glad about it…until she looked over and saw the wolf-princess and her fur ball dancing close, very close. *Stupid mated, married ginger,* she thought, but chuckled all the same at how happy Jacque and Fane were. When the song ended Decebel stopped, but didn't let go of her.

They stood like that, looking at each other. Jen had no idea how long they would have continued it but Damion showed up, requesting that dance he had asked her to save. As Decebel reluctantly stepped away Jen thought, *Well, if we just sort of dance together but not touch, it should be okay.* Yeah, that idea flew out the door, nearly smacking her in the face on its way, when a slow song came on. She groaned inwardly, and groaned again when she realized what song it was. "Fall for You," by Second Hand Serenade.

Damion pulled her quickly into his arms as Decebel backed away, never turning or taking his eyes off of them.

Jen finally pulled her eyes away from Decebel when Damion spoke.

"You're an amazing dancer."

Jen smiled, hoping it looked genuine. "Thanks. I love to dance. To just let go and lose yourself in the music," she was rambling. Well, anyone would ramble if they were in the arms of a werewolf while the werewolf you wanted to be with stared daggers at you. *Who am I kidding?* Jen thought. *No one else is dealing with wanting a werewolf. Nope, other girls my age are swooning after the jocks, or the artsy guys who play in bands, normal guys.*

She looked over at Decebel again when Damion turned them. She watched his strong jaw tense and his chest flex as he crossed his arms. *But who wants normal when you can have that?* She grinned at her thoughts. That smile was wiped off her face quickly as Jen watched another female walk up to Decebel. She was standing much too close for Jen's liking. Just then, Damion turned them again and she lost them briefly. When she had them in her sights again she watched as Decebel led the girl by the hand to the dance floor. Jen was beginning to see red. She hadn't realized she'd stopped dancing until Damion spoke.

"Jen, are you alright?

Jen couldn't take her eyes off of Decebel as she watched him take the brunette in his arms. She felt like she had been punched in the stomach. She was trying to breathe but she couldn't seem to get any air in.

"Jen?" Damion's voice was beginning to sound worried.

"Damion, what's wrong?" Jen heard Sally's voice but still could not respond. Decebel must have felt her stare because his head snapped up and their eyes locked. Jen didn't want him to see her jealousy or the hurt inside at seeing another in his arms. She knew she didn't have a right to be mad. She had been dancing with a guy, after all, but that didn't matter at the moment. Her better judgment was out on a coffee break.

"Jen!" Jacque snapped her fingers in front of her face.

Sally followed Jen's stare and shook her head. "This is not good, Jacque, so not good."

Finally Jen pulled her eyes away from the offending sight.

"I think I'm going to call it a night."

"Jen, don't let him ruin your evening," Jacque pleaded.

"I'm not, Jac, really. I'm just tired." Jen's excuse was weak at best, but there was no way she could stay here and watch Decebel dance with other girls. *Nope, not happening,* she told herself. Before her friends or Damion could stop her, she turned and quickly left the dance floor, making a beeline for the exit.

Chapter 15

Decebel watched as Jennifer left the dance floor at a brisk walk. It was obvious to him that she really wanted to sprint but was trying to be inconspicuous, and failing miserably. He stepped away from Sasha, the female who had asked him to dance.

"I'm sorry, Sasha, but I need to be excused." Decebel turned before she could say anything in return.

He was cut off from following Jennifer when Sally and Jacque stepped in front of him, hands on their hips and eyes narrowed. They were not happy with him.

"I need to speak with her," he told them, knowing they'd watched the whole scene on the dance floor.

"Why?" Sally challenged, and it made Decebel's wolf perk up. "So you can tell her how you don't want to pursue these feelings between you? So you can flirt with her only to tell her you aren't interested? So you can tell her not to look elsewhere even though you don't want her!" Sally was fuming by the end of her speech.

"I WANT HER!" Decebel growled. Everyone around them got quiet and Decebel realized his canines had lowered. He took several deep breaths and pulled himself together.

Fane walked up and looked at Decebel and then the girls. "I think we should step out." He motioned towards the door and all of them filed out.

Once in the entry way Decebel turned to Sally. "I apologize for raising my voice at you, I just -" Decebel didn't want to bare his soul to Sally or Jacque or Fane. He wanted Jennifer. He wanted to tell *her* that she nearly ripped his heart out when she looked at him like he had betrayed her when he took Sasha in his arms. He wanted to tell her that his skin crawled at the contact of another and it took everything in him not to push Sasha away. He wanted to make her understand that he was going mad seeing her touching other males. But there were no mating signs. The Alphas would consider them unmated and that made them both fair game.

Most Alphas did not allow pack members to fraternize with someone who was not a true mate. They saw it as purposeless. So their argument would be that if he and Jen pursued each other with no signs that they were true mates then they might be keeping the other from meeting their mate.

Decebel hadn't been at The Gathering for twelve hours and already he knew he wouldn't be able to do this.

"Decebel, maybe you should just give her some time," Jacque was telling him, pulling him from his thoughts. But he knew that if he left Jennifer to think on this all night she would not cool off. No, he had to talk to her. Now.

"I'm sorry, Jacque, but I have to disagree. She needs to hear what I have to say." Decebel walked around the baffled Jacque, and past Fane and Sally. He took the stairs two at a time, moving silently towards Jennifer's room.

He didn't really know what he was going to say to her. All he knew was that somehow he had to smooth this over. He arrived at her door and didn't bother knocking, he figured she was used to it by now and loved to see the spark in her eyes when she got irritated with him about it.

However, when Decebel stepped into her room Jennifer was nowhere to be seen. He walked over to her closet and gently knocked on it, there was no response. He pulled the door open to find it full of clothes, ones that even at first glance he could tell he wasn't going to like her wearing out in public, but Jennifer was not there. He stepped back and debated on whether he should wait or go looking for her. He decided he was going to go look for her when her door opened and in she walked.

They both froze when their eyes met, and Decebel swore his heart was going to beat out of his chest.

"Dec," she began.

"Come take a walk with me," Decebel interrupted her and surprised himself by his invitation at the same time.

"What?" she asked, clearly confused by his request.

"Please." Decebel took a step towards her. He thought it a good sign that she didn't take a step back, so he continued to move towards her.

When he reached her side he gently took her arm and tucked it into his.

They walked in silence, neither really knowing where to begin. Decebel led her to the indoor garden room that he was sure she didn't know anything about, but felt she would really like. He opened the door and gestured for her to enter. He wasn't disappointed by her response.

Jen stepped into the room as Decebel held the door for her. She didn't know why she had accepted his invitation to walk with him. *Yeah, Jen. Just keep lying to yourself if it helps you sleep better at night,* she chided herself.

Jen couldn't help the breath that escaped her lungs as she entered what felt like a whole other world. There were plants everywhere – tall plants full of big leaves, small plants with delicate flowers blooming in every color you could imagine. There was even grass, thick, plush dark green grass. There was a pebbled path that wound through the indoor garden and she lost sight of it as the vegetation swallowed it up. She continued on down the path, curious as to where it would lead. She could feel Decebel's eyes on her from behind as he followed her but she didn't bother to look back at him. Jen felt like a kid in a candy store. Her head turned from side to side, trying to absorb every little thing. She saw that along the right side of the garden a small brook bubbled and water flowed gently down over rocks and plants. She came around a curve and there in the center was a gazebo with a swing hanging in the center of it. There were deep green vines growing all around the gazebo, holding it like a lover's embrace.

She followed the path to the steps of the gazebo and climbed them. Finally she turned and faced Decebel as she sat down on the swing. Decebel slowly climbed the stairs and the look in his eyes made Jen feel like prey. She shivered and noticed his lips quirk up ever so slightly. *Cocky fur-ball,* she growled inwardly.

He sat down on the swing and the next words out of his mouth took her breath away.

"I want you."

Jen stopped breathing. Not by choice, she just couldn't. It was like his words had flipped a switch in her and everything that required her brain to run just shut off.

"Jennifer." Her name on his lips, the intensity in his voice had her looking up at him. "Breathe, Jennifer."

"I don't understand, Decebel."

"I don't either," he admitted. "I'm sorry if my dancing with Sasha hurt you."

Jen's mouth tensed at the name of the other female on his lips.

"I don't have any right to be hurt." Jen tried to act like she didn't care but then decided she wasn't going to do this. She wasn't going to play games, not with Decebel. "Okay, it hurt." She angled her body so that she was more fully facing him. "In my mind I know that it shouldn't matter who you dance with. In my mind I get that I have no claim on you, okay? Honestly, I do. But damn if my heart could care less what my mind is telling it." Jen knew she was running the risk of sounding like a needy girl, but it was day one of hell week and if they were going to make it to day seven in one piece, then it was time to lay it on the line. She started to continue but Decebel stopped her with a finger to her lips.

"I need you to know this because when you see me touching, dancing, or talking to another girl, I need you to remind yourself that I've told you – I want *you.*" Decebel paused and took a breath. He had decided during the walk from her room to the garden that he was just going to be honest, no more holding back, no more trying to deal. He was too old to leave things to chance and regardless of his fears he knew that he wouldn't leave Jennifer's safety in the hands of another, "Despite how we feel towards one another, the Alphas are looking for mating signs. The closest thing we have to that is the strong pull we both feel and the way you smell."

Jen jerked. "I smell?"

Decebel chuckled. "Not bad, I assure you." He sounded slightly disappointed by this fact.

"You want me to smell bad?" Her brow furrowed. She really didn't know where he was going with this.

Decebel leaned towards her and pressed his nose to the flesh of her neck and took a deep breath. Chill bumps broke out all over Jen's skin and she was trying, mildly unsuccessfully, not to hyperventilate at his close proximity.

"You're scent is intoxicating to me," Decebel growled as he drew away from her reluctantly. "Mates have a certain scent that they only smell on one another. I only just noticed that your scent changed, became stronger. Do I have a scent to you?" Decebel asked curiously.

Jen could have stopped the blush that seeped into her cheeks about as well as she could stop a freight train with her bare hands.

"Woodsy and spicy," she admitted.

Decebel looked thoughtful. "Hmm, interesting."

"So you're saying the Alphas won't allow us to opt out of The Gathering just because of our attraction to one another?" She asked.

"Right." Decebel leaned back against the swing and draped his arm over the edge. His eyes were drawn to Jennifer's bare back and his mind couldn't help but imagine his markings on her beautiful, pale skin. Before he knew what he was doing he was tracing a pattern on her back gently with the tip of his finger.

Jen froze as she felt Decebel's warm finger tip on her back. *He's trying to kill me,* she decided. *He figures if he just tortures me to death then I'll be out of the picture and poof, problem solved...although death by Decebel doesn't sound too bad at the moment.* Jen snorted at her thoughts, but thankfully Decebel didn't stop the swirling stroke of his finger.

"So what I'm telling you, Jennifer," Decebel's voice was deep and raspy, "is that I want to see where this goes between us. I want to get to know you better and spend time with you. But we are both going to have to endure the other being in the company of more than one suitor. As it is, we have both demonstrated that it is more than difficult for us."

Jen closed her eyes. The combination of his deep voice and finger making swirly patterns on her back was pure torture. Exquisite, perfect, wonderful torture. She heard his words but couldn't bring herself to acknowledge them at the moment.

"Jennifer?" Her name was nearly a whisper on his lips.

"Hmm?" Her head lulled around on her neck until she had swung it around to look back at him. "If you want me to be able to hold any semblance of an intelligent conversation with you then you are going to have to quit that."

Decebel's smile was as wicked as any she herself had dished out to him. "Quit what, micul meu lup?" he asked as he continued to touch her.

Jen growled and jumped up. She turned to look at him, but she wasn't angry. "So what do we do?"

"I think you Americans call it hooking up." Decebel raised one eyebrow at Jennifer.

"Do you really want to go there again?" she teased. "It would be more like hanging out, B. Hooking up tends to imply a more physical involvement, if you catch my meaning."

"Consider it caught." He winked, which only succeeded in causing her heart to nearly stop.

I have got it bad, Jen thought to herself.

"So we just hang, talk, and see what happens?" she asked him as she leaned back against a post on the gazebo.

"Sounds about right." Decebel stood and walked up to her. He left a little space in between them. A little more would have been better for Jen's comfort but she tried to act as if it didn't bother her.

"I'm going to ask something of you, Jennifer," he told her seriously.

"I'm listening." Jen tilted her chin up and gave him her full attention.

"My wolf is not coping well with the idea of others near you, touching you. *I* realize that there is no getting around it, but *he* doesn't. For all intents and purposes he has claimed you, mating signs be damned,"

Jen's breath caught at his declaration.

"So what I'm asking is, for lack of a better term, reassurance in your -" Decebel searched for the right word. Jennifer beat him to it, as she often did.

"Intentions, interest, attraction?" Jen grinned, she tended to go overboard on the vocabulary when she was nervous, which she was. Nervous, that is.

"All of the above."

"Okay. So I scratch your back, you scratch mine, right?"

Decebel's head cocked to the side as he drew even closer. Jen realized that she had unleashed a monster with her unabashed flirting. The question was no longer could he handle what she dished, but would she survive what he poured out on her? If she were honest with herself she would say she didn't yet know the answer to that question. *But where's the fun in being honest with myself?*

"I take that this saying means that you will need the same reassurance from me." Decebel placed his hands on her hips and pulled her away from the post and close to him. Jen gasped as her hands came up to his chest. Her breathing quickened and she watched his eyes follow her movement as she licked her lips.

Is he going to kiss me? Am I ready for him to kiss me? Jen laughed at that question. *Has Joan Rivers had enough plastic surgery to qualify as a plastic figurine? Enough said.*

"I wish the answer to that was no," she told him. "I don't like being the clingy, insecure chick."

Decebel chuckled and she felt the rumble vibrate through her hands clear to her soul.

"You are anything but clingy and insecure, Jennifer. Mysterious, confident, playful, beautiful, too sexy for your own good? Definitely. But never clingy or insecure."

"Are you trying to rack up brownie points, wolf?"

"Is it working?"

"I'll never admit it." She winked at him.

He squeezed her hips one time with his strong hands and looked into her eyes. "You will not doubt at any moment my intentions or interest in you. Are we clear?"

"Crystal," she said absently as she watched his amber eyes begin to glow. It took everything in her not to grab the front of his shirt and pull his lips to hers. Decebel must have seen it written all over her face. He lifted one eyebrow in a silent challenge. She wouldn't be the one to make the first move, not with her wolf. Decebel chuckled, and much to her disappointment dropped his hands and stepped back.

"I suppose I should escort you back to your room," he told her as he once again tucked her hand into his arm and began walking down the steps.

Jen grinned. "You don't want to go back and dance?"

Decebel looked at her from the corner of his eye. "I think we've both endured enough for the night. Don't you, *micul meu lup?*"

"Oh, come on, B. Surely you aren't one to run away from a little excitement?" she taunted.

"Being close to you is quite enough excitement for me, I assure you."

Jen blushed. *Okay, that is just going to have to stop. I am not some fainting violet,* she growled in her mind.

Decebel chuckled as if he could hear her inner monologue. The crazy thing was that she wanted him to hear her inner dialogue as bad as she wanted him to finally pull her to him and kiss her senseless. *Oh, how the mighty have fallen,* Jen laughed at herself.

Decebel dropped her off at her door, but before he left he pulled her to him, wrapping her up in a snug embrace. He tucked his head into her neck and took a deep breath. She let out a contented sigh. If this was what Jacque experienced when Fane held her, she didn't know how she ever let him let her go.

"Are you planning on taking a shower tonight?" he asked her, taking her completely off guard.

"Moving a little fast, aren't we?"

Decebel actually blushed. "I'm being selfish and a little underhanded, actually," he explained.

"And what does me taking a shower have to do with it?"

"Have you noticed how much Fane touches Jacque? Especially before they were bonded?"

"How could we not? They were attached at the hip. Well, when she wasn't being fought over or abducted, that is."

"Remember, we aren't human, Jennifer. When I touch you, because there is a certain amount of attraction between us, and because my wolf has claimed you, I leave my scent on you. It's kind of like a calling card to other males. I hugged you that close to put as much of my scent on you as possible without," he cleared his throat before finishing, "getting more physical."

Jen made an "ahh" motion with her mouth. Then her head cocked to the side. "Do I leave a scent on you?"

Decebel grinned. "Like my own personal perfume," he teased.

"So you want to know if I'm going to take a shower because it will wash your scent off?"

"That's correct."

"I really would like to," she admitted reluctantly, because truth be told she liked the idea of having Decebel's scent surrounding her.

Decebel released her. He placed two fingers under her chin and lifted her face to look at him. "Then I will come see you early before we go down for breakfast. We can't be seen as being overly interested in one another. Although Vasile understands, the other Alphas do not."

"Gotchya. So I'll see you in the morning, then?"

Decebel nodded. "Sleep well, Jennifer," he told her as he raised his hand and gently ran his thumb across her lips, almost as if he were imagining what they would feel like if he kissed her. She wanted to dare him to find out but instead she smirked. *Fat chance, that.*

Decebel smiled as he left her staring after him like a love struck teenager. "That's what you are, dummy," she muttered as she turned and went into her room.

Sally and Jacque were lounging on her bed. No surprise there.

"Spill the goods, Jen. Where have you been and why do you have that goofy ass grin nearly splitting your face open?" Jacque quipped.

Chapter 16

Jen spun in a circle. "I'm basking in the glow. Don't ruin my buzz."

Sally sat up. "You've been with Decebel," she accused.

"Been working on your sleuthing, Watson?" Jen asked with raised eyebrows.

"Not really. There's just nothing, or anyone, who could make you look so smitten."

Jen began undressing, not even caring that she had company. She was the immodest one and they were used to it.

"Decebel told me he wants me and that his wolf has claimed me as his mate," she threw out there without any warning.

This time it was Jacque who sat up abruptly. "Just like that? No *'hey, want to see a movie?'* or *'I'm thinking we might have some intense mojo going on'*? Just bam," Jacque smacked her hands together, "you're my mate?"

Jen grabbed a pair of boxers and t-shirt. She figured she wasn't going to get a shower until she spilled every detail to these two – not that she hadn't once demanded the same of Jacque.

"I think we both just don't want to play any games. Well, not ones that are going to hurt us. You know I'm still going to make him work for it, but at least we both know where we stand."

"So what else did he say?" Sally asked eagerly.

Jen proceeded to go over – verbatim, she might add – her and Decebel's conversation. Jacque and Sally hung on every word.

"So did he kiss you?" Jacque asked.

"No," Jen's face fell, " he put his hands on my hips and pulled me close. And bloody hell, Jacque, you could have helped a sister out and prepared me."

Jacque grinned. "It's good, isn't it?"

Jen smiled wistfully. "Better than eating Godiva chocolate and watching Johnny Depp and Brad Pitt while taking a hot bubble bath. Which, yes, I have done…all of the above…at the same time."

Sally laughed, "Only you would chance putting a television so near a bathtub."

"We all have our vices, Sal," Jen said unrepentantly.

"So the verdict is basically y'all are going to pursue this behind the Alphas' backs." Jacque more stated than asked.

"I just love a good scandal." Jen beamed.

"Especially when you're right in the middle," Sally added.

"Don't you know it." Jen stood up from the chair she had been occupying while she recapped her evening. "Oh, one more thing," she added absently as she headed towards her bathroom to shower, "He told me he wanted his scent on me. So he's coming by in the morning early before breakfast."

"Shut. Up," Jacque sputtered.

"And how exactly is he going to accomplish this, Jennifer Adams?" Sally's motherly tone was sharp. Jen found it quite amusing when Sally got all protective.

"Why Sally, how dare you." Jen laid on the thickest southern belle accent she could. "You imply that I would allow that wolf to put his paws on me."

"Oh, honey, I'll do more than imply it," Sally retorted.

"Then you know me better than I thought." Jen winked.

"Jennifer!" Sally said, outraged. "I thought you wanted to wait."

"Oh chillax, Polly Prude. All he's going to do is hug me. Geez, here I thought my mind was the only one that lived in the gutter. I didn't realize you were looking for real estate, Sal."

Jacque jumped up off the bed. "Alright. Well, don't do anything I would do." Jacque winked. "Of course, I'm licensed to,"

This time Sally yelled Jacque's name. "What is with you two?"

"We've got to get you a man, Sally," Jen threw out as she shut the bathroom door.

"I don't need a man," Sally growled. "I have my hands full enough as it is with you two."

"Well, maybe it's time you got your hands full of something else," Jen yelled through the door. They heard the rush of the shower starting.

Jacque cackled. "Nice."

Sally followed Jacque out of the room, and Jacque laughed more as she heard Sally mutter under her breath, "I'll show you need a man. Puuuhlease, you two need your mouths washed out with soap, or better yet bleach. No, no, actually. Bleach *and* soap."

Jen emerged from the bathroom, clean and completely de-Decebeled, to a knock at her door. She told the little part in her that hoped it was said wolf to pipe down.

She opened the door to find Crina and Marianna standing outside her door.

"Hey ladies, what's up?" Jen asked and stepped back so they could enter.

"Hope it isn't too late to come by," Marianna told her as they walked in.

"I'm a night owl, so no worries."

"Marianna and I were bored," Crina started.

"Translation," Marianna interrupted, "Crina's bored. I'm dragged along."

Jen grinned.

"So we were thinking, you know how tomorrow we're supposed to go to the gym to learn self defense from the Serbia pack males?"

"Yeah," Jen said, already interested in a possible scheme – oh, how she loved schemes.

"There will be another group of females there as well, so I figure they'll probably introduce our packs. I – well, we," Crina said, looking at Marianna, who just snorted at her, "were thinking how funny it would be if when they introduce our pack we did some sort of cheer or dance or something. Like what you Americans do for your sports teams."

"You're wanting to stick it to the man. I'm totally digging it."

"Sticking what to what man?"

"It's just a saying, when you want to rebel against authority."
Marianna nodded.

"You realize Vasile will be upset about this, right?" Jen asked.

Crina gave a very Jen-like smile. "Never stopped us before."

"Nice." Jen smirked.

"For the record I'm usually the innocent bystander," Marianna added, but winked at Jen afterward.

"Uh huh, sure you are. Okay, so let's do this." Jen paused. "Um, where are we going to do this exactly?"

"The gym. It was empty when Marianna and I checked on our way here," Crina told her.

"Lead the way, Thelma."

"Who's Thelma?"

Jen shook her head. "I can see a major movie night is in order."

The girls made it to the gym without encountering anyone, for which they were grateful.

"So Jen, were you a cheerleader in school?" Marianna asked.

"No, I was usually one of the ones making fun of the cheerleaders. But I'm really good at rhyming and songs, so I'll come up with the cheer. Crina, I saw your moves on the dance floor. You and Marianna put together some moves, okay?"

They nodded and got to work.

An hour later, Jen had composed a complete cheer and Crina was perfecting the dance moves to go along with it.

"Alright, let's do it from the top," Crina told them.

They each got in their designated spots and on Jen's count, they started.

"Shimmy, shimmy, shake, shake,
We know you want some, of this cake.
Shimmy, shimmy, bye, bye,
Still others want, some of the pie.

Careful boys don't get too near,
It's not our Alphas you should fear.

Grubby, Grubby, paws, paws
You know you want to, break some laws.
Double, Double, dog dare,
You pant and growl, while you stare.

Sorry but, we're not that easy.
Turn around, if you want sleazy.

Get it, get it, Got it, Got it,
Too bad you can't, get up on it.

Wolf, wolf, big, bad,
Turn us down and we'll be mad.

We may be fine, and smokin' hot,
But gentle she-wolves we are not.

Run, run, male, male,
We know you want some of this tail.
Hit it, hit it, tap it, tap it,
You could not find it, if we mapped it.

We told you once, now that's twice,
We don't play fair, we don't do nice.

Growl, growl, drool, drool,
No pups with us, you silly fool.
Watch us, watch us, run, run,
Try to catch us, if you're that dumb.

You can look, maybe even touch,
We promise not to hurt you much.

Boys, boys, don't run away,
We've more games we want to play.
Challenge, Challenge, Fights, Fights,
Who will get, my Blood Rites.

We know you each, have a plan,
Catch us, catch us, if you can."

The girls were panting by the time they finished. They actually all had a pretty hard time keeping a straight face as they pulled off the moves. Jen was cracking herself up with her lyrics.

As the girls continued to practice, changing up different moves to make it flow better, they were completely clueless to the gathering audience outside the gym doors. A couple males from the Serbia pack had been coming to work out in the gym when they heard the girls' cheer. They stopped to look in before they entered and were surprised to see three of the unmated females from the Romanian pack.

"We really should leave," one of the males said as he continued to watch.

"Yeah, we should," his pack mate answered.

There was a pause.

"Go get some of the other guys. Oh, and grab my phone. Let's get this on video."

Decebel lay in his bed after reluctantly taking a shower. He hadn't wanted to wash Jennifer's scent from his skin. But he took solace in knowing that he would see her, touch her again in the morning.

After he dropped her off at her room he had gone to the workout room and ran off some of the adrenaline flowing through his veins after having been in such close proximity to Jennifer. He had to admit that he felt lighter, more in control now that they had talked and put all their cards on the table. He was relieved to hear that Jennifer felt as strongly towards him as he did her. Sometimes he wasn't sure. It felt so strange to him to feel insecure and worried that a female wouldn't like him. He grinned to himself. She did like him. A lot.

The issue hadn't really changed. He was still going to have to deal with other wolves showing interest in her. But it made him feel better knowing that she wasn't interested in them. That in her heart, it was him. He figured maybe he should be worried that she would indeed find her true mate among the other packs, but truthfully, regardless of the lack of mating signs, Decebel would bet his life that Jennifer Adams was his true mate.

There it is, he thought. *I'm admitting it and accepting it – better than that, I'm embracing it.* Decebel felt his wolf settle down for the first time in months. Finally, man and wolf were in harmony again.

Just as he began to close his eyes and drift off there was pounding on his door. Urgent pounding, not just an average knock. Decebel was at the door in one bound.

Costin was on the other side, looking a little nervous.

"What's going on, Costin?"

"Beta, it's 11.30. Do you know where your female is?"

Decebel might have appreciated the little joke, but Costin was referring to Jennifer, and implying she wasn't where he had left her.

"Tell me." Decebel's voice was a knife.

Costin's eyes widened and he started talking very fast. "I was going to the gym to work out and when I got down there I saw a bunch of the males from other packs looking in the gym windows. I heard voices, cheering female voices. When I got close enough to see...well, there was Jen, Crina, and Marianna."

Decebel pushed past Costin and was trying hard not to run. He needed to calm himself before he got there.

"What exactly are they doing?" he asked as Costin tried to keep up with his Beta.

Costin hesitated, but the cutting look Decebel sent him loosened his tongue. "They're doing some sort of cheer and dance," he said vaguely.

"Do I want to know what she's wearing?"

"Probably not."

"Bloody hell."

Costin remained silent the rest of the way.

Decebel heard snickers and male voices as he rounded the same corner Costin had only minutes before. He walked right up and the wolves parted like the red sea.

They all stared at Decebel, waiting for him to come unglued. Instead he plucked the phone from the nearest wolf, then looked at them all with glowing eyes.

"If you have been recording this you have five seconds to delete it."

There was sudden movement all around as buttons were pushed on phones.

"If I hear that any of you have not deleted it and are showing it to others, I will call you out, I will challenge you, and you will lose."

Decebel met the eyes of the wolves and each dropped theirs quickly.

"Are we clear?"

"Yes, Beta," they said in unison. The power coming off Decebel was raw and strong. It took even the more dominant wolves effort to not collapse under it.

"Good. Now go before I decide that I don't care about keeping the peace between our packs."

The wolves were nearly all gone before he had even finished speaking. *Smart wolves,* he thought.

Before Decebel opened the gym door, he looked at the phone he had taken and pushed the play button on the video. Decebel's eyes grew wider with every word, every hip gyration, every bend, every come hither look he watched his mate perform. After standing in shock for a moment, he pressed the delete button and handed Costin the phone.

"When I open this door, Costin, I want you to escort Marianna and Crina to their rooms. You are to stay outside their doors the remainder of the night."

"Yes, Beta," Costin complied.

Decebel reached for the gym door. He took a deep breath and told his wolf to cool it, but he knew his eyes still glowed.

"Okay, this will be the last time," Jen panted, it had been a while since she'd gotten this much exercise. "Then I think we can call it a night."

"I'm pretty sure the night has been called."

The three girls froze at the sound of the voice behind them.

"Crap, crap, crap," Jen muttered to herself.

"Crina, Marianna." Decebel's voice was not harsh, but firm. He meant business. "Costin will escort you to your room. Do not leave it until it's time for breakfast in the morning."

Neither girl spoke as they walked towards Costin.

Crina looked up as she passed Jen and mouthed, "Sorry."

Jen gave a shrug, then took a deep breath and turned to face her Beta.

"Fancy meeting you here," she flirted.

The look in his eyes said that wasn't going to work. One thing Jen was quickly learning about Decebel – his emotions very rarely ruled him. With her, they occasionally broke free of their cage. And in times like this, when he'd decided he was right and that she was going to obey, nothing could sway him.

"I distinctly remember dropping you off at your room, Jennifer,"

"Well...I wasn't really tired and Crina and Marianna said they wanted to get some exercise, so -"

"Why is it that you did not procure an escort to the gym? Why exactly did you think it a good idea to prance around in your sleep attire without any sort of protection in a mansion full of unmated male wolves?" Decebel took slow, measured steps towards her as he spoke. "Please tell me, because I know there has to be an earth-shattering reason for why you did something so haphazard and dangerous."

"Did you just use the word procure?" Jen asked incredulously, the hint of a smirk across her lips.

"Jennifer." Decebel's voice was deathly low.

Jen unconsciously took a step back at the glowing eyes boring into hers. "It's not a big deal, B. Nobody came in while we were in here. I don't see why you're giving me grief."

Decebel chuckled. It was not a good sound.

"Not a big deal. Right. Well, maybe you can explain why I just had to run twenty wolves away from those doors. Who, I might add, were recording your little performance on their phones. So tell me again how it's not a big deal." Decebel was once again moving towards her.

Jen continued to back up until the backs of her legs hit the foldaway bleachers. She nearly fell back on her butt, but caught herself with one hand. Irritated with her clumsiness and the slight fear she felt at being stalked by Decebel and his eerie calm, she reverted back to the "gives a rats ass" Jen. Call it a defense mechanism, but it helped her keep her cool.

"Only twenty?" she asked as she cocked her hip to the side and propped her hand on it. "I would've thought that little dance would pull in quite a bit more." She made a show of looking thoughtful, tapping her chin with her finger. "Hmm, maybe we needed a bit more hip action. Although, I don't think we were giving it our best. It'll definitely be better when we do it for real."

Decebel growled and took a final step closer. They were less than a foot apart. Jen still had her hand propped on her hip, but now she was having to lean back a bit to look up at his nearly painfully gorgeous face.

"I hate to be the one to break it to you, baby, but you will not be performing *that* little number for anyone. Ever."

Jen's eyes narrowed. "I have a feeling one day I'll change your mind about that. By the way, don't think that calling me baby will help you get away with being a pushy, furry dictator."

"Look, I know girls don't understand how guys' brains work." He actually looked bashful as he continued. "I'm over a century old and my brain still works that way. Guys don't just see hot chicks doing a hot dance."

"What else could they possibly see?" Jen asked, revealing just how innocent she was despite all her big talk.

"When you dance like that, and look at them like you were...they – we," he corrected, "see it as an invitation."

Jen couldn't stop the disbelieving laugh that emerged. "Man, you guys really are messed up in the head if that's what you get from a dance and cheer that's actually insulting towards unmated males. Which, if they listened to the words, they would understand."

Decebel grabbed her hand and tugged her to him. He wrapped his arms around her and inhaled her scent deep into his lungs.

"You already stand out with your beautiful blonde hair, long legs, and stunning eyes. Could you please not draw more attention to yourself?" he pleaded.

"You left out one of my best attributes," Jen began but Decebel cut her off.

"Jennifer." His voice was a growl.

Jen laughed. "You just outed yourself, wolf."

Decebel couldn't stop the grin that spread across his face. Only she could calm him and make him forget he was even angry.

"I'm going to take you back to your room and I want you to stay there until I come for you in the morning."

Jen stepped out of the shelter of his arms. She rolled her eyes. "Fine, geez. Always cramping my style."

Decebel walked her back to her room. Right before she went inside, he stopped her with a hand on her arm. He leaned in close and Jen's breathing quickened. He skimmed his nose against her neck, causing a shudder to ripple through Jen's body. He pulled back and said the last thing Jen ever expected.

"As much as I hate for you to take another shower now that you bear my scent, it would be best. Apparently your little dance made you hot."

Jen grinned wickedly. "If it got me hot, it most certainly got you -"

Decebel laid a finger against her lips. He shook his head, letting her know he knew exactly what she'd been about to say.

"Keeping your words in check is becoming a full time job," he teased. She stuck her tongue out in response, bringing a chuckle from him. "Sleep well," he told her as he turned to go.

Jen blushed heatedly as she began to push the door to her room open, but before he got too far she muttered, "Wouldn't be such a hard job if my mouth were busy with other things." She knew with his wolf hearing he would hear her.

Decebel didn't turn around. "Look forward to scenting – I mean *seeing* you in the morning, Jennifer."

Jen quickly closed the door. Grinning as she leaned back, she said out loud, "You are seriously poking the beast, Jen. And if I were a betting girl I would say you want to get bit." She laughed breathlessly. "That about sums it up, Sherlock." She shook her head and once again headed for the shower.

Cynthia's head rose at the sudden knocking on her door. She looked at her watch and wondered who would visit her at midnight. She got up and opened the door to find Sally on the other side.

"Sally." Cynthia didn't hide the surprise in her voice. "Is everything alright?"

"Yes," Sally said initially, but quickly recanted. "Well, honestly, I don't know. Can I talk to you for a minute? I realize it's late." She couldn't stop wringing her hands and shifting from one foot to the other.

The girl's behavior did not go unnoticed by the doctor.

"Sure. Come on in." Sally scuttled through the door and Cynthia shut it softly. "So, what brings you here at this hour?" she asked, though not unkindly.

"It's about Jen and Decebel..." Sally started.

"Ah, yes. The celebrities of the ball," Cynthia joked.

Sally smiled. "You can always count on Jen to either make an entrance or an exit. One of them will always be epic."

Cynthia waited patiently for Sally to continue.

"After Jen left the dance, Decebel followed her and they talked."

"Only talked?" Cynthia's eyebrows lifted as she leaned forward.

Sally nodded. "Yeah, there was no funny business. Contrary to her appearance and big talk, Jen actually has high standards when it comes to being physical in a relationship."

Cynthia had to admit she was surprised. Jen's mouth often suggested otherwise.

"When Jen came back to her room, Jacque and I were waiting for her. We wanted to make sure she was okay, ya know?" Sally continued to fidget with her hands as she spoke. "Jen said that Decebel just came out with everything."

Cynthia sat up abruptly. "What do you mean 'everything'?"

"He told her he wanted her and that his wolf had claimed her as his mate. Of course, we all saw it a mile away, but I'm just wondering what would've made him change his mind about pursuing it so quickly."

Cynthia crossed her legs as she leaned back and watched Sally. It was obvious that the girl really cared for Jen, and even Decebel. *How good it must be to have that kind of friendship,* she thought. "Well, there could be a couple of reasons for his abrupt change of heart. I know that Alina and Vasile have tried to impress upon you all the differences between Canis lupis males and human males, as well as dominant Canis lupis males from non-dominant."

Sally nodded.

"Because of that, I will try not to be too redundant. So the dominant male is controlling, obsessive, protective, fiercely loyal, extremely intense, and very, very possessive. Sometimes these traits are an absolute inconvenience and frankly, a pain in the – well, you get my drift. There are other times, however, that these are necessary traits in our world. These qualities can be the difference between life and death in some situations." Cynthia paused, gathering her thoughts. "I will tell you that, at times, a dominant male might seem a bit bipolar in personality because they can switch at the drop of a hat. They are conditioned to think quickly and under pressure, to make snap decisions for the good of the pack and those they love. So what they think might be the right thing to do one minute can be nullified in the next by a change in circumstances or players on the field. With me so far?" she asked.

"Yeah. I'm beginning to see how those things could have made Decebel decide he needed to get over this fear of not being able to protect Jen."

"Exactly," Cynthia agreed. "Tonight Decebel saw how the game was going to play out, so to speak. I think he realized even more how intensely he feels towards Jen. He hasn't had to compete for her attention until now. Decebel is intelligent, he is very strong, and at his core an Alpha. Being an Alpha takes all the traits I mentioned to the extreme. Personality also can make them react more strongly. Decebel's personality is much more intense than Fane's. He is an observer, not a talker. Tonight I would bet that he realized what his limit was in regards to not pursuing Jen, and he reached it. When he saw another wolf show considerable interest in her whatever was holding him back snapped."

Sally rubbed her face, obviously tired, but she wouldn't leave just yet. She wanted to try to understand the dynamics between Jen and Decebel. Something in her felt compelled to watch out for them.

"I know that was a long explanation, and I think probably the correct one. But there is a second possibility as to why Decebel changed his mind about his relationship with Jen. Decebel came to me today and told me Jen's scent has changed to him. He said he was sure it was the mating scent."

Sally's brow furrowed. "Oh, yeah. I remember Fane explaining the different mating signs – scent was one of them."

"Her scent might have finally pushed his wolf over the edge, allowing him to take control from Decebel, even if briefly. I really think that because Jen's a dormant the mating signs are just going to require an increase in emotional attachment and, even more annoying, patience. Simply being patient to let nature do its thing. It's almost as if her wolf needs to be awoken."

"Good analogy, doc." Sally smiled tiredly. "Okay. Well, I just wanted to get your take on the situation. But one more thing – do you think Decebel will change his mind?" Sally's voice took on a sharp, serious tone. "Cynthia, Jen – strong, capable Jen – would not handle it well if Decebel walked away from her. Not after his declaration tonight."

"There is one thing a wolf cannot change – his feelings towards his mate. If Decebel has accepted that his wolf has claimed Jen, if he has accepted that sometimes the wolf in us is much more perceptive than we are, and he is choosing to trust that, then there is no going back. Decebel couldn't walk away from Jen even if, by some miracle beyond miracles, he wanted to. Not only that, but it goes against every fiber of his being to cause Jen such pain, physically or emotionally. His wolf would never stand for it. Decebel is over a century old, Sally. He knew all that when he decided to really pursue Jen. I can assure you he did not go into this lightly."

Sally nodded and took a deep breath, letting it out slowly. "Okay, that makes me feel better. Jen is one of those people who, once she commits, once she declares that you are hers, she goes all in with her whole heart. Jen would take a bullet for Jacque and me without a thought. She dragged Jacque out of that burning car, not caring if she made it out alive. So I just wanted to make sure Decebel understood that since he's given Jen the green light to claim him, he needs to be prepared to accept the consequences. Those consequences just happen to be called one very bossy, but also severely loyal, Jennifer Adams."

Once Sally left, Cynthia sat back on her bed and recapped their conversation. She wasn't really surprised that Decebel had made his move. Not after what she and everyone else had witnessed tonight. Cynthia decided it would be important that she try and keep up with any changes they experienced, especially Jen since she wasn't full Canis lupis. She knew Decebel wouldn't like the idea. He would consider it as prying on something very private, but this was important and could help future dormant relationships.

Chapter 17

Jen sat on her bed as she slipped on shoes. She'd decided on a comfortable, yet flattering outfit. It definitely had to be comfortable since self defense class was today. So she donned black yoga pants, a blue long sleeved tee, and her Nikes. Standing in front of the mirror, she examined the result and grinned. *Not too shabby.*

Jen wasn't really vain, but she did appreciate the attributes God had given her. Long, shapely legs, a small waist, and a large bust. Admittedly she was glad for being ample in that area, but there was the annoying problem of guys often talking to her chest instead of her face. Sometimes she thought they really expected them to respond, seriously. She had long, thick blonde hair – although blonde wouldn't have been her first pick – and bright blue eyes. She was often mistaken for a dumb blonde, but sometimes it was better to let people underestimate her.

Jen glanced at the clock on her phone and took a deep breath. Decebel would be here any minute, or at least he should be. Unfortunately there was that tiny voice – that most of the time she was able to tell, *"bite me"* – trying to tell her that he'd probably changed his mind. He'd probably lain in bed last night cursing himself for reacting in the heat of the moment and making a commitment that was beyond what he wanted.

He wouldn't do that, she told the voice.

Are you positive? it responded.

Jen shook her head. *What the – I'm arguing with my subconscious. Stop, Jennifer. Just stop.* She took a couple deep breaths and felt a little more grounded. "Okay, I got this. No problem," she said to the empty room…then nearly jumped out of her skin when there was a knock at the door. "Yeah, you are all over it, Wonder Woman," she muttered sarcastically as she went to open the door.

She held her breath as she pulled it open. No matter how she tried to prepare herself, she was always affected by his presence –

the sheer size of him, the level of intensity always in his amber eyes when he looked at her. Okay, so "affected" was putting it mildly.

They both stood there looking at each other. Jen got the distinct feeling that he too had expected her to bail. Decebel was going to learn that Jen didn't bail. Once she was in, she was in for the long haul.

"Can I come in?" Decebel finally asked, breaking the intense moment.

"Oh, yeah. Sorry," Jen fumbled. And then, as he walked into her room she realized it.

"You knocked," she said. The words almost sounded like an accusation instead of an observation.

Decebel turned to look at her, a small grin on his ruggedly handsome face, "Are you disappointed?"

"Yes. No. I mean, it just caught me off guard," she finally admitted. Although she had given Decebel a hard time about the knocking, she found now that she'd felt special. *Yes, you heard right*, she thought. Ridiculous as it sounded, him barging in made her feel like he just couldn't wait to see her, or check on her. The urgency in him every time he just waltzed in uninvited was a rush of adrenaline to her. She hoped he couldn't see through the poker face she had perfected – *not*.

"I don't like knocking," Decebel told her, sounding like the dominant he was. "I shouldn't have to knock on *your* door."

Jen felt a smile threatening to morph her face. "You shouldn't have to?" It didn't go unnoticed by her that he'd just given her a way to maintain her pride but still get what she wanted. *Smart wolf.* "If that's how you feel, then why did you?" she challenged.

"I thought I would try it out, see if I liked the fit." He cocked an eyebrow at her.

"You were test driving the knocking concept." Jen kept a straight face as she spoke. She felt very proud of herself for that.

"That's a good way to put it," he agreed. "I'm returning it to the dealership. I wasn't impressed with the outcome."

Jen laughed. "The outcome? So you didn't like how I answered the door?"

Decebel chuckled with her. "I prefer the annoyed look you give me when I come in uninvited."

"Well, I suppose on your next entrance you will get full compensation for having wasted your time on an unsuccessful test drive. I will be sure to be doubly annoyed."

Decebel grinned at her playfulness. It was that grin that made Jen realize that only with her did he ever look like that. Only with her did he let down the hard outer exterior.

"You're the only one who makes me feel like this," Decebel told her, having once again guessed correctly at the direction of her thoughts.

"Tell me again why we need to have that mental connection thing, because you already know what I'm thinking most of the time."

"Your face is very expressive. I would never choose you as a poker partner." Decebel laughed at the glare she sent his way. But his wolf was pacing inside, tired of the bantering, ready to move onto the scent marking. His eyes must have started to glow because she swallowed hard.

"I'm sure your partners in crime will be arriving any minute. Come here, Jennifer," Decebel's voice was a growl. He was trying to tone down the possessive gleam in his eyes, but judging how she looked like she was ready to bolt, he was unsuccessful.

"I would never hurt you," he tried to reassure her.

Jen mentally slapped herself at her reaction to Decebel's possessive demeanor. *It's Decebel, dimwit,* she admonished. *He would die before he hurt you.* Sufficiently scolded, she pulled her shoulders back confidently and walked over to stand in front of him.

Jen knew this was probably the only time he would touch her today, and she was going to savor it and burn it into her memory. Once they were out of her room, under the scrutiny of the Alphas, they wouldn't be able to show serious interest in one another. It was bad enough that they'd already brought attention to themselves to the extent at which they had in less than twenty four hours. You would never be able to accuse Jen or Decebel of being subtle – it definitely wasn't either one's middle name.

He gently wrapped his large hand around the nape of Jennifer's neck. He watched in fascination as her eyes fluttered closed, as if she relished the feel of his skin on hers. He pulled her close. Her arms wrapped around him and she laid her head on his chest as if she had done it a thousand times. Decebel growled deeply, his wolf was basking in his mate's touch.

Mate, Decebel thought. Every fiber in him said she was, and yet a small part of him still worried that the lack of mating signs was confirmation that she did not belong to him. He felt a howl of rage welling up in his throat at the thought of her being another's. He had to get a leash on his wolf.

He laid his cheek against the top of her head and blew gently into her hair. Jennifer shuddered in his arms, making him pull her tighter. After standing that way for what felt like seconds, although he knew it was longer, he pulled back enough to lean down and placed his nose on her neck, the sensitive place where it met her shoulder. He took a deep breath and again blew out gently. This time Jennifer's knee's nearly buckled and had his arms not been around her, she probably would've fallen to the floor.

Decebel smiled to himself as he continued to breathe close to her neck. It was taking every ounce of control left in him to keep from biting her, even just nipping her. Showing her where she would wear his mark. He kissed her neck gently and when he heard a breathy moan come from her, he quickly stepped away. He kept his hands on her arms until he knew she was steady on her feet.

Jen stood there, dazed as Decebel abruptly stepped away from her. *Did I do something wrong?* she wondered. She looked at Decebel and saw that his breathing had quickened. His jaw was tense and his eyes were brighter than she had ever seen them.

"Are you okay?" she asked him tentatively, afraid she'd startle him.

"I just need a moment." His voice was rough.

"Did – did I do something wrong?" Jen stammered out her worry. She suddenly couldn't stop rubbing her hands down her pants. They weren't clammy or sweaty, but she felt like she needed to do something with them.

"No, beautiful. You didn't do anything wrong. You did, however, do something right. Very, very right." Decebel let out a deep breath as he ran his hands through his hair.

"Then what's wrong?" she asked, cocking her head to the side and folding her arms across her chest, effectively drawing Decebel's eyes to her now pushed up breasts.

Decebel's head snapped away just as quickly as his eyes had landed on her. He cleared his throat, unmistakably uncomfortable and embarrassed by his actions. Jen couldn't help the smile she felt inside at his obvious attraction to her. *Well, a girl likes to know,* she thought defensively.

"It's not that there is something wrong. It's just...well, you see..." Decebel was seriously flustered.

That's a first.

"I'm attracted to you," he finally blurted out.

"Well, I hope so," Jen shot back.

"I'm not saying that's bad, Jennifer. I'm saying it's intense and...when you make sounds like you just did -"

Jen's hand flew to her mouth. A muffled, "What sound?" came around her hand.

"The moan," he said matter of factly. "Baby, you can't make sounds like that. It's like handing a man an invitation to a banquet made just for him."

Although Jen heard all his words, she was stuck on the *"baby"* endearment.

"Did you just call me baby?" she asked him sweetly.

"Jennifer, did you hear what I said?"

"Yeah, but did you call me baby?"

Decebel stared at her and confusion filled his expression. "Yes. Is that a problem?"

Jen shook her head. "No, I kinda like it," she admitted shamelessly. "I just never pinned you for the *baby* type."

"I have a feeling there's quite a bit about me that will change because of you," he confessed.

"Huh. Well, I like it. Don't stop." She winked at him.

Decebel chuckled and shook his head, once again running his hands through his hair. "You're going to be the death of me, Jennifer Adams."

"So will I see you today?" she asked.

"Yes. I will be in all the groups you are in. It was arranged beforehand since I've been assigned to keep you safe."

"But is it safe? I mean, for you to be with me?"

Decebel didn't look at her when he answered. "For you."

Jen didn't respond and he walked back over to her. Reaching up, he stroked her cheek and promised, "I will try to keep it together."

"I don't like seeing you with anyone else either. I'll be trying to hold it together just as much as you."

"We are quite the pair, are we not?" he said, grinning.

Jen smiled back.

There was a knock at the door and Decebel automatically stepped in front of Jen. She pushed around him.

"Chillax, wolf. It's probably the girls."

Decebel followed close behind and before she could open the door, asked, "Who is it?"

They both heard giggles on the other side. Jen rolled her eyes and pulled the door open. Jacque, Sally, Crina, and Marianna all stopped and wiped the grins off their faces.

"Ladies." Jen eyeballed them sternly.

"Jen, I would like it noted that I did not participate in the giggling." Fane spoke from behind the pack of hyenas at Jen's door.

"Noted, fur ball," Jen acknowledged.

Jacque smiled sweetly. "We came to see if you were ready to go down for breakfast."

"Yeah, sure ya did." Jen felt Decebel's hand on her lower back and she relaxed, allowing her annoyance to fade. "Let's do this," she relented with a smile.

"Let's get our grub on, ladies," Jacque spouted as the group headed downstairs.

"Jacque, I thought we discussed not using that saying," Jen reminded her.

"No," Jacque responded. "You talked about me not using it and I ignored you."

"Good to know you value my opinion," Jen muttered.

"Most ardently, Jen." Jacque's response brought a snort from Jen.

The room they were to eat in was much smaller than the large ballroom they had been in the night before, but it was every bit as nice.

They all took their seats and Jacque sat on Jen's left side and Sally on her right. When Jacque noticed that Decebel sat across from Jen, not beside her, she looked at Jen, brow furrowed. Her eyes plainly said, *"What gives?"*

Jen leaned over and whispered close to Jacque's ear. "We have to keep things on the DL."

"Got it."

Vasile and Alina soon arrived and the other pack members slowly ambled in. Jen nodded at Cynthia when she showed up. She'd apparently arrived late last night after all the drama. Jen guessed that she and Decebel were going to have to fill her in on what they'd decided last night.

Dorin and Cami arrived and smiled at Jen. She returned with a smile of her own and watched as Anton and Delia acknowledged her. Once the entire pack was present, Vasile motioned for the meal to be served.

Breakfast consisted of ham, bacon, some sort of bread that was supposed to be a biscuit, eggs, and pancakes if you wanted them. Most of it was spent in silence as everyone concentrated on eating.

Vasile finally addressed them. "Each of you knows what you are to do today. Represent us well." His eyes landed on Decebel and Jen tried really hard not to snicker. Jacque, Sally, Crina, and Marianna weren't so successful. Decebel glowered at them and they immediately shut up.

"I don't really understand the point of these activities," Crina said, adding quotations when to *activities*. "I mean come on, Alpha. The TFFs are going to be working on self defense with the males from the *Serbia* pack. What is that?"

"The TFFs?" Vasile asked before addressing her question.

"Yeah, as in The Fabulous Five." She motioned to herself, Sally, Jen, Jacque, and Marianna.

Decebel, Fane, Costin, and even Sorin coughed their laughs into their hands. Crina shot them a look that promised retribution if they didn't cease and desist.

Vasile smiled at the name she'd derived for the group, and at the friendship that had grown. It meant that there was camaraderie, which was vital to a healthy pack. He knew that a pack with vehement females carrying petty jealousies could be ripped apart.

"Crina, as silly or ridiculous as it seems, these activities are designed to keep from having idle wolves with nothing to focus on but beating the competition for a mate. We can't very well stick you all in a room and allow the males free reign."

"Talk about a 'mate fest'," Jen joked.

Sally and Jacque grinned.

"I so did not need that visual, Jen," Sally admonished although the smile never left her face.

"Oh, come on. You know you all were thinking it," Jen whined.

Costin smiled and winked at her. "Guilty as charged."

Decebel shook his head at the young wolf. *Was I ever that goofy?* he asked himself, then answered his own question. *No, definitely not.*

Vasile continued, ignoring the banter among them. "The point today is that you will get to meet other males but your time will also be put to good use. You all need to learn self defense and we've killed two birds with one stone."

When no one else objected, he went on. "If you are so blessed to find your true mate, I would ask that you come speak with Alina and I immediately. This setting is quite different from ours, and the pair will be required to prove their mate status."

"What kind of proof?" Decebel asked, an undercurrent of something very dangerous in his tone.

"The most obvious would be the markings." At Vasile's words, several of the unmated males – including Costin and Decebel – spoke up.

"You can't be serious," Decebel growled. "How dare the Alphas ask us to parade our mate in front of them like she's a piece of meat. And to ask to see what should be for her mate's eyes only – they cross the line, Alpha."

Alina touched her mate's arm and Vasile looked over. "You would never have allowed them to see my marks."

Vasile was silent as he observed the faces of his pack. The males were all tense, ready to react at a moment's notice. Even the mated males were appalled at the idea of anyone seeing a female's markings. He took a deep breath. This gathering was truly going to test his leadership and the loyalty of his pack.

"I'm not saying I agree with it, nor am I saying I would force you to comply. That is why I ask that you come to Alina and I first."

"Why can't they just have one tell what the other is thinking?" Marianna asked.

"Because they claim that the pair could simply plan beforehand what they would say, therefore making it appear that they have a mental connection when they do not," Vasile explained.

Sally raised her hand to speak. Vasile smiled at her warmly. "Sally, you have a question?"

"Um, yeah. Why would someone pretend to be true mates?"

"You know of our longevity. You have seen the extent some males would go to have a mate through what Jacque experienced." Vasile paused and Sally nodded her agreement.

"There are females who are just as desperate for a mate. There are some who think that if they both consent then they should be allowed to be together, regardless of the consequences. What they don't understand, or don't remember because they have been alone for so long, is that no one on this earth, human or Canis lupis can fill the hole inside them. No one, no matter how you may love them, can give you the other half of your soul. And should you choose to take one who is not your true mate and your true mate comes along, there is nothing that can stop you from going to them. You will walk away from any life you have built, children you have sired, and person you have married without so much as a glance back. It is our job as Alphas to protect our pack. As a parent guides his child, so an Alpha guides his pack. The Alphas that have brought us all together want to make sure that no one makes the mistake of thinking they can find what they are looking for in someone who does not truly belong to them. That is why they insist on proof."

The room was quiet when he finished speaking. Vasile knew that understanding the why of it didn't necessarily make it any easier to accept. His pack would just have to trust him.

Decebel looked across the table at Jennifer, imagining her with his markings. Then the thought of another seeing them. Quite simply that just wasn't going to happen. He would be dead before anyone saw Jennifer's back.

Feeling his eyes on her, Jen looked up and saw the intensity of Decebel's stare. She figured he was contemplating the idea of her bearing his marks and the possibility of someone else seeing them. She wasn't completely sure but she guessed that Decebel's answer was a big, fat "when hell freezes over." His eyes were glowing, his jaw tense. He'd crossed his arms across his chest and she could see his muscles flexing. Yep, pretty sure pigs would have to fly, hell would have to freeze, and George would have to sell his oceanfront property before another person saw her markings.

If they ever come, she thought solemnly.

"If no one else has anything to say..." Vasile waited. When no one spoke up he dismissed them.

Chapter 18

Jen sat in the gym with the rest of the TFF – she had to admit she loved Crina's designation of their little group. Dorin and Cami were on one side of the room and Anton and Delia were on the other. Their eyes roamed the gym constantly, waiting to see if any of the wolves would become a problem.

Jen had the feeling some of the mated males were itching for a fight and wouldn't mind if taking down a wolf or two. To the far right sat another group of unmated females. Some looked eager, eyes wide, scoping out the males on the floor. Others looked as if they'd just found out they were headed to the taxidermist.

Decebel and Fane were sitting a couple rows behind the TFF on the bleachers, scanning the crowd with equal concentration. Even with his eyes roaming over the room, Jen knew Decebel was acutely aware of her. He would know if she moved an inch from where she sat now. He would know if her breathing changed at all, or her heart rate increased. She smiled to herself, thinking how nice it was to have the one she had been pining for, how nice it was to have accepted this thing between them.

Marianna, who sat on Jen's left, nudged her and nodded in the direction of the doors. They watched as a man, a very large man, walked into the gym. He stopped in the very center and his presence immediately brought the room to silence. Jen looked closer and realized it was Skender. It was then that she realized she hadn't seen him or Boian since arriving at The Gathering.

That's odd, she thought.

"Did you notice Skender and Boian have been MIA since we arrived?" she asked, leaning over to Jacque.

Jacque nodded. "I hadn't thought about it 'til seeing him just now."

Jen watched as Jacque's face took on that weirdness it got when she talked to Fane through their bond. She thought, *Note to self: practice using bond while looking in the mirror.* That way she could make sure she kept a normal face when and if Decebel and she ever got to that.

"Fane says that Vasile has both of them leading a couple of the activities to help minimize the risk of Decebel getting in a situation where he could offend the other pack females."

"How could he offend them?" Jen asked.

"If he flat out refuses to participate with a female in a solo or group activity, it's considered a slap in the face."

Jen nodded as she turned and glanced up at the one who occupied her every thought. He was looking at her, as he often was when she looked at him. She smiled and the slight upward curve of his lips would not have been caught by just anybody. But Jen was learning his subtle expressions. In their current situation, he was trying to keep from holding up a sign that said: "I'm after Jennifer Adams," but at the same time he didn't want her to forget what he'd said.

He wanted her.

"Welcome Serbia pack," Skender announced. "My name is Skender and I'm a member of the Romanian pack. I will be leading today's lessons." Then, turning to the bleachers where the two female groups sat, he pointed to the right. "We welcome the females from the Bulgaria pack."

All of the guys clapped respectfully but their eyes were wild and eager.

"We also welcome the females from the Romanian pack."

Again the males clapped.

"That would have been the perfect entrance," Crina muttered, referring to the cheer that had been thoroughly shut down my Decebel.

Spoil sport, Jen growled inwardly at him.

"Today the males will be teaching self defense and some combat moves. The Alphas feel it is important that all members of the pack know how to defend themselves. Those of you who have already been training will be paired up with an advanced instructor." Skender looked past the TFFs and pointed again. "Decebel, why don't you and Crina come down and demonstrate some of the moves we will learn today."

As Decebel made his way down the bleachers, he walked right behind Jen and the other girls. As he passed her he ran a finger lightly on the nape of her neck, so quickly that nobody picked up on it. She smiled.

I want you. She heard his voice in her mind and wished it wasn't just a memory.

It was then that Jen really understood why Skender had been made leader. He knew that Jen would feel less threatened if Decebel sparred with one of the females from their pack. She was thankful for that, but knew it was only a brief reprieve because he was majorly advanced at fighting. He would be placed with a non-pack member at some point, but definitely never with Jen as she had as much self defense skill as she did in basket weaving. That would be a gigantic none.

The girls watched as Decebel and Crina made some impressive combat moves and then demonstrated some basic – what Jen considered "get the hell out of dodge" – moves. These were moves designed to disable an attacker long enough to book it to safety.

When the demonstration was done Skender started calling out names, announcing the pairs. He explained that every twenty minutes the females would rotate clockwise to spar with a different male.

Great, Jen thought. *It'sKarate Kid speed dating.*

She heard Decebel's and some girl's names called. She didn't even look to see who it was. She couldn't. Instead she started muttering, "I want you. I want you. I want you."

Jacque looked at Jen, shaking her head at her best friend's weird tactics. "Well, if you insist," Jacque responded. "Although, Fane might get a little jealous."

Jen shot her the finger.

"Why are you muttering that? You've gone from '*not an option*' to '*I want you.*' What gives?"

Jen looked at Jacque and Sally, who watched her questioningly. "He told me to remember, when he has to be with the other girls, that he wants me. I can't look at him with another girl. I wish it wasn't such a big deal but I've never been so screwed up over a guy."

"He's not just any guy," Jacque told her.

"Maybe," Jen said softly.

Sally smacked her leg. "Don't talk like that. It's obvious he's crazy about you, like certifiably. Trust him, Jen."

Jen nodded and her head snapped up as her name was called. She looked over to the mat Skender had indicated, where a tall guy was standing. He grinned at her and the look in his eyes made her feel like he was trying to see her soul. It made her feel naked and vulnerable, and there was only one wolf she was okay with making her feel like that.

She started down the bleachers. "This is going to suck."

Marianna gave her an encouraging smile. "Hang in there, dormant."

"Thanks, she-wolf." Jen tried to smile back, but it didn't reach her eyes.

Decebel watched as Jennifer walked over to the wolf she'd been paired with. He nearly snarled when he realized it was the guy he had taken the phone from last night. That pup had been recording the girls' dance. He ripped his eyes away, trying to get his wolf under control.

It didn't escape his notice that Jennifer hadn't looked at him a single time since he'd been paired with the short brunette in front of him. The girl smiled tentatively and Decebel had to force his lips to turn up. By the look on her face it didn't quite make it to a smile.

"Let's get this over with," he muttered as he stepped towards her. She looked ready to run, and as Decebel began to walk her through basic self defense moves he could feel her trembling. He wished he could bring himself to care enough to at least try to put her at ease, but it was taking every ounce of willpower for him to not go throw Jennifer over his shoulder and carry her off to perform the Bonding Ceremony.

His eyes kept straying towards her, and when Skender finally announced it was time to switch, he let out a slow breath. At least she was getting away from the wolf who'd been drooling over her last night. But as Decebel looked to see who was next in Jennifer's row, he realized they had almost all been there last night. They'd watched his mate sway her hips suggestively, things moving that would only lead a guy's mind in the wrong direction. The flirty, come hither look that had been plastered on her beautiful face... *Bloody hell, it's going to be a long day,* he thought as he turned to face the next female he didn't want to be near.

An hour and a half into the self defense training, Jen was feeling slightly encouraged. She'd finally allowed her eyes to land on Decebel. Each time he had been working with a girl it was painfully obvious he was trying to touch her as little as possible.

Jen wished she could say the same about the guys she had been working with. She felt like she was constantly having to steer clear of an accidental – yeah, right – grope or grab. She was just glad Decebel hadn't seen.

The guy she was now training with turned her around to teach a move that would disable an attacker pinning her from behind. Jen stood still as he wrapped an arm around what she thought was going to be her neck. He stepped even closer so that their bodies touched from his chest to her calves. But instead of her neck his arm wrapped over her chest, his hand not quite making under her arm. He basically had a handful of boob. So not good.

Jen would've overlooked it if the idiot hadn't squeezed. She gasped in shock and instantly heard a growl somewhere beyond her. She knew that growl.

The wolf who held her tightened his grip painfully and Jen tried pulling away from him, which only caused what felt like his claws to descend.

That's going to leave a mark, she thought.

The growl, Decebel's growl, turned into a snarl. Her head snapped up as she tried desperately to get out of the wolf's groping hands. She saw Decebel look at her, then at the hand that was planted on her chest.

Decebel phased, faster than she had ever seen a wolf phase, and launched himself across the room. Suddenly everything a flurry of movement. Jen was pulled from the offending wolf's arms and into Dorin's.

"Get her out of here now.," he told Cami. "And get the Alpha. He's the only one who can call Decebel down."

Cami nodded and turned to Delia. "Go get Sally and Jacque. Fane and the other guys are going to have to try to pull Decebel off the idiot."

Jen and Cami turned when she heard bodies slamming together. They froze. To their horror, the other guy had phased into a motley grey wolf and he and Decebel were circling each other. Decebel was much, much larger with a shiny grey pelt and four white paws.

They watched as Decebel snarled and snapped at the other wolf, trying to slip him up. Decebel got his chance when the wolf stumbled back just a little. Decebel took advantage of the mistake and launched himself forward. His teeth sunk into the smaller wolf's neck and in an amazing show of strength, Decebel raised the wolf upward and slammed him onto his side.

The other wolf struggled briefly before submitting. Decebel stepped back, releasing him. Had Jen not been scared witless, she would have laughed when he slapped the other wolf across the head, effectively knocking him unconscious.

Decebel raised his head and howled, and as if beyond their control, the other Romanian pack males howled with him.

Suddenly Jen felt a pressure fill the air that nearly drove her to her knees. The howls cut off. She watched as the full blooded wolves all knelt and a very, very pissed off Vasile thundered through the gym doors.

When Jen looked back at Decebel, she could see him struggling under the weight of his Alpha's power. A couple of times he stumbled, but continued. *Stupid barbarian.* She rolled her eyes and closed the rest of the distance between them.

 She shook her head. "What were you thinking?" Jen snarled, "Do you want them to separate us? Because that's what they're going to do if you can't keep it together."

She stopped talking when Vasile came up beside her. His eyes were glowing a deep blue. He snapped a hand out and someone placed a pair of sweat pants in it.

"Phase back." His voice was low, but no less commanding than a shout would have been. Decebel phased back and Jen quickly turned. When she no longer heard the ruffle of clothes, she turned back around to see Decebel's eyes on her, not Vasile.

"Are you all right?" he asked her.

Jen hesitated as she thought about how the wolf had grabbed her – violated her, even. She'd felt his claws pierce her skin... Deciding it was probably best for every person in the vicinity if she didn't mention that little tidbit, she lied – only a little. "I'm fine."

Vasile turned to Skender. "Please give the Alphas my apologies and let them know I will discipline my pack accordingly. We will take our leave until tonight's events."

Skender nodded

Vasile looked at the other members of his pack. One by one they dropped their eyes, baring their necks.

"Pack, meet me in the room we had breakfast in. Now."

Marianna came up beside Jen. Sally and Jacque had already appeared at her side.

"You okay?" Marianna asked.

"I'm not really sure how I am at the moment," Jen admitted.

She could feel Decebel's eyes on her as he walked behind them.

"What happened, Beta?" Fane asked.

"Not now," Decebel answered gruffly.

One by one the pack members filed into the breakfast room. The tables and chairs had been put away. In their place were lounging chairs. Vasile didn't sit. Alina joined him and looked just as angry. Jen watched as all the males eyeballed each other. None would concede and sit until Vasile commanded it. Once everyone was inside, Dorin pulled the door closed with an ominous click.

To Jen's surprise it was her that Vasile addressed first.

"Jen, please explain to me in as much detail as possible what happened."

She took a deep breath before she began.

"The last wolf I was training with felt me up," Jen said frankly.

Decebel snarled, even Fane and Costin snarled at her words.

Vasile took a deep breath. "That's as detailed as you can be?"

"At first his hand just landed on my chest, that I would've overlooked. The clincher was that he squeezed and didn't let go." She shrugged uncomfortably. "So, it wasn't an '*oops, my bad*' or a passing '*hello*,' it was more like '*I'd like a room for the night, please,*' kind of gesture."

Decebel was visibly shuddering in the corner as he attempted to keep his wolf under control.

"Decebel, calm yourself." Vasile commanded.

"Did he leave any marks on you?" Vasile turned back to Jen.

Inwardly, Jen cussed because she'd really been hoping to avoid this part.

"When you say marks..." Jen started vaguely.

Before Vasile could comment Decebel was at her side, turning her to face him. Although he was very gentle with her, his touch was firm, determined.

His hand, now steady, came up and stroked her face.

"The truth, Jennifer. Did that mongrel leave any marks on you?" Decebel's words were so soft. She could tell he didn't want to have this conversation in front of everyone.

"I'm not sure. I haven't really had the opportunity to check."

"Check," Decebel said simply.

Jen's jaw dropped open. "W-what, here? Now?"

Alina walked over to Jen and pulled her to the side. Decebel looked back at every male in the room and growled. They instantly all turned their backs. He glanced back at Jen. Alina was helping her lift her shirt. When Jen noticed him, she stopped her shirt from going any higher.

She cleared her throat. "Wolf, you haven't earned any special privileges. So unless you're handing out Benjamins, you don't get to watch the show."

At the moment his thoughts about her were far from inappropriate, no matter what part he saw. But he understood she didn't feel comfortable with him seeing her unclothed. He relented and turned around.

The other girls walked over to form a semi-circle around her while he waited impatiently. He nearly spun when he heard Sally's gasp.

"Damn," Sally murmured.

Alina looked up at her mate; she was growling. "She's bruised and she has claw marks."

"Bloody hell," Jacque gasped as she leaned around Alina.

Crina covered her mouth to keep from blurting out the f -bomb.

Marianna shook. "That's going to be there for a while, Jen."

Jen rolled her eyes as she watched Decebel twitch as he tried to keep from looking.

"Your play by play is really helping keep everyone calm, guys," Jen said sarcastically. "Just chill out. It's not like I'll have his marks on me forever."

She realized the mistake of her words a second after they were out of her mouth. Decebel's wolf would consider that as the other wolf marking her, claiming her. Jen knew he hadn't been – he was just a perverted guy.

Decebel pushed all the girls out of his way and was standing in front of her faster than Jen could blink. She froze as she looked up at his face, his dark features accentuated by anger. She felt him pull her shirt down to cover her. She still couldn't move.

"Once again, Jennifer, you make light of something that is serious." Decebel's eyes narrowed dangerously. "Why?"

"I'm not saying what he did was okay, but I could have handled it. He was just being a guy. He saw an opportunity to get some free action and took it. I'm perfectly capable of kicking a guy in the balls, B. I didn't need you to go all fangs and claws on him."

Every guy in the room cringed at Jen's words except Decebel. He was unmovable at this point.

"He was just *being a guy*? He was just BEING A GUY?" Decebel roared. "He touched you! He had his hands on you, on your -"

"Girly bits?" Jen offered oh so helpfully.

Decebel's mouth tightened. "Yes, Jennifer. He had his hand on your girly bits. That is not 'just being a guy,' that's being an ass. An ass who touched what is mine!"

Jen should have just shut up and cut her losses, but backing down had never been her strong suit.

Jacque watched, fascinated by the argument ensuing in front of her. She didn't think either of them truly realized how passionate they were about each other. Though, she wasn't sure they were going to survive their mating without one of them strangling the other. The words that Jen was spewing at the moment were seriously taking the odds of survival out of her corner.

"Are you mad because he got there first, wolf? 'Cause if that's the case I feel it necessary to remind you that your opportunity is coming."

The sputters, coughs, and curses that rippled through the room were punctuated by Sally surprising everyone with a loud, "What the HELL, JEN? Shut up."

Jen didn't take her eyes off of Decebel as she answered what was certainly rhetorical. "What? I'm just reminding him that, ultimately, I'm his."

"Yeah, well, emphasizing that another wolf had his hands on you at all, not just that it happened in front of your mate, is not really helping matters," Sally shot back.

Decebel's hand came up as he squeezed his eyes closed. He pinched the bridge of his nose, holding on by a thread.

"Alpha." The word was a plea.

"Mated pairs, please take the girls back to their rooms. The rest of you head back to your rooms."

Everyone was in motion except Jen and Decebel. Vasile was the last to leave the room. Before he closed the door he looked back at Decebel, who didn't look away from Jen. "I understand why you did it, Beta. It may be that because he left marks on her skin you won't be punished for your impudence."

Decebel watched Jennifer return his stare without flinching. He couldn't remember a time in his long life that he had been this angry. He started to shake with the urge to phase, remembering the wolf's hand on his mate.

Jennifer took a step towards him, completely undaunted by his lack of control. She placed her hands on either side of his face and before he even realized it, stood up on her tiptoes and pressed her lips to his.

Decebel wished he could say that he hesitated to consider the consequences of their actions, but in that moment nothing could have calmed his wolf the way that intimate touch did. His arms went around her small waist, pulling her closer. As her body met his Decebel tilted his head to deepen the kiss. He heard her moan and growled in response. When their tongues met he nearly smiled. She hadn't hesitantly tried to slip it in his mouth, not his woman. She plunged confidently, daring him to respond.

He felt her wince when he pulled her closer, her chest tightly pressed to him. That brought his thoughts back to her injury. Possessiveness surged forward, muddling his brain, and his kiss turned desperate. He lifted her by the waist and pressed her against a wall, never once taking his lips from hers.

Jen wrapped her arms around his neck and pulled herself up, then wrapped her legs around his waist. This bold move allowed him to push through the fog. He gentled the kiss and after a few small lingering ones, pulled back.

Decebel noticed how beautiful she looked, her lips red and swollen from his kiss, her eyes half closed as she tried to catch her breath. Slowly she unwrapped her legs and lowered herself to the ground. He couldn't deny the attraction he felt at her confidence. She didn't blush or apologize for having become so passionate, she didn't try to hide the desire that filled her eyes, and she didn't drop her arms to grant them some space. She held on tight and sultrily smiled.

"That was yummy."

Decebel chuckled. "Of all the things you could say: passionate, amazing, incredible, unbelievable, and you come up with yummy?"

"It was all of those things," she agreed. "But none of those describe how you taste."

"Jennifer." Her name was a groan pulled from his chest.

"How would you describe it then?" she challenged.

"Which part? Your taste? The feel of your lips on mine? Having your body pressed so close to me? What would you have me describe, baby?"

"The look in your eyes says enough," she answered gently.

Jen dropped her arms and Decebel immediately felt cold and empty.

"Are you better," she asked hesitantly.

Decebel thought about it for a moment. "Yes. Thank you. I just couldn't calm my wolf," he paused, "or myself."

"So you're calm now?"

"Somewhat." His smile faded, replaced by a clenched jaw and furrowed brow. "I just need some time with you. Just you."

Jen watched as Decebel allowed the wall he always erected in front of others to come down. She took his hand and led him over to one of the love seats. Kicking off her shoes, she pulled her legs up on the couch and leaned into his side as his arms came around her. She closed her eyes and she felt him lay his cheek against her hair. There was a low rumble in his chest as she snuggled closer.

Decebel closed his eyes as he held Jennifer. This was what his wolf needed. He was beginning to realize why Fane touched Jacque all the time. It was like he couldn't not touch her. The reassurance, comfort, and peace that came from Jennifer's touch was a drug. A drug that he was fast becoming addicted to.

Gladly, he thought.

"Let's just stay here for a little while, okay?" Jen asked him sleepily.

"Ten thousand could not pull you from my side."

Chapter 19

"You are asking me to allow you to retaliate against the Romanian Beta?" Thad asked the wolf who stood before him, the same wolf who had grabbed Jen.

"Yes, Alpha. She does not belong to him. He had no right to attack."

"Maybe she isn't his mate, Dragos, but she is a pack mate," Thad reminded him.

"He still could have handled it differently, he didn't have to draw blood."

Thad was quiet for a few moments while he considered his options. This situation could actually work in his favor – if he played it just right. He turned back to Dragos. "Why not attack the one who allows Decebel such liberties?" The other wolf peered up at him, betraying his interest. Thad went on, "Why not take out the one who controls Decebel?"

Dragos couldn't deny that taking out the most powerful Alpha in a century appealed to him. "How could I take him out? He's too strong and protected."

Dragos watched Thad pull a small vial from the obviously expensive blazer he wore.

"Two drops of this in his drink and the big, bad wolf crumbles."

It was then that Dragos realized what was in the vial. "Menispermum," he whispered.

"Otherwise known as Moonseed," Thad concurred. "Well done. You must know, then, that the juice that comes from it is fatal."

Dragos nodded.

"So your task is to get this into his drink. I have simplified this by inviting the Alphas to dine with me privately. They will each have their own place setting with their names. You will be one of the wolf caterers that night and you *will* make sure Vasile gets the special drink. Then you can watch in satisfaction as the great Alpha withers away slowly. You see, unlike Kamalah, Moonseed kills slowly, makes the victim suffer."

Dragos smiled at the idea of bringing one so great to his knees.

"When is this dinner?"

"In three days' time. Be here at 5.30 p.m."

Thad dismissed the wolf. He then sent a text on his phone: "*Have orders for you.*"

A few minutes later his contact from the Romanian pack entered the room.

"I have a plan set for Vasile's death. Your job will be to lead Jen off on a wild goose chase to find the antidote for Moonseed. While you are out searching, somehow Jen will fall into one of those pesky cracks in the mountain."

"The antidote for Moonseed is Wolfsbane." The contact's brow furrowed. "It grows all over. How will I lure her so far away?"

"I will make sure to have all the Wolfsbane closest to the estate destroyed, thereby forcing you to wander out to find more. The reality is, I don't really want the Wolfsbane, but I will need some of the plant to fool them when we administer the so-called antidote. You see, when in their liquid form they are nearly impossible to tell apart. In fact, the only person I know that can tell them apart are gypsy healers. But, conveniently, there isn't a gypsy healer around," Thad explained with a satisfied smirk.

He watched as his contact thought about the plan, then nodded. "Okay. When?"

"Vasile will be poisoned in three days. Jen strikes me as the hero type. You will be able to convince her to go with you, no problem."

The contact said nothing more and left.

Thad smiled. His plan was coming together quite nicely. It was pure dumb luck that Dragos had come to him seeking revenge. Now the blame for the poison would fall on his shoulders. Thad would be left in the clear and even be able to act like he was helping. In three days' time he would watch the Romanian Alpha brought to his knees and, ultimately, his demise.

Vasile and Alina sat in a small gathering room with the other Alphas and their mates, the exception being Dillon, who was spending time with Jacque. Vasile had been the one to call the meeting, feeling like it would be best to meet the consequences of his Beta's actions head on.

"Did you find out exactly what provoked your Beta?" Victor, Alpha of the Bulgaria pack asked.

"The wolf training Jen was touching her inappropriately. Apparently Decebel saw the wolf touching her before Jen could *handle* it on her own." Vasile waited to see if any would contradict him. No one spoke so he continued. "As you know, Decebel is Beta of my pack. Jen is an unmated female, making it is his job to protect her since she has no mate to do so."

"I agree that he should protect her," Dragomir spoke up. "The question is, did he go too far?"

"I don't think her unmated status should decide the amount of defense she is allowed," Alina addressed Dragomir. "If any mated female had been grabbed so hard that bruises and claw marks became visible, her mate would kill the offender. There would be no fight to submission as Decebel did. The wolf who would touch a mate in that way would be signing his death warrant. Are our unmated females worth so much less?"

"No. No, Alina. I didn't mean that at all," Dragomir backtracked, clearly uncomfortable with the picture Alina painted.

"If they are not worth less then Decebel was lenient. Do you agree?"

Vasile tried to hide the smile that threatened to spread across his face as he watched his mate bring the Alphas to heel.

"I have to agree with you, Alina," Victor stepped in. "I don't think any disciplinary action is necessary. It's been dealt with. Decebel put the pup in his place, and I'm sure the young wolf has learned his lesson about what happens when one touches a female inappropriately."

Vasile stood, pulling Alina up along with him. "I appreciate you all discussing the matter. If we are done..." He left the sentence hanging.

"Vasile, you are still planning on joining us for the dinner for the Alphas, yes?" Thad asked as Vasile and Alina headed for the door.

"Yes, thank you. We will be in attendance."

"So how are you liking pack life, Jacque?" Tanya asked as she, Jacque, Dillon, and Fane sat together in one of the many small sitting rooms in the mansion.

Fane had his hand across the back of the couch he and Jacque were sitting on. He worked his hand underneath her hair and his fingers traced the markings on her skin – he knew them by memory. Jacque tried not to shiver at her mate's touch.

"Could you please behave?" Jacque asked, using their bond.

"I'm only rubbing your neck, love. It's not like I'm touching -"

"Fane, don't you dare," Jacque threatened before he could finish his sentence. It didn't help that he pictured what he'd been about to say. Jacque just knew her face was beet red.

"Are you taking notes when you're around Jen?"

Fane sent her another picture and Jacque about jumped up and left the room at that.

"If you could only see the beautiful shade of red your skin is glowing with right now. You look quite luscious."

"I've really been enjoying it. I'm learning a lot about pack history, which I find really interesting," Jacque answered, more tersely than she intended. Fane was going to pay for his fool's play.

Jacque spent the next hour talking with her dad and Tanya, all the while trying hard to ignore her mate's words and images, ones that would've made even Jen blush.

"I want you to know that this means war," Jacque promised as they were saying their goodbyes.

Fane chuckled as he placed his hand on the small of her back. "Do you want to go check on Jen?" he asked her.

"That's probably a good idea. Do you think Decebel is allowing her to have visitors?"

Fane laughed. "Are you saying he's going to be a little overprotective now?"

"No." Jacque looked at him from the corner of her eye. "I'm saying he's going to be completely unreasonable and we'll be lucky if he doesn't make her wear sack cloths when she's out in public."

"Was I that bad?"

"Uh, Fane, you didn't let me leave your sight except to take care of personal stuff for over a month. So, yes. Yes you were that bad and then some." Jacque bumped him with her shoulder.

"It appears we weren't the only ones concerned about her," Fane said as they joined Sally, Crina, and Marianna at Jen's door.

"We've been knocking for about five minutes. Either Decebel has her tied up and won't answer the door, or she isn't here," Sally told them.

"You think they're still in the meeting room?" Jacque asked.

"Worth a try," Crina piped in.

"Ten bucks says they made up and are smooching," Jacque announced.

"I'll take your bet and raise you five. I say they made up but smooching has come and gone on the agenda." Crina winked at them.

"You're wicked bad." Jacque grinned. "Jen would love it."

Decebel awoke when he felt Jennifer moving. At some point she'd taken a pillow and laid her head in his lap. He had stroked her hair until he himself had finally fallen asleep. He couldn't remember a time he had slept so well – even sitting upright on a love seat.

Jennifer had his wolf practically purring. He was so content at having her so close, so relaxed in his presence. He glanced down and could tell she was beginning to wake. He ran the back of his fingers across her cheek and her eyes fluttered open. She looked up at him and smiled. At that moment she could have asked him for anything and he would have toppled empires to make it happen.

"Hey," he murmured.

"Hey yourself."

She stretched her arms up and arched her back like a cat waking from a long nap in the sun. Decebel made sure to keep his eyes plastered to her face and off her beautiful form. When she looked at him again, he brushed the hair away from her face and leaned down to capture her lips with his. When he moved back, she was grinning like the Cheshire cat.

"More," she ordered.

Decebel chuckled as she wrapped her hand around the nape of his neck and pulled him back to her. He placed his hands on her hips and was fixing to drag her onto his lap when the door behind them flew open.

"I win!" Jacque hollered.

"No you don't," Crina countered. "Look at his hands. They were absolutely not *just* smooching. There was some definite hand action."

"Oh, I wouldn't say definite," Marianna piped in. "More like the possibility of hand action."

Sally turned. "My respect for you is growing in leaps and bounds."

Marianna grinned and winked.

Jen's head snapped up to look over Decebel's shoulder.

"What the hell are y'all yapping about?" she growled, clearly not happy about the interruption.

"They had a bet," Sally offered.

"A bet? A bet on what?"

"Your virtue," she answered dryly.

Jen's mouth dropped open. "I've already been felt up once today and look what that got me. You really think I'm up to more?"

Decebel growled. He pulled her closer so he could whisper in her ear. "Not a good subject to bring up, baby."

Jen kissed him on the cheek. "Sorry, B."

Jacque looked at Sally, who was as dumbfounded as her.

"She has a gentle side?" Jacque muttered.

"Did she just use the word 'sorry' and 'B' in the same sentence?" Sally countered.

"I guess every creature has their weakness. Hers is similar to mine." Jacque smiled. "Hot, sexy, furry men."

Crina and Marianna laughed.

"I like mine with whipped cream," Jen said conspiratorially to the two she-wolves. Then she looked at Jacque. "What do you like yours with, Red?"

Fane spoke up quickly. "Don't answer that, Luna."

Decebel busted out with a loud laugh at the firmness in Fane's voice, and the girls all fell in line behind him. Fane didn't even crack a smile.

"So what brings the motley crew to see us?" Jen asked once the laughing was under control.

"We went to your room to check on you, but you weren't there," Sally told her.

"All of you?"

"You're pack." Marianna answered as if that was all that needed to be said.

Decebel's phone rang and Jen climbed up so he could reach his pocket. Since they were all super unnosy, they made sure to be as quiet as possible while he answered the call.

"They didn't?" Decebel asked.

The room was silent as he listened.

"Okay. Yeah, I got it. Thanks, Vasile." He closed his phone and looked up to find six sets of eyes glued to him.

"So is there a plan for this evening?" he asked casually.

Jen rolled her eyes. "Spill it, wolf."

Decebel grabbed her wrist and pulled her forward. She fell against his chest. He wrapped his arms around her, enjoying the freedom to touch her.

"That was Vasile," he said finally.

"Yeah, we sort of got that when you thanked him and used his name." Jen's eyes narrowed. "Try again."

"Testy tonight, aren't we?" Decebel teased.

"I think I liked it better when you were broody," Jen muttered, which only made him chuckle and squeeze her closer.

"Vasile informed me that the Alphas have decided to not subject me to any punishment for my actions against the mongrel who touched you." Decebel's words became rougher as he spoke.

"It would have made no sense for them to punish you," Fane told him.

"Why do you say that?" Jacque asked her mate.

Fane took her hand and tugged him to her, tucking her under his arm. "Any mated female who had been touched that way would have watched as her mate tore the offender limb from limb."

Jacque shivered at the menace in his voice.

Jen cocked her head at Decebel. "Aw, would the little furry wolf make a chew toy of the pervert for me?" she teased, squeezing Decebel's cheeks like she would a baby's.

Decebel gently removed her hands and took her face in both of his. "I will kill the next male who touches you. I'm done playing nice," he said, snapping his teeth together as his canines descended.

"Sally, get a hose." Jen grinned wickedly. "Because that was *so* freaking hot and I'm on fire."

Decebel rolled his eyes, but softened it with a smile.

"Ohhh nooo," Sally groaned. "I thought it was bad before the nympho had an outlet. Now she has her very own boy toy."

Decebel growled. "I'm not a boy toy," he said, clearly offended.

"Don't mind her, B. She's just sexually frustrated," Jen placated.

Decebel shocked the room into silence when he looked at Sally and dryly quipped, "Join the club."

Jen's face turned eight shades of red.

Jacque recovered first. "Bloody hell, I didn't know Jen had that color in her skin repertoire."

Crina and Marianna snickered while Jen tried to recover herself. She hid her flaming hot face in Decebel's neck. He rubbed her back soothingly and murmured to her in Romanian.

Note to self, Jen thought. *Find out what he's saying... Correction, throttle wolf for joking about his needs in front of my friends, then find out what he's saying.*

"So what are we going to do tonight?" Fane asked.

Jen sat up, having finally composed herself. "Isn't there some sort of something going on tonight?"

"Yes, but my father thinks it best that we lie low. Just until things simmer down."

"Well, my vote is that we hit up the mess hall first and foremost," Jen announced.

Sally rolled her eyes. "Here we go with the military lingo."

"Where does she get that?" Jacque asked, shaking her head.

"I can't decide if she was in special forces in a past life or if she was dropped on her head as a child." Sally shrugged.

"I definitely wasn't dropped on my head, Sally dear. My head is perfectly rounded, free of any discombobulation," Jen said haughtily.

Marianna, who usually stood quietly and observed, chuckled. "Only an American would describe the shape of her head as if it were some sort of special art form to be prized."

Jen stood up from the couch, straightening her clothes and tugging at her ponytail. She smiled brightly at Marianna. "Seriously, she-wolf. Are you looking at the same head I see in the mirror?" she asked as she made a circular motion around her head. "This is God's way of showing that he is indeed capable of creating perfection."

Jacque and Sally snorted as Fane and Decebel chuckled.

Jen looked down at Decebel as she heard him mutter, "Niciodata nu inceteaza sa el (she will never cease to amaze)."

"Have something to tell me, B?" Jen asked sweetly.

"Just that I have never beheld a head possessing such utter flawlessness, baby," he told her, dramatically bowing at the waist.

Jen narrowed her eyes. "Definitely liked you better as an ominous, brooding, fur ball."

His response was a wicked grin and a wink.

Chapter 20

"Ugh, if I eat another bite I'm going to be sick," Jacque groaned as she looked at the feast they'd all heartily dug into.

" I have to agree, Thelma." Jen leaned back in her chair, rubbing her belly. "I'm as full as a tick stuck to the flesh of a bull mastiff on a hot summer day."

Jacque shook her head. "I swear, Louise, you really know how to ruin a good carb-induced buzz."

"I aim to please, wolf-princess."

Crina stood and stretched as she looked around the room. "What do you guys say to a swim? There's bound to be a pool in this breeding facility."

"Good one, C. 'Breeding facility,' like it." Jen grinned.

Jacque sat up and looked at Fane, "What do ya say, wolf-man. Up for a swim?"

Fane nodded but didn't answer out loud. *"You in a bathing suit – like I could ever turn that down."*

Jen watched the play between Jacque and Fane and knew they were using their bond. Something in her heart tugged. She wanted that intimacy, longed for it with Decebel. She turned to look at him and found him watching Fane and Jacque as well. He must have felt her eyes on him because he turned and met her gaze. Something unspoken flowed between them. Almost as if she could hear him say not to worry, their time would come. Her response was, *"are you so sure?"* at which he growled, this time out loud. Jen shook her head, amazed at how in tune they were with each other, and yet there seemed to be a vast chasm between them.

"I could go for a swim," Marianna spoke up.

"Yeah, I'm in." Jen stood up, stretching her stagnate form.

As they made their way out into the hall, Fane and Decebel both perked up.

"What do you hear?" Jacque asked just as Costin came around the corner, nearly plowing into Marianna.

"Oh. Sorry, Marianna," he told her as he caught himself. He looked nervous and he wouldn't meet Fane's or Decebel's gazes.

Decebel stepped forward. "What's all the noise about?"

Costin shook his head as he looked at the floor. "Why do I always have to be the one to find things out," he muttered.

"Costin," Decebel warned.

Finally Costin looked up. He didn't address his Beta, instead he spoke to Fane. "I think we should get your father and a few other males."

Fane nodded. Costin took off at a run while Fane turned to Jen. "Distract him."

Jen looked confused for a second, but quickly caught on as soon as Decebel moved in the direction of Costin, the direction of the noise.

Jen didn't know what to do to distract a six foot four inch male wolf that was ten times stronger than her. She wracked her brain as Decebel continued to move forward – he did so slowly, as if he were afraid of what he'd find. Fane was standing in front of him, trying to coax him to stay.

Then inspiration hit. *He's male,* Jen thought. She grinned.

"Hey, fur ball!" Jen hollered. There was a wicked gleam in her eye as she grabbed the hem of her shirt and tugged it over her head, leaving her in a sports bra.

"This is so not good," Sally muttered to Jacque.

Jacque shook her head as she pinched the bridge of her nose. "I swear we're going to have to duct tape her mouth and put her in a straight jacket."

Jen mock-sighed. "The sacrifices we make for our men."

Decebel turned at the sound of Jen's voice and she winked.

"Don't you want to hang around?"

Then she flashed him.

Costin was banging on Skender's door when Vasile stepped out of his room.

"What's going on?" Vasile asked.

Costin met his Alpha's eyes briefly. "We need all our males. Now."

Alina heard the wolf's worried voice and followed Vasile out. "What happened?"

"Decebel is going to go on a killing spree if he sees what I just saw without us to stop him."

"What have you seen?" Vasile took a step forward.

Costin quickly explained about Jen, Crina, and Marianna dancing while the males of the other packs videoed them.

"Alpha, it was not an innocent little dance. But our females didn't know they were being watched so they definitely weren't tempering their moods, if you know what I mean."

Alina was shaking her head in frustration. "So even though Decebel ordered them to delete the video, someone did not?"

"Correct. They are showing it in one of the movie rooms at this moment. It's packed with males. I think their thoughts are 'strength in numbers.' They figure Decebel cannot retaliate with so many of them present."

"They do not know he is an Alpha in his own right." Alina's voice was low.

"No, Luna. Decebel purposely allows others to underestimate him." Vasile's eyes snapped up as Skender, Boian, Dorin, Anton, and a couple other males ran up the stairs.

"You are aware of the situation?" Skender asked.

"Costin has just informed me. Since there hasn't been widespread panic, do I correctly surmise that Decebel hasn't yet made it there?"

Skender and the males with him couldn't stop the chuckles. "He has been momentarily... distracted."

"Do I even want to know what with?" Vasile asked dryly.

"No, Alpha. You most definitely do not want to know," Skender replied.

"Fine," he snapped. "Let's go. Alina, please come and retrieve the females. And call Cynthia. We're probably going to have to tranq him."

It'd been a long time since Vasile had subdued one of his males in such a way, but Decebel was powerful, and he had found his mate and couldn't bind her to him. That was a deadly combination even without adding unmated males to the mix. Vasile had underestimated Decebel's feelings towards Jen. That wouldn't happen again, if they all survived this.

The wolves followed their Alpha as he made his way down the stairs with a single, determined thought: he had to stop his Beta from destroying an entire pack…or two.

Jen's bra came up just as Skender and a slew of Romanian pack males rounded the now infamous corner. Fane cursed and turned away.

Skender and the other males' eyes hit the floor faster than humanly possible as they continued to run, but Jen heard Skender loud and clear as he passed by.

"Keep up the good work, dormant."

Decebel was so stunned that he hadn't moved. His eyes were glowing and he looked angrier than Jen had ever seen him. *Okay,* she thought. *At least it's working.*

"Um… Kinda getting cold here, Dec." Jen squirmed.

Decebel moved faster than her eyes could track. He grabbed her around the waist and hauled her into an empty room. He gently, but quickly set her down. Then he turned and stepped out.

Before he pulled the door closed, he growled, "Cover yourself, woman, and pray that I have regained control when I return for you." Then he slammed the door so hard it nearly came off the hinges.

"That went well," Jen grumbled as she pulled her sports bra back down. She stilled as the door opened, thinking that maybe Decebel had decided to punish her now – but Jacque, Sally, Crina, and Marianna walked in. Jacque tossed Jen the shirt she had discarded.

Marianna walked up to Jen and placed a hand on her shoulder.

"I just wanted to touch the one who would purposely provoke the wrath of an Alpha," she told her, then stepped back with a shake of her head.

"He's Beta," Jen corrected as she pulled her shirt on.

"No," Crina disagreed. "He's an Alpha, he just chooses not to take that title. He definitely has all the power of one. Some wonder if he would be as powerful as Vasile if he decided that was his path."

Jen let out a deep breath. "Well, Fane said to distract him. What else would you suggest to stop an Alpha with deadly retribution on his mind?"

"We're not saying your method wasn't effective. We're just saying you are one brave she-wolf." Crina's voice actually held awe in it.

"So, do we know exactly what hell-like situation made it necessary for me to bring out the big guns? Pun naturally intended." Jen laughed.

Jacque snorted. "Only you, Jen. Only you."

After Decebel pulled the door shut, he closed his eyes and took a slow breath. *I have got to get it under control,* he told himself as he tried to pull his wolf back. His mate was going to get every male in her vicinity killed. How many of his pack mates had just witnessed her little stunt? He squeezed his eyes tightly, only to see the bruises and claw marks that marred her skin. His wolf snarled. Okay, that was not something he needed to think about.

Opening his eyes he began moving in the direction of the noise he'd heard earlier. Fane was trying to keep up and reason with him at the same time.

"Beta, don't you think we should maybe heed Costin's advice and wait for our Alpha?"

Decebel didn't respond. The closer he got the clearer the noise became. Fane's head snapped up when he heard Jen's voice.

"We may be fine, and smokin' hot,
But gentle she-wolves we are not."

Decebel stopped dead in his tracks. The images of Jennifer and that dance flashed through his mind. Fane watched Decebel's canines descend – his claws grew, his eyes glowed feral. Fane moved quickly to get in front of his Beta, which was probably the dumbest thing he could have done.

Fane tried being forceful. "Decebel, stop."

Decebel batted him aside as if he were no more than an annoying fly. Fane wasn't using all his power – he didn't want to provoke the already enraged wolf. When Decebel reached the room where all the noise was coming from, Vasile was already there with the others.

Fane looked in horror as a room full of males whistled and hollered as his female pack mates danced oh so very suggestively on a huge cinema-sized screen.

Vasile turned to Fane. "Stop that from playing."

Fane didn't wait to see what would happen. He walked into the room, shoving other males out of his way in order to look for the source of the video feed.

Decebel growled so loudly the room silenced. Every head turned to watch as the Romanian Beta took on his full Alpha power, drawing it from his pack mates.

"DECEBEL!" Vasile roared. He might as well have been yelling at a wall.

Decebel lunged.

"Grab him," Vasile commanded his pack. Eight males descended on Decebel as he surged forward. The males grunted against his brute strength. It was taking all of Vasile's power to keep Decebel from phasing. If he phased, the only way Vasile would be able to stop him would be to phase as well and take him on in his wolf form. He didn't even want to consider the consequences.

They all struggled as Decebel pushed, slashed, and even bit to get free of their grasp. Vasile eyed Cynthia running through the hall towards them, Alina and the others behind her. The Americans' defiance was rubbing off on his mate, he thought dryly.

"Hold him still," Cynthia snarled as she lifted a very large syringe and grabbed Decebel's arm.

She sunk the needle into his arm. He didn't even flinch, if he even noticed. The plunger depressed, pushing the powerful sedative into his system.

Decebel continued to struggle – he was on the verge of getting free when he collapsed.

Jen watched as Decebel, struggled against his pack. She couldn't suppress a scream as she watched him, powerful, massive Decebel crumble. Jen took off and pushed several males out of her way.

"MOVE!"

Jen gently placed his head in her lap, placing two fingers against his neck. She let out a strangled breath – his pulse was strong.

"We have to move him now," Cynthia said firmly. "That won't last long."

"Jen," Vasile's voice was calm, gentle, "you have to let us take him."

Jen looked up at the man who had become her Alpha. "Where are you taking him?" Jen's voice was smaller than she had ever heard it.

"We are going to have to detain him until I can talk to the Alphas about your unique situation," Vasile quickly explained.

"Lock him up?" Jen's eyebrows nearly rose to her hair line. "Can I see him?"

Vasile shook his head. "Not until I talk to the Alphas. Jen, Decebel cannot control his wolf where you are concerned, and these unmated males will not relent as long as you appear available. I have to do this to protect him from himself, but also from them."

Jen finally relented. She leaned down and kissed his lips before letting Decebel go.

She watched as nine people carried the man she loved away to be locked up like some criminal. Jen's eyes narrowed as her lips thinned into a tight, straight line.

"Jacque," Sally nudged her friend, and nodded in Jen's direction, "look at that face."

"Shit," Jacque muttered as she watched the evil wheels turning in Jen's brain.

"I would say it's hit every fan in this monstrosity they call a house," Sally replied automatically.

They watched as Jen walked over to Crina and Marianna.

"What's she up to?" Jacque murmured.

"I need y'all to do me a favor," Jen told the two she-wolves briskly.

"What do you need, pack mate?" Crina asked.

"I want to know the names of those who planned this."

"You have a plan?" Sally asked as she and Jacque joined the group.

"You bet your furless ass I do." Jen's eyes nearly glowed.

Marianna looked at Jen apprehensively. "Should we be afraid?"

"As long as you're standing on this side of the Jennifer Adams treaty line, you're safe."

"Duly noted."

"Can y'all find out?" Jen asked again.

Marianna nodded. "I think I can. There's been a male eyeballing me. I think a little reciprocation might go a long way."

Jen's smile grew. It was beginning to become a very unnerving look.

"Excellent."

Chapter 21

Decebel felt groggy as he awoke. Shaking his head, he ran his hands across his face.

In a mad rush, memories flooded him and he jumped up with a snarl. But there was no one to respond, only four stone walls. Decebel walked over to the one with a door. He grabbed the handle and pulled. It was locked. He turned, taking in his surroundings. The room wasn't large but it was nicely furnished. A large, plush four poster bed with a deep green comforter and elegant gold drapes around the frame stood against the far wall. Across from the bed were two wing-backed chairs in the same green as the comforter. Above the chairs was a large mirror framed in antique gold with a wolf head carving at the top. There were no windows in the room.

Decebel growled. *A gilded cage,* he thought.

The mirror drew his eyes again.

"Why would a prisoner need a mirror?" he wondered out loud. The closer he got, the more he allowed himself to use his wolf eyesight. Finally, his face inches from the glass, he realized it was double paned glass. Someone was watching him.

Decebel snarled and hit the glass so hard that a small crack formed where his fist connected.

"Beta, calm down."

Decebel looked up as he heard his Alpha's voice. The speakers in the ceiling became obvious.

"Why am I locked in a room, Alpha?" Decebel growled.

"You aren't controlling your wolf."

"Control my wolf when those mongrels lust after my mate?" Decebel snarled, interrupting Vasile.

"You have no visible proof she is your mate. Let me handle this, Decebel."

"How is locking me up, keeping me from protecting her, handling it?" Decebel sneered.

Suddenly the door was thrown open and Vasile walked in. Decebel felt his Alpha's power pushing him to submit.

"I understand that you are only my Beta out of choice, not lack of strength. You chose this, Beta. You will submit to me, you will not disrespect me." Vasile's voice was deadly. "I love you like a brother, Decebel. I understand your need to protect her, but you have got to trust me. You don't have to like it, but you will obey my commands."

Decebel was shaking with rage. He was torn for the first time in his life. His wolf's only thought was to get to their mate, protect, claim, bond. But Decebel the man could use logic. He finally sunk to his knees and bared his neck. Vasile let out the breath he'd been holding and walked over to him.

"I'm not trying to defeat you, Decebel, I'm trying to protect you. You are strong, my equal, but I doubt either of us could take on four Alphas and their packs. Which is what will happen if you attack their males for ogling your pack mate."

"MATE," Decebel snarled.

"To us, yes, she is yours," Vasile said calmly. "Not to them. She doesn't carry your scent in her blood, she doesn't bear your marks or your bite, there is no mental bond. All of those things are strikes against you two."

"Perform the Bonding Ceremony, Vasile. Allow me to complete the Blood Rites. Then everyone will see that Jennifer belongs to me."

Vasile shook his head. "Allow me to speak with the other Alphas. There have been three true mates found today – maybe they will be willing to allow you and Jen some time to explore this without any other males in the picture."

"Why is it their business?" Decebel snarled. "What say do they have in my or her fate?"

"Normally, they wouldn't. But we came to a gathering where wolves are specifically looking for their true mate. The Alphas are looking out for the best interests of their males. If you keep Jen from the other males and she isn't your mate, then you might be dooming one of their males to a dark existence." Decebel started to interrupt but Vasile stopped him. "They don't see her as your mate, therefore they won't let you keep her to yourself. It's as simple as that. You claiming that there is some feeling between you and her is not enough for them."

Decebel's shoulders slumped in defeat as reality sunk in. He understood now why his Alpha had him locked up. Regardless of what the other Alphas thought, regardless of the lack of mating signs between him and Jennifer, he and his wolf had claimed her. No mated Canis lupis male would stand for another touching, ogling, pursuing, or flirting with his mate. He couldn't be trusted around the others. At the same time, the idea of Jennifer out there without him, as his mate would say – *that is so not good.*

"What of Jennifer?" he asked Vasile.

"She's with Alina and the other females. We will protect her, Decebel."

"I don't want another touching her. Can't you keep her from participating in these stupid *activities*?" Decebel spat the word as if it were the most repugnant thing.

"I'll see what I can do," Vasile relented. "I need you to get control."

Decebel nodded once. He didn't look up as Vasile left.

After several deep breaths, Decebel finally stood. He began to pace just as his wolf paced inside of him, thinking, plotting. The wolf was cunning and would not be caged, would not be kept from his mate.

Jen lay in her bed, staring up at the ceiling. She was restless, angry – *No*, she thought, *I'm pissed. Angry doesn't begin to cover what I'm feeling.*

She turned from side to side, repositioned her pillow a hundred times, and tried counting every animal that'd come out of the Ark. Nothing helped. She couldn't sleep, not when she knew Decebel was locked up. Vasile wouldn't tell her where. *Smart wolf*, she thought. Surely he wasn't in some dungeon or crude prison. Vasile would never allow one of his to be treated that way. But still, wolves were meant to be free, to run and roam. Decebel wouldn't handle being caged well.

Growling out loud, Jen reached for her iPhone. She plugged the headphones in and put them in her ears. Without scanning through her music, she just hit shuffle and waited. She grinned when Jason

Derulo's "Fight for You" came on. Her grin widened when she thought about the plan she was putting into motion.

Oh, yeah. She'd fight for Decebel. Heaven help those who found themselves on the wrong side of the battle field.

The next morning, Jen watched as Marianna moved through the room over to where the Serbian pack was eating breakfast. She kept strict track of Marianna's progress as the she-wolf started up a conversation with the interested male.

Jen had asked why a wolf would show interest if the mating signs didn't appear. Her jaw nearly hit the floor when Marianna and Crina explained that in the past few years, when true mates had been found, it sometimes took several days for the signs to show up. When Jen started to go postal about it, Crina quickly added that it had never taken longer than four days. Decebel and Jen had been around each other for months.

Jen had then asked why no one had bothered to divulge that little morsel. Crina said that Alina had told them the Alphas didn't want the males being overly forward to any one female, just from attraction, for days with a hope that the signs would appear.

Jen's response: "Maybe it would be better to just neuter the males and nip all the posturing and peeing in the bud."

Costin had been within earshot and growled, then paled when Jen had looked at him and made scissoring motion with her fingers. As she did, she sang to the tune of Wheels On the Bus: "Scissors on the wolf go snip, snip, snip."

But now, Marianna was talking with the wolf who'd eyeballed her yesterday. He was handsome enough, tall and strong, like all Canis lupis.

"Hey," he said with a sly smile.

"Hi," Marianna answered with her own sweet smile. "What's your name?"

"Jovin. Yours?"

"Marianna." She batted her eyes. "So, you want to go somewhere?"

Jovin's face lit up. "Sure."

As he stood up and bid farewell to his pack mates, Marianna turned to the TFF and gave them a thumbs up. Now to get him to give up the goods. She rolled her eyes. *I'm talking like the Americans now,* she groaned.

She quickly schooled her face as Jovin took her hand and led her from the room.

"So, oh great evil one, what's your plan?" Sally asked Jen dryly.

Jen rubbed her hands together and grinned. "Well, it starts with strip poker,"

"Ahh, good grief. It always starts with strip poker."

"You remember what happened the last time she played strip poker?" Jacque added.

"This sounds good," Crina piped, folding herself down on the floor in Jen's room.

"Oh, come on. That was one time. I mean, seriously, lose one little game of strip poker..."

"Jen, it's always *'I only did that one time'* with you." Sally sighed.

"See, that's good. Means I learn quickly." Jen shrugged.

"Unbelievable." Jacque threw her hands into the air. "She finds a way to justify anything."

"Do you want to hear my brilliant plan or would you just like to list all of my transgressions?"

"No." Sally held up her hands now. "We go digging in that bag-o-worms and we just might find something worse than the brilliant plan you're fixing to enlighten us with."

Jen glared at Sally. "If you're finished..."

"By all means."

Crina looked over at Jacque. "Are they always like this?"

"Believe it or not, this is good. They've considered counseling, but I think they're trying to work out their differences on their own."

"Okay, you hussies, listen up." Jen stood with her hands on her hips, steel was in her eyes. "As I was saying, it starts with strip poker. We need something that's going to keep them distracted for a while. That way, Jacque and Sally will have plenty of time to go through said wolves' rooms.

"Whoa, whoa. You lost me at Jacque and wolves' rooms." Jacque backed away.

"Well, if you think Fane will be okay with you playing strip poker with a bunch of unmated wolves, then by all means..."

"Okay, good point," Jacque conceded. "But what are we supposed to be looking for in their rooms?"

"Clothes," Jen stated. "All of them. I don't want them to have a stitch of clothing to put on. Linens, too. Sheets, towels, comforters. Gone, all of it."

"Won't they be able to just phase to their wolf forms? They won't need clothes." Crina put in.

"That's where things get complicated."

"More complicated than confiscating a bunch of men's clothing and somehow carrying it away without being seen?" Jacque asked sarcastically.

"Complicated because I'm going to have to talk to Cynthia. I'm figuring if they've got drugs to subdue werewolves, then maybe they have drugs that will prevent them from phasing."

Jacque grinned. "You wicked, wicked woman."

"I don't want anyone to get hurt, but I don't want them to think they can mess with what's mine and get away with it. So, although it may seem slight, they are gonna be humiliated."

Crina, who had been listening intently, raised her hand. Jen looked at her. "Whatchya got, she-wolf?"

"How do you know you'll win at strip poker?"

"Jen never loses," Sally said matter of factly.

Jen shrugged. "What she's trying to say is, I never lose."

"Okay," Jacque said slowly. "So, strip poker and a mass exodus of all forms of coverings." She cocked her head to the side. "What are we going to do with said clothes, towels, etcetera, etcetera?"

"How do you girls feel about a bonfire?" Jen winked. "Fire is my specialty, after all."

Sally groaned again. "Strip poker and fire. Does she ever learn?"

Jen started to pace. They were going to need help. There was no way Sally and Jacque could get all of the things from those rooms on their own. *Think, Jen. Geez, you're supposed to be the schemer in this posse.* She racked her brain. She needed someone who could move through the mansion freely. Someone they wouldn't pay any mind to. There was no way they would let any of the females walk unbidden through the halls. No females, but a male could go where he pleased. *Bahh, it's like we're back in the eighteenth century or something.*

"We need a dude," Jen announced, then her head snapped around to Jacque. "Are you letting your fur ball hear all this?"

Jacque shook her head, even though she knew as soon as Fane found out he was going to be eight shades of pissed.

"Good, don't. You know he would lock us all up until this whole thing was done." Jen tapped her chin. "Who would be the easiest sell? Costin or Sorin?" she thought out loud.

There was a knock on the door. Jen walked over and pulled it open to see Costin's sweet smile. *Costin it is.*

"I was just checking to make sure you ladies were okay." He grinned. If Jen hadn't already been smitten with a certain out of control wolf she could see having the hots for Costin.

"Costin, the fates have chosen you," Jen said dramatically, reaching her arm out to indicate him to enter.

Jacque rolled her eyes.

"What is she doing?" Sally muttered.

"Getting all our asses hung out to dry," Jacque responded.

"Good to know."

Costin stepped in warily. "The fates have chosen me, huh? Should I even ask?"

"Well, you'll probably be deemed guilty by association anyway. Might as well dive in head first." Jen smiled sweetly at him. "Besides, I always say if you're going to do it, do it big."

He looked at the other girls in the room.

"Yes, she is for real," Jacque offered dryly.

"What do you need?" Then he huffed, "Just for the record, I will swear that you black mailed me into this."

Jen grinned. "I knew you were more than just a pretty face."

Costin snorted, raising a single eyebrow at her.

"We need you to help Sally and Jacque steal clothes, bedding, towels. Pretty much anything they could attempt to cover their glorious nakedness with." Jen was pacing the room as she spoke still trying to figure out the logistics of her plan. When Costin gave her a confused look, she added, "Oh, from the wolves who planned that little movie adventure."

"Okay... First. I just want to say not only do I think this is a bad idea, but I think this is a seriously bad idea."

"Seriously bad," Jen repeated. "Okay, noted."

"Alright, say I go along with this and help. How exactly are we supposed to get all of those items out of their rooms?"

Jen stopped her pacing and blew out a loud breath. "This is what I've got. All of the rooms have windows in them, right?"

Costin nodded.

"Okay, so what if Jacque and Sally were to throw the items out the window to you? Then you could take them and make a pile out in the main yard."

"Okay, then what?"

"Then we light a match and watch 'em burn, baby." Jen's eyes narrowed and the smile that slid across her face made chills run down Costin's back.

The room was quiet for several minutes.

"So when are we supposed to do this and where are these wolves going to be?" Costin finally asked.

"Oh, yeah. You missed that part," Jen grumbled, then perked up. "Well, it starts with strip poker,"

"Here she goes," Jacque muttered.

Costin's eyes widened. "Oh no, Jen. Huh uh, no freaking way. Decebel will rip my head off if he thinks I let you play strip poker with a bunch of males. There is no way that's happening. You can just forget your plan and wait for De -"

Costin was abruptly cut off when Jen stepped so close to him their chests touched. He tried to back up, but she grabbed the front of his shirt and held him in place.

"You listen up and listen good, fluffy," Jen snarled. "This is how my day has gone. I spent the morning dodging grubby paws, literally, only to have a grubby paw land on my boob and squeeze the hell out of it. I watch the wolf that is probably my mate fight said grubby paw dude and get all bloodied up. Then I got to lift my shirt in a room full of wolves to show off the oh so beautiful additions to my already glorious chest. Are you with me so far?"

Costin was smart and didn't so much as breathe.

"To top it all off, these walking flea motels videoed me and my girls without our knowledge when we were being less than ladylike – our bad. Then, after being told by Decebel to trash it and let it go, they put it on the freaking big screen and had a party – not our bad. I had to flash the whole damn pack to try to keep Decebel from killing the idiots, which means he saw the bruising and whatnot, and it will likely get me locked in a room until he decides he can handle other males being around me again. They got Dec locked up because he went all postal on them, which means I don't get to be with him. I'm a girl. I can't challenge those idiots, they would wipe the floor with my ass. But I can get even. Hell hath no fury like a woman scorned, Costin. You would do well to remember that." She let go of his shirt and stepped back, but held his stare. "I'm tired, I'm pissed, I want to see my wolf, and my chest hurts. You don't get to tell me that I can't retaliate against those who have wronged me. Are we on the same page yet?"

Costin rubbed his face and let out a deep breath. He looked back at Jen and a big grin spread across his face. "I'm so glad you're the Beta's mate.

Jen cocked her head to the side. "Why do you say that?"

"Because somebody needs to keep his head from getting any larger than it already is and I have a feeling you're just the wolf to do it. That, and you will keep him busy," Costin waggled his eyebrows suggestively, "and out of the rest of our hairs."

"Huh, he does have ego-mania," Jen agreed. "Back to the issue at hand, are you in or out?"

Costin's eyes softened. "I'm in. Someone has to make sure you girls come out of this alive. Aahh, this is such a bad idea." He groaned.

Jen grinned. "So glad to see that you are seeing things our way. We would've hated to have to tie you up and stuff you in a closet somewhere."

Costin's head snapped around to the other girls.

"Once again," Sally said dryly, "yes, she's for real."

Chapter 22

Cynthia was sitting at her desk, continuing to search the archives for any documentation on the mating of dormant and full blooded Canis lupis. Her door suddenly opened.

"Doc, we need your help," Jen announced as she and Sally walked in.

Cynthia sat back in her chair and smiled. "How can I be of service, girls?"

"First I need your word that you will keep an open mind and let me finish before you freak out." Jen held Cynthia's stare, waiting for the doctor to agree before she continued.

"Alright, I'll go along. I promise to keep an open mind and not freak out until the appropriate time."

"Great." Jen took a seat in one of the two chairs in front of the desk and Sally took the other. "I'm declaring war on the males who were stupid enough to provoke my mate."

"Your mate?" Cynthia interrupted.

"Ah ah, doc. You promised to keep a lid on it 'til I finished." Jen cocked an eyebrow at her.

Cynthia held her hands up in surrender.

"As I was saying, I'm declaring war. I don't want to hurt anyone but I do want to send a message that the females in this pack won't take crap from anyone, nor will we put up with them pissing our males off." Jen paused waiting to see if Cynthia was going to saying anything. She didn't. "So I've cooked up a plan, that although harmless, will be quite humiliating."

She went on to explain the details of her plan. All the while, Cynthia's eyes kept getting wider and wider.

"Now, one issue I was trying to figure out was how to make sure everyone gets to see the Chippendales. I think I've come up with the answer. Crina and I will be the ones to invite them to come play cards with us. We'll tell them that we need to play in the gym after everyone has left because we can't have their scent in our rooms or our males will freak. Then, after Jacque, Sally, and Costin do their part, they can take fliers – made by yours truly – and go door to door handing them out." Jen smiled, obviously pleased with herself.

Sally looked at her, brow creased. "What exactly is the flier going to say?"

"To come to the multi-pack after hours party in the gym. How you like them apples?" Jen held up her hand for Sally to high five.

Sally gave her a reluctant slap to the hand. "But when they get to the gym instead of a party they're going to get an eyeful of -"

Jen interrupted, "Bare ass were-wolves." Then she laughed.

"You are really beginning to scare me," Sally said wearily.

When Jen looked at Cynthia expectantly, she leaned forward and placed her elbows on her desk. Taking a deep breath, she asked, "And what exactly do you need me to do in this crazy, albeit somewhat ingenious, evil plan?"

"We were hoping that maybe you knew of a way to keep the wolves from phasing," Jen explained. "It would be kind of pointless if they could phase into their wolf forms."

"Wow. No pressure, huh?" Cynthia's smile was slight, but she wasn't kicking them out of her office…yet. "I don't know of any drug developed for this purpose. An Alpha can prevent their wolves from changing, but I take it you don't want any of the Alphas aware of this plan of yours?"

"You would be correct."

Cynthia tapped her chin as she thought about all the things she knew in regards to medicine and wolves. Suddenly, Sally jumped up.

"Holy crap."

"Uh, Sally dear, would you like to share your obvious epiphany?" Jen asked.

"Nepeta," Sally whispered.

"Nep-whata?"

"Nepeta," she repeated. "Don't ask me how I know this because I have no freaking clue. I'm just sitting here thinking about how crazy you are -"

"Gee, thanks for the vote of confidence," Jen muttered.

"- and then, BAM! It's just there in my brain. Nepeta. It keeps wolves from phasing."

Cynthia was sitting with her mouth wide open, staring at Sally.

Sally looked up at the doctor. She threw her hands in the air. "I'm telling you I don't know what the hell it's all about, but there it is."

Jen got up and went around to the doctor's computer, pushing against Cynthia in order to get access to the mouse and keyboard. "Move your stunned butt over and let me do some research, doc."

Cynthia absently rolled her chair out of Jen's way while she went to tapping on the keyboard.

"What are you doing?"

"Looking up Neptun," Jen answered.

"Nepeta," Sally corrected. "N-e-p-e-t-a."

She looked up. "You even know how to spell it?"

Sally nodded and swallowed hard.

Suddenly Jen laughed. "Oh, this is rich. The more common name for our little phase-freeze is cat nip." Sally actually let out a few chuckles while Jen slapped the desk. "I don't know if it gets much better than that."

Cynthia was finally knocked out of her momentary shock when Jen jolted her with the slap to the desk. She looked over to Sally and smiled.

"Uh, doc. You're kind of freaking me out," Sally admitted reluctantly.

"I think you're a healer," Cynthia told her with awe. "A gypsy healer."

Jen looked from Cynthia to Sally and back again. "Come again?"

"Every century or so, a gypsy healer appears to a pack of Canis lupis. There's no rhyme or reason to it. But it's a huge honor and pushes the power scales majorly into that pack's corner," she explained.

"What do you mean 'appears'?" Sally asked.

"Just that whoever she is – and the healer is always female – wherever she is, fate brings her to the pack she is to serve. You were destined to be Jacque's friend because Jacque was the key to leading you to this pack. Just as Jen was destined to be Jacque's friend, because she too was to be a part of the Romanian pack."

"How is that even possible?" Sally asked dubiously.

"There's no explaining the Fates, Sally," Cynthia told her honestly. "Everyone has a destiny and no matter how many times they wander, they will always find their way back to the path that will fulfill their purpose."

"So how do you know I'm a gypsy healer?" Sally sat back down in the chair she had bolted from.

"We'll have to make sure you are, but gypsy healers are blessed supernaturally with the knowledge of herbs, medicine, healing arts, things you couldn't possibly know without years of studying."

"How do you know all this?" Jen asked.

"I didn't just study human medicine when I went to medical school. I learned as much as I could about how to care for Canis lupis as well. Although, I would never be able to learn all that the healers know. I studied the history of gypsy healers within the packs a few decades ago. There hasn't been a gypsy healer, at least documented, in nearly two centuries." Cynthia shook her head in disbelief and smiled. "Wow. If we confirm this, Vasile is going to be thrilled."

"Okay, so congratulations are in order," Jen announced. "Sally, congratulations. Now we gotta move along and come back to this revelation at a later date and time."

"By all means, Jen, I just find out I'm some sort of rare commodity, but please let us plan the demise of some perverted Canis lupis." Sally rolled her eyes at her snarky best friend.

"Outstanding." Jen nodded. "So, catnip. As I was saying, that rocks mega boulders, but where can we get some? It says here that it's commonly found in Europe. And we just happen to be in Europe. Coincidence?"

"Yes," Sally interrupted.

"I think not," Jen continued, undaunted. "Cynthia, I have a mission for you should you choose to accept it."

"Oh, brother," Jacque muttered.

"Let me guess. You want me to hunt down some catnip and figure out how to make the concoction?"

"Preferably something liquid so we can spike their drinks," Jen said absently.

Cynthia sat in silence, contemplating the ramifications of being party to Jen's little scheme. She wasn't going to lie and say she was above such pettiness, because honestly, she wanted to get those little punks for thinking they mess with their females. Vasile was most assuredly going to be pissed, but then again she was already in the proverbial dog house so what the hell.

"Okay, I'm in." She clapped her hands eagerly, feeling younger than she had in a long time.

Jen winked. "I love it when a plan begins to come together, especially one that involves strip poker, bonfires, and naked werewolves. Really, what more could a woman want?"

Sally groaned as she slumped back in her chair. "This is going to be a disaster, I can feel it."

Jen's head snapped around to Cynthia. "Can gypsy girl over there tell the future?"

"No, they aren't clairvoyant."

"In that case, no, Sally. What you are feeling is the exuberant joy that comes from being a participant in one of the life-changing Jen experiences."

"Oh, is that what that is? I thought it was gas," Sally said wryly.

Ignoring Sally's remark, Jen addressed Cynthia once again. "So you've got operation phase-freeze. It's," Jen looked at her watch, "nine o'clock now. We're going to need to test it before the op commences, so we need it to be ready by tomorrow night."

"When are you planning to have this little party?" Cynthia asked.

"Day after tomorrow. Fane mentioned to Jacque that the Alphas and their mates are having a private dinner then. With them distracted, I think it will be the most opportune time to get our revenge."

"Okay," Cynthia said, standing. "I'm going to head out and see if I can't sniff out some catnip outside the estate grounds. You girls try to stay under the radar."

"Will do, doc-a-roo." Jen gave her a thumbs up and left the office.

Sally looked back at Cynthia, who smiled. "Don't worry, Sally. I'll do some research on the gypsy healers, and you and I will figure this out."

Sally returned the smile. "Thanks, doc. I appreciate it."

Chapter 23

"So the Beta has been taken out of the picture," Damion told his four pack mates. "That means the blonde won't be as protected."

"You really think she could be your mate?" Vilim asked.

He narrowed his eyes. "I don't know. I know that if she is, I'm going to rip your hands off for touching her the way you did during the training.

"Like you wouldn't have taken the opportunity," Vilim accused. "It's not like they were easy to avoid. She's rather well endowed, in case you hadn't noticed."

"Just keep your hands to yourself from now on," Damion growled

"Yes, Beta," he conceded reluctantly.

"Thad didn't say he was going to punish us for the video?" Sava asked.

Damion shook his head. "He said he didn't feel like we did anything but show our interest in the Romanian females. None of those females in the video are mated. That makes them up for grabs."

Marianna knocked on Jen's door and waited, looking around nervously. She'd gotten the information Jen asked for, although she had to make it appear that the girls weren't mad, but actually flattered by the attention from the video showing.

The door opened and Sally smiled at her. "How'd it go?" she asked.

Marianna walked in to find Jen, Jacque, Crina, and Costin all on the floor with paper spread out, holding markers. The only word she saw just at a glance was *party*.

She held up a piece of paper she had been holding and smiled. "Got the names."

Jen jumped up. "I knew you could do it!"

Marianna grinned, glad to have been helpful in some way. She was surprised at how much the Americans had started to grow on her. She felt a sadness settle over her at that thought, but quickly shook it off as Jen read the names out loud.

"So, Costin. You're a guy,"

"I'm glad you noticed." Costin grinned.

Jen rolled her eyes. "Do you know who these guys are? Other than Damion and Adrian, we met them already."

He growled. "They're all Serbian pack. Damion is the Beta. Vilim is the wolf who..." Costin paused uncomfortably.

"Got a handful," Jen added helpfully.

"You do have a way with words, Jen. I know what all of them look like."

"Perfect," Jen breathed out. "Now, to invite them out to play."

"That shouldn't be hard," Costin told her. "They're always together."

"We could talk to them at breakfast tomorrow," Crina offered.

"Good call, she-wolf," Jen praised, then looked down at the floor. "I think we've got enough fliers. Let's call it a night."

They all let out a collective breath.

"Oh, come on. Y'all act like I've just made you sign your souls over or something."

"Might as well have," Jacque muttered.

"I heard that, Jacque Pierce. Oh, and remember not to let your fur ball slip in and pick your brain, or our plan will go to sh -"

"I've got this, Jen," Jacque interrupted as she headed to the door.

Jen held up her hands and took a step back. "Alright, I know when to back off."

"Since when?" Sally's mouth quirked up at her.

Jen gave her the finger and started gathering up the scattered fliers. Everyone filed out one by one, muttering good nights.

Costin was pulling the door closed when he stopped and turned back to Jen.

"Hey, I wanted to let you know that I scoped the outside parameter of the mansion, and even found a wheelbarrow in one of the work buildings." He grinned. "I found kerosene as well. We're going to light up the night, little dormant."

Jen laughed, "Man, when you go in, you go all in, don't you?"

"I figure I'm probably going to die for helping you girls out, might as well go out with a bang."

"A wolf after my own heart," she teased. "Thanks, Costin. Really. Decebel is going to be mad."

"Understatement," Costin added quickly.

"Of the millennium," she agreed. "But whether he's my mate or not, I don't take crap from anyone. I defend myself and those I love when I can. He'll throw a major hissy fit and beat his chest, but eventually he will understand why I had to do this."

His face was serious, his voice thick with emotion. "He's blessed to have such a mate, and Alpha in every sense of the word."

Jen grinned and winked. "Bet your hot, furry ass I am."

Costin chuckled as he shut the door.

Jacque opened the door to her and Fane's room to find him lying across their bed, reading.

"You've been quiet today," he said, referring to their bond.

Jacque hated the idea of lying to Fane, even if it was a lie of omission.

"Just been with Jen and the girls. You know she's mentally exhausting. I missed you." Jacque climbed onto the bed and stretched out next to him. Hoping to distract him, she coyly added, "In more than one way."

Fane chuckled. "You won't get off the hook that easy, Luna."

Jacque nuzzled his neck as he continued to look at his book. Her hands began rubbing his back, moving up to his neck, then running through his thick dark hair.

Fane let out a deep rumble in his chest.

"Jacquelyn," he warned.

"Yes, mate?" she asked innocently.

Fane shut the book with a snap and set it aside. He rolled onto his side, propping himself up on one arm, effectively evading her roaming hands. Jacque frowned at him.

"I will admit that I am new to relationships, and obviously new to being mated. However, I've seen enough American television to understand that women think they can distract a man with sex when they are trying to avoid something."

Jacque knew her face was turning red because she could feel the heat creeping up her neck.

"So, as I spent most of the day in a semi-state of shock from the direction your thoughts have been going, which is normally not something you are super comfortable with, I came to the conclusion that you must not want me to know something." Fane narrowed his eyes. He wasn't angry, but he was slightly annoyed. "Is my assessment of the situation accurate, Jacquelyn?"

Jacque groaned and rolled onto her back, throwing her arm across her eyes.

"Luna, what's going on?" Fane asked matter of factly.

She took a deep breath and let it out. "I can't tell you."

He growled."We are keeping secrets so soon?"

Jacque's head whipped over to look at him. He saw the gleam in her emerald eyes and knew he had succeeded in ticking her off.

"It's not really my secret to tell, Fane. I'm not trying to be sneaky." Okay, that wasn't absolutely true. *But still*, she thought. "I promised not to tell you."

Fane held her stare, frustrated, but also understanding of the fact that she didn't want to break her promise. He admired that quality.

"Luna, I've let you -" He stopped and closed his eyes, pinching the bridge of his nose. "I mean, I've been willing to have you spend the majority of your time with your friends, while we've been here. Mainly because I know that I get you at night." Jacque blushed. "I understand that Jen needs you. I understand that they are very important to you. But just as my family and friends no longer come first in my life, yours do not in your life either." He reached across the space between them, hating the distance. He ran his fingers across her cheek, down her neck, shoulder, and arm, landing on her hip. He pulled her to him. "I don't mean for that to sound mean, or bossy, but your safety comes first. Jen has a tendency to throw safety out the window, along with her sense of survival."

Jacque grinned at his words, but she knew that although he was teasing, he was also telling the truth.

"I love you. I hate keeping something from you, but I need you to trust me." Jacque winced inwardly at her words, knowing she was asking him to give the trust she did not deserve at the moment.

Fane brought his hand up to the nape of her neck and pulled her face to his. He pressed his lips firmly against hers and loved that she moaned and relaxed against him. He loved that he had that effect on her. He nearly growled when he felt her tongue sweep out, seeking entrance. He opened his mouth, deepening the kiss, and listened as her heart sped up – music to his ears.

He slowed the kiss down and finally pulled away. He grazed her thoroughly loved lips with his thumb and chuckled when she nipped it. His breath caught when he saw that her canines, which only made an appearance at certain times, had descended. His eyes began to glow in reciprocation.

Fane watched in fascination as Jacque flicked her tongue against one of the sharp canines and grinned wickedly at him.

He was ready for the conversation to be finished, at least for the night. "I will trust you, love. But if something happens to you because of this secret -"

"Shhh," Jacque cut him off as she nipped his bottom lip gently. Fane growled and pulled her impossibly closer.

"It's been a while since I've had your blood," she said in response to his jest.

Fane's face sobered. *"You know you don't even have to ask. It's our wolf's way of wanting to reaffirm our mark, our claim on each other."*

"I know." She had dropped her eyes from his and was fidgeting with his shirt collar. *"It's just...embarrassing."*

Fane let out a loud laugh, throwing his head back.

Jacque looked at him, her eyes narrowed and mouth tight. "Why are you laughing at me?"

Fane's laugh finally wound down. He tugged at her ponytail to pull her hair free. He ran his hand over the wild curls and continued to grin at her. "After the thoughts you were sending me today, you little vixen, I don't see how anything can embarrass you."

Jacque rolled her eyes. "Are you going to kiss me or tease me all night?'

Fane grazed his teeth along the flesh of her neck where his mark was, his own canines descending. *"Who said anything about kissing, Luna?"*

Decebel stood up after finishing several hundred crunches and pushups. He was restless; his wolf was getting very edgy. He paced around the room, flexing his hands as his claws kept descending and retracting. He had been in a state of partial phase all day and knew that at the moment, he was more dangerous than ever.

All he could do was hope to the fates that Jennifer was staying out of trouble and that Vasile was keeping a close eye on her. Because he knew that when he got out of confinement, and found her in any less safety than being locked in her room with the door guarded, he was going to lose the minuscule amount of control he was grasping onto with both hands.

He was still fuming over the wolf who had dared to touch what was his. Then his mate had pulled that little stunt in the hall for every one's enjoyment. He wasn't going to lie to himself, Jennifer had a beautiful body. He just hadn't planned on seeing it along with the rest of his pack. Maybe he needed to explain to her that the Blood Rites performed after the Bonding Ceremony was generally where the clothes came off – in private. He would make sure to emphasize the *private.*

Her little exploit had allowed him to see the evidence of the wolf's hand on his mate's body. The bruises where his fingers had pressed hard, and the angry cuts where his claws had penetrated her flesh. To top off the day from hell, Decebel had watched – in a haze of red – a room full of unmated males lust after his mate and two of his pack mates. He snarled at all the memories, realizing that at that moment he would have killed any and all of the wolves responsible.

There was only one thing that would calm him and his wolf – Jennifer.

"Alpha," Decebel spoke into the open room. "I need to speak with you, please." His voice was guttural, so close to phasing.

Less than a minute after he spoke, the door to his room opened.

"Decebel," Vasile said his name as an Alpha in pain for one of his own's suffering.

"I need her," Decebel said honestly.

"I can't bring her to you."

"Then at least give me a phone so I can talk to her." Decebel had never been one to beg, but he was on the verge of groveling just to hear her voice.

"They will hear if you talk to her." Vasile's brow furrowed. "But...they wouldn't be able to see a text."

Decebel felt a smile spread across his face – not really a happy one, more like a "I just got away with sneaking a cookie from the cookie jar" smile. Six months ago, he wouldn't even have considered texting, but since Fane and some of the other young wolves had started to, he had sort of been forced to, and learn the lingo on top of that.

Turned out, Decebel preferred texting to talking any day. Except with his mate. *But it will have to do for now*, he thought.

"I'll return in a moment. I will have to get Jen's number."

"Hurry," Decebel growled, but added, "please."

Decebel paced and paced as he waited for his lifeline to be brought to him. If he'd any doubts about Jennifer being his mate, they had been abolished while he felt his rage grow at being apart from her.

Eventually Vasile walked in, holding out his phone. Decebel forced himself to retract his claws so he would be able to text unencumbered.

He didn't acknowledge Vasile as he left.

Decebel found her name in his contacts list and pressed the text button. A blank screen came up with a key board below it.

Decebel txt: Jennifer

He waited, growling when she didn't respond immediately. His phone finally vibrated as her text appeared.

Jennifer txt: Fur ball

Decebel growled, but grinned at her smart mouth. His phone vibrated again before he could respond.

Jennifer txt: r u ok?

She cared. His heart was in his throat as he read the simple text.

Decebel txt: slightly grumpy

Jennifer txt: so ur ok then

Decebel laughed, feeling his wolf settle, if only a little. It was enough to keep him sane.

Decebel txt: how r u?

Jennifer txt: miss n u

Decebel txt: I miss u 2 baby

Jennifer txt : r we agreeing?

Decebel txt: never

Jennifer txt: r u mad at me?
Decebel txt: idk
Jennifer txt: :(
Decebel txt: ur mine
Jennifer txt: yes
Decebel txt: only mine 2 c
Jennifer txt: didn't know how 2 distract u
Decebel txt: mission accomp
Jennifer txt: lol
Decebel txt: keep ur clothes on
Jennifer txt: blunt much?
Decebel txt: keep ur clothes on
Jennifer txt: that can make things difficult
Decebel txt: Jennifer. Keep. Ur. Clothes. On.
Jennifer txt: fine, I'll keep some clothes on
Decebel txt: I need u
Jennifer txt: V said no
 Decebel txt: u asked him
Jennifer txt: of course, ur mine
Decebel txt: grrr
Jennifer txt: a good grrr?
Decebel txt: definitely
Jennifer txt: excellent
Decebel txt: r u bn good
Jennifer txt: hmm more specific
Decebel txt: Jennifer
Jennifer txt: im always good at whatev I do
Decebel txt: not reassuring
Jennifer txt: do u disagree?
Decebel txt: can't
Jennifer txt: ?
Decebel txt: been on the other end of ur good
Jennifer txt: ur b n wicked bad
Decebel txt: ur fault, I was innocent b 4 met u
Jennifer txt: im sure u were squeaky clean
Decebel txt: I shld let u sleep
Jennifer txt: LET? really

Decebel knew the only way he was going to get her to go to sleep would be reverse psychology. As much as he wanted to sit and text her all night, she needed her rest.

Decebel txt: I need sleep baby

Jennifer txt: ur a quik learnr

Decebel txt: dream of me

Jennifer txt: I'll think about it

Decebel txt: mate, grrr

Jennifer txt: hmmm yummy

Decebel txt: Woman! Go 2 bed

Jennifer txt: alone?

Decebel txt: hell yes alone!

Jennifer txt: such a big bed, lonely n it

Decebel txt: Jennifer

Jennifer txt: I evr told u ur sexy when ur bossy?

Decebel txt: yes, u were drunk off ur cute ass

Jennifer txt: blushing

Decebel txt: u should b, go 2 bed

Jennifer txt: can't txt u if asleep :(

Decebel txt: ur kill n me

Jennifer txt: assure u that's not what I want 2 do 2 u

Decebel txt: blushing

Jennifer txt: LMAO!

Decebel txt: Go. To. Bed.

Jennifer txt: join me?

Decebel txt: phone will b by my heart

Jennifer txt: tears

Decebel txt: don't cry baby

Jennifer txt: why here? why now?

Decebel txt: don't know Jennifer

Jennifer txt: sucks

Decebel txt: I'm holding u

Jennifer txt: more tears

Decebel txt: wolf gettn restless

Jennifer txt: sorry, I'm ok

Decebel txt: hold me 2

Jennifer txt: all nite long

Decebel txt: nite baby xoxo

Jennifer txt: nite

Decebel txt: no lovin 4 me?

Jennifer txt: didn't want 2 get u all worked up

Decebel txt: thanks 4 ur concern

Jennifer txt: nite, deep intense kiss, hands in your hair, bodies pressed together

Decebel txt: GRRRRRRRRR

Jennifer txt: what? 2 much?

Decebel txt: i'll dream of u

Jennifer txt: I bet u will, lol, nite B

Decebel txt: nite baby

Decebel scrolled through their texts, smiling at her playfulness. It wasn't enough, but it would get him through the night.

Jennifer curled into a ball in the bed that she'd told Decebel was too big to be in by herself. All day she had kept herself busy. Now here, in the dark, she could feel the hole that was widening with every moment away from Decebel.

She had been thrilled when Vasile had told her she could text him. She smiled to herself, remembering his texts. Decebel had a sweet, romantic side. And bloody hell if it wasn't the sexiest thing ever. She closed her eyes and thought of him. His handsome face, dark hair, amber eyes.... She fell asleep to the memories of her mate's deep, soothing voice and strong body holding her.

Chapter 24

Cynthia yawned as she sat at the table with her pack, eating breakfast. She'd been out searching until two in the morning. She had phased when she went out looking for it, knowing her wolf could move much faster. Finally, over ten miles away from the estate, she found the Nepeta, a.k.a. catnip. She was still working on perfecting it in liquid form – the hardest part was that it needed to be potent enough, but also dissolved so the plant's little particles weren't visible. People tend to get suspicious when there's stuff floating in their drinks.

Cynthia caught Jen's eye across the table and nodded, a subtle motion for her to follow her out of the room.

Cynthia was waiting in the hall when the five girls came out, Costin at their heels. *Yeah, this doesn't look suspicious,* she thought.

"Whatchya got, doc?" Jen asked.

"I found the Nepeta ten miles out. I've been working on it all morning, and the only thing I'm not sure about is its potency while making it undetectable in the drink."

"You found something that will keep the guys from being able to phase?" Costin spoke low, so as not to be overheard.

Cynthia, Jen, and Sally all nodded but didn't elaborate.

He lifted his eyebrows. "Ooookay, how did you find out about it?"

Sally looked over at Cynthia who gave a nearly imperceptible shake of her head.

"We just did some digging and it sort of fell in our laps," Jen told him vaguely.

"Uh-huh, just fell in your laps." Costin eyed them suspiciously. "Well, if that's your story..."

"Finalized, illustrated, and edited." Jen gave him a sharp nod. "Alright. Moving along, people. Doc, we need test subjects for your mojo."

"That would be the most accurate way to determine if it's effective," Cynthia agreed.

Jen smiled sweetly at Costin.

Costin watched the gleam in Jen's eyes as she smiled at him. Realizing what she was thinking, he put his hands up. "No way, Jen. Come on, you can't ask me to do that. I can't protect you guys if I can't phase. No. I'm putting my foot down."

Jen didn't argue, realizing that no amount of flirting, groveling, pushing, or bribing was going to work on Costin. She watched each member of their group, all trying to think of a wolf to test this concoction on.

Finally, Cynthia spoke up. "I'll do it. It's my creation, I should be the one to test it."

"Are you sure you want to do that, Cynthia?" Sally asked.

"Yes, definitely. I'll take Jacque, Sally, and Costin with me while you three go bait your prey."

Jen held out her fist to Cynthia's. Cynthia picked up on what Jen was after and balled her fist and bumped it to Jen's.

"Let's get this party started, ladies."

Costin cleared his throat and look pointedly at the evil schemer.

"Oh, for crying out loud. Let's get this party started, ladies *and* hot werewolf. Happy?" Jen asked.

"You think I'm hot?" Costin grinned and winked.

"You don't hold a candle to B, so don't get too excited."

"Ouch. I'm hurt, Jen." Costin smiled, placing his hand over his heart.

Jen shook her head and turned to Marianna and Crina, "You two ready?"

"Totally." Crina smiled.

Marianna gave a weak, "Yipee," her eyebrows raised as she made pom-pom motions with her hands.

"That's the spirit." Jen laughed. "Let's go find the rat pack."

Damion looked up from his table to see the blonde American and the two female Romanian wolves coming towards him. "This day is looking up boys."

The other four turned in their seats to watch as the girls walked confidently to their table.

They stopped a foot away and looked each of them over.

"I hear you boys are the ones who put that wicked cool video together." Jen smirked as she folded her arms across her chest – not by accident.

Damion's eyes wandered south of her neck before returning to her face.

"That was us." Damion winked. "We wanted to share all that beauty with everyone."

"Aw, that's sweet." Jen glanced back at Crina and Marianna. "Isn't that sweet, girls?"

"Very sweet." Crina raised an eyebrow at the wolves.

Marianna silently nodded with a sweet smile.

"Is there something we can do for you, ladies?" Adrian spoke up, drawing their attention.

"Actually, we came over to invite you guys to a friendly game of cards tomorrow night. There will be refreshments."

Damion leaned back in his seat and folded his arms. He unabashedly eyed Jen, starting at her feet, going all the way to the top of her blonde head.

"Who else will be there, beautiful?"

"You five studs and us." Jen indicated herself and the two girls with her.

He raised his eyebrows as a smile slid across his face. "And what kind of cards will be played?"

Jen leaned forward, resting her hand on the table so she could whisper closely, "The kind that rhymes with lip stroker." She winked and then stood as she watched Damion's brain deduce what she had just told him. "If you wanna play be in the gym tomorrow night at ten o'clock. It's our little secret, if you get my drift."

Damion watched as she walked away with a very appealing swing in her hips. He heard several of his pack mates give low whistles.

"So are we in?" Adrian asked his Beta.

"Like I would ever pass up playing strip poker with some fine women." Damion rolled his eyes. "Yes, we're in," he reiterated when Vilim and Josif looked at him blankly.

"Strip poker!" Vilim suddenly announced.

"Shhh."

"Shut up, you idiot." Damion and Adrian waved him off.

"I didn't realize that was what she was talking about," Vilim continued.

"What else would rhyme with lip stroker?" Damion asked his pack mate, voice filled with exasperation.

"You four keep your traps shut," Damion warned. "I don't want any other males catching whiff of this. Those she-wolves are ours."

"That went well," Jen said enthusiastically. She felt her phone vibrate and pulled it from the back pocket of her snug jeans.

Decebel txt: morning beautiful

Jen knew the grin that stretched across her face probably looked ridiculous, but she didn't care. Decebel thought she was beautiful, and was thinking about her. The only thing that could make it sweeter was if he were to tell her himself.

Jen txt: morning yourself

"You think they'll show up?" Crina's voice brought Jen back to the present.

"Honey, their eyes were roaming all over us. They'll be there." She looked at her phone as she said, "Let's head to Cynthia's office and see how things are going."

Decebel had texted her again.

Decebel txt: what r u do n 2day?

Jen knew that Decebel didn't want her participating in any more of the activities that were planned, but Vasile couldn't justify her not being there. She had to answer this carefully – if she couldn't be honest she would just redirect his attention.

Jen txt: basket weaving

They reached Cynthia's office and opened the door without knocking. Costin, Jacque and Sally were already there, sitting and staring at the doctor.

"Sooo, how's it going, guys?" Jen asked carefully.

"We're waiting," Jacque whispered.

Jen looked at each of them and then at Crina and Marianna.

"Waiting for what?"

"To see if she phases," Sally answered her.

"Why are we whispering?" Crina asked.

"Don't know. Just seems like we shouldn't be loud or make any sudden movements," Jacque replied absently.

Costin rolled his eyes and looked at Jen. "It's been fifteen minutes and so far she can't phase." He spoke in a regular volume.

"How much did you drink, doc?" Jen asked.

"I put about one third of a cup in eight ounces of liquid. So far I just feel stuck. Like my skin is just stuck. I don't really know how to describe it."

The other full blooded wolves in the room all cringed at Cynthia's description.

"So we just sit and wait?" Crina asked.

"Pretty much." Costin nodded.

"What time is the group activity we're supposed to be doing today?"

"Eleven," Jen answered, looking at her phone. It was nine now, and she had another text.

Decebel txt: why do I not like the sound of that

Jen grinned. *Smart wolf.*

Jen txt: basket weaving is perfectly safe

Decebel txt: so it's an all girl class?

"Sneaky wolf," Jen snickered.

Jen txt: define all

Decebel txt: entire, every one, total, whole

Jen txt: cute

Decebel txt: answer

Jen txt: I gotta use the girls room, b back

Jen txt: fyi, the girls room is all, entirely, totally, wholly girls :)

Decebel txt: Jennifer!

Jen ignored the last text. She didn't want to flat out lie to him. He would just worry and probably tear something up. She leaned back against the wall and slid to the floor. Closing her eyes, she prepared to wait with the others to see how long it took until Cynthia could phase. Her phone vibrated several more times. She didn't look at the texts, but she knew would they'd probably be in all caps.

Bad Jen, she thought to herself.

Jacque walked into the dining room and straight into Fane's arms.

"That's better," Fane murmured in her mind.

"I missed you, too." She snuggled into his chest and let out a deep breath. Dealing with all the drama of Jen's scheme and Cynthia's magic potion was wearing her out. Although, they were all a little less stressed on discovering it took Cynthia over three hours to phase after drinking her catnip concoction. At least they knew that part of the plan would work.

"I hope you don't mind, but your father asked if we would eat with them and I said we would."

Jacque smiled at the worried look on Fane's handsome face. "That's fine, wolf-man."

As they walked out, Jen passed by.

"I'll meet you in your room later, Jen," Jacque said with a calm demeanor.

"Okay, have fun." Jen winked at them and smiled at Fane. "Hey, hottie. Taking care of my girl?"

Fane chuckled. "Always."

"I mean that in many ways," Jen tossed at them as they continued out. "Just in case you didn't catch that."

"Where are they going?" Sally asked she sat down next to Jen at the table.

"I'm assuming to eat with Dillon," Jen told her. "But I've been known to be wrong on rare occasions. There's the distinct possibility that this is one of those occasions."

Sally rolled her eyes. "It must be exhausting being you, Jennifer Adams."

"It's a big responsibility, no doubt," Jen said seriously. "I mean, the expectations would make a weaker woman falter."

"Oh, definitely."

"I'm just saying, Sal, it ain't easy being green."

Sally snorted. "You're not green."

Jen waved her off. "It's all relative, chica."

Crina and Marianna ambled in, then Costin. Cynthia trailed in last. They were trying to break up their "together time," so that it didn't look suspicious. It probably wasn't working since they all looked as guilty as Professor Plumb in the conservatory with the candle stick.

They ate quickly, all of them eager to finalize the plans for the next night. Jen was ready to have some alone time. She used the word alone loosely – she would quasi-be with Decebel. He'd been texting her all day, most of them the equivalent of growling her name. She hated to leave him hanging, but she'd had to do the stupid pool lessons.

Yes, she thought. *You heard right. We had pool lessons, as in billiard tables.* The last thing she needed was Decebel imagining her leaning over a pool table with a bunch of unmated males surrounding her…which was exactly what had happened. She would conveniently leave that little bit out tonight when she texted him.

Before Jen could leave the table, Vasile spoke up. "You all remember that tonight is another pack gathering?"

"Crap," Jen muttered and was followed by several others in their little posse muttering similar expletives.

Vasile lifted an eyebrow. "Plans?"

Jen's eyes widened and she was frozen in the stare of the Alpha. Her brain just stopped, the only thing she could hear was a little voice screaming, *Busted.*

"Oh, um," Sally started. "I think Jen was wanting to sit this one out, with all that's happened."

Jen looked at Sally and willed her to see the gratitude in her eyes.

"Well, I suppose I could say that you aren't feeling well," Vasile said thoughtfully. He looked back at Sally, "Am I correct in assuming that there are several other females who are wanting to sit this one out with Jen?"

Sally nodded. "Yes, Alpha. Sir."

Alina smiled at Sally's nervousness.

"Fine, then. But you are not to leave Jen's room. For anything." Vasile stared pointedly at each of girls.

"Yes, Alpha," they all said in unison.

As Jen stood to leave, she caught Costin's eye and mouthed, "Later."

He gave a slight nod.

Cynthia also nodded.

Disaster averted, Jen thought with a sigh.

Chapter 25

"Okay let's go over it one more time," Jen announced as she laid back on her bed. There was a collective groan throughout the room.

"Jen, it's nearly one in the morning," Costin complained.

"One more time, then I promise I'll let you go."

Jacque scoffed. "How kind of you, oh great one."

Jen turned her head and smiled at her. "I know, right?"

"Come on, Jen. I'm tired, cranky, and I have a hot werewolf waiting in my bed."

"Okay, at ten o'clock Crina, Marianna, and I will be..."

"In the gym," Crina supplied.

"I will make sure the spiked drinks will be on the side the guys are going to sit," Marianna explained.

"And Jacque and Sally will be..." Jen looked pointedly at the two girls.

"Making our way to the suckers' rooms," Jacque said dryly.

"Such enthusiasm, Jac. Thank you."

"Cynthia and I will be outside below the windows of the rooms waiting for the bonfire donations," Costin added.

"Great. Then..."

"Jacque will go to the gym and watch to see when the guys have thoroughly lost. Then we'll go door to door passing out the fliers," Sally continued.

"Right." Jen looked at Cynthia. "And you..."

"Will be waiting to hear from Jacque via text that the party has started, then torch the loot."

"Superb! I think we've got it, boys and girls."

"Finally," Jacque groaned as she stood up and stretched. "I'm out." She waved to Jen and headed out the door. Costin, Cynthia, Crina, and Marianna were all right behind her.

Sally stood at the foot of Jen's bed and looked down at her friend.

"You doing okay, Jen?"

Jen smiled up at Sally. "I'm better now that Decebel and I can communicate, even if it is just texts."

"And you're sure you want to go through with this?"

"I'm sure," Jen said simply.

Sally nodded once. "Okay then, Lucy. I'll see you in the morning."

"Sleep tight, Ethel."

Jennifer jumped up and went about getting ready for bed. All she wanted in that moment was to crawl under the covers and then spend time with a certain brooding werewolf.

Throwing on sweats and a long sleeved t-shirt, she hurried into the bathroom, brushed her teeth and washed her face. As she patted her face dry with a towel, she paused to look in the mirror. Something was different, but she couldn't put her finger on what it was. Her hair was as long and blonde as ever, her eyes crystal blue, skin fair and smooth, and yet there was still something. She shrugged her shoulders and tossed the towel on the counter.

As she climbed into the soft, big bed she snagged her phone from the bedside table. She propped herself up against the headboard with the many fluffy pillows that adorned the bed and hit the text message icon on her phone.

"Oh boy," she muttered as she saw text after text from Decebel. *I knew it was going to be bad,* she thought as her fingers began moving deftly across the small onscreen keyboard.

Jen txt: Hello?

Jen held her breath as she waited for his response. And waited, and waited. She frowned at her phone. "Okay, maybe he's asleep," she spoke into the darkness. A few more minutes went by with no response.

Feeling bereft and very empty, she snuggled down into the pillows and laid the phone beside her. She knew she should have answered his texts, but she also knew he was going to be upset and worried if he knew she was out among the other males. *Could have handled that better.*

Jen had just begun to drift off into a restless sleep when her phone chirped.

She looked at the screen through sleep-filled eyes. She nearly cried when she saw it was a text from Decebel. She didn't care if he yelled at her, she just needed to hear from him.

Decebel txt: Hey baby

Now she did cry. She was expecting him to rant and rave, but instead he sent her a simple *"hey baby."* She could hear him in her mind, and see the half smile that would be on his lips. She sat back up and wiped her tears away before replying.

Jen txt: No yelling?

Decebel txt: r u ok?

Jen txt: physically yes

Decebel txt: did anyone touch u 2day?

Jen txt: no

Decebel txt: no yelling

Jen txt: I'm sorry 4 not responding

Decebel txt: I understand why

Decebel txt: doesn't mean I like it

Jen txt: I worried u

Decebel txt: yes

Jen txt: I shouldn't have

Decebel txt: I'm not mad Jennifer

Jen txt: thank you

Decebel txt: I miss u. I feel empty

Jen txt: me 2

Decebel txt: I will see u 2moro nite

Jen shot straight up at the words on her screen. He was getting out? Tomorrow night? "Not good," she muttered. Okay, she was going to have to get Costin to intercept and stall him somehow. She snorted. "Yeah, that'll go over real well."

Jen txt: ur get n out ;)

Decebel txt: Vasile is talking with the other As, explaining our situation

Jen txt: that's good

Decebel txt: r u happy?

Jen txt: of course! I have no 1 to growl at me w/u gone :)

Decebel txt: It's late

Jen txt: is that ur way of telln me 2 sleep w/out b n bossy?

Decebel txt: it's my job to take care of u Jennifer

Jen txt: hey B, it's late and I'm tired, think I'll call it a nite

Decebel txt: lol, that's my girl
Jen txt: miss u, nite xoxo
Decebel txt: miss u more, nite baby xoxo

Jen set her phone on the bedside table and snuggled back into the covers. She was exhausted, but rest would elude her because now she had to figure out how she was going to keep Decebel from finding out about her plan. She knew that after it was said and done he would be angry, but her motto had always been "it's easier to ask for forgiveness than for permission."

Looked like that motto was finally going to bite her in the butt.

Decebel lay back on the bed in his temporary prison and thought about Jennifer's response to his release tomorrow. He'd expected a little more than *"that's good"* and since he didn't doubt her feelings for him, that only left one other explanation. She was up to something. He smiled to himself. His mate was going to keep him on his toes, no boring life for him. Oddly enough he looked forward to the havoc she was sure to wreak.

Decebel closed his eyes and chuckled to himself. Now, only to get out tomorrow and stop whatever plan she and her cohorts were implementing without killing some innocent – or not so innocent – males.

"How is Decebel doing?" Alina asked her mate as she curled up next to him in their bed, her head on his chest.

Vasile stroked her long dark hair gently. Even after centuries there was still nothing better than his mate in his arms, her scent surrounding him.

"He seems to be a little better since he can communicate with Jen."

Alina laughed. "I can't see Decebel texting like some enamored teenager."

Vasile smiled and chuckled with her. "I've no doubt she is his mate and like all of us males is utterly lost without her."

"So you admit that you would be lost without me," she teased.

"Mina, ma vad (see me)," he whispered.

Alina leaned back so she could look into his eyes, a privilege few had.

"Eu sint nimic fara tine (I am nothing without you). Fara tine nimic in viata aceasta ar insemna nimic (Without you, nothing in this life would mean anything)." Vasile pulled her up so that he could place both hands on either side of her face. Gently, he stroked her cheeks and loved the way her skin flushed under his gaze.

"Without you, Alina, colors would not be as bright, fragrances would not be as sweet, and food would be bitter ash in my mouth. For two centuries you have been by my side. Not behind me, but by my side, as my equal. During these two centuries I don't know if I have ever truly expressed to you what you are to me, what you mean to me."

Vasile wiped the tears that had escaped from her eyes. He leaned forward and kissed her softly, then pulled back just enough so that when he spoke his lips brushed hers. "If Jacque and Jen are even half the woman you are, Fane and Decebel will be blessed beyond all measure. So never, ever doubt that without you I would wander through this world in darkness and hopelessness. I would be a shell of a man, unable to lead, unable to care for my pack. I love you, Alina mine."

They sat quietly, forehead to forehead, lips barely touching. Breathing in each other's air, literally being life to the other. When they finally turned out the light, wrapped in each other's arms, Alina whispered into the darkness the words she had spoken during their long ago Bonding ceremony.

"Sufletul meu pentru dumneavoastra, inima mea pentru dumneavoastra, viata mea pentru dumneavoastra (My soul for yours, my heart for yours, my life for yours)."

"Always, Mina," Vasile whispered into her mind.

Chapter 26

"Look alive, people." Jen clapped her hands as she walked into the small room she had requested, via text, they all meet her in.

"What's going on, Queen o' drama?" Sally asked.

"Decebel texted me last night. I'll spare you the sappy details, but -"

"That's a first," Jacque muttered.

Jen made a hand motion like a mouth closing and shushed Jacque.

"What I will share is that he said he's getting out tonight."

Mutterings rippled across the room: "Crap." "Great." "Perfect."

"I knew this would happen," Costin growled. "Do you know what he's going to do to me when he finds out I helped you, Jen?"

"I have a fairly good idea. But we aren't going to freak out like a bunch of amateurs."

"But we are amateurs, you -" Before Jacque could finish, Jen interrupted.

"Uh-uh, no need for name calling."

"Puulease, I know you've called me much worse." She rolled her eyes.

"Jacque dear, that's the past. This is the now, and right now we need to figure out how we are going to keep the big bad wolf from finding out about the three little pigs' scheme."

"Did you just refer to us as the three little pigs?" Sally asked incredulously.

"Oh, good grief. Fine. Three little, hot as hell, give Ms. Piggy a run for her money, pigs. Better?" Jen batted her eyes.

"You're in rare form, Jennifer Adams."

"Okay, so what I'm thinking," Jen continued, "is that Costin or Cynthia will have to be the ones to be on the lookout for Dec because y'all will be able to smell him before you ever see him."

Costin groaned. "I knew I should have just stayed in my room. Kept to myself. But nope, I just had to hang around the hot unmated females. I just had to be my usual charming self."

"No self esteem issues on that side of the room, huh?" Sally interrupted.

He looked up at her and grinned. "I have a weakness for beautiful women and they seem to have a weakness for me."

"Definitely no self esteem issues."

Jen continued on, ignoring their play. "I don't think we need to change any of our plans at this point. I think we just need to be extra vigilant."

"Did you just use the word vigilant?" Jacque laughed.

"Jacque!" Jen growled.

"Okay, okay. I'll shut up. I realize your evil plan is stressing you out."

"Honestly," Jen agreed. "Who knew it would be so exhausting being the villain?"

"Haven't you ever watched any Disney movies?" Sally asked as they all stood up to go to breakfast.

Jen looked at her questioningly.

"Seriously, Jen, do you think all those wicked witches look like they've been ridden hard and hung out to dry because it's easy being evil?"

Cynthia, Crina, and Marianna, who'd been sitting quietly through the meeting, lost their composure at that.

Jacque and Jen were grinning from ear to ear.

"I do believe we have managed to corrupt our sweet little Sally." Jacque high fived Jen.

"It's about time, too." Jen nudged Sally with her shoulder. "I was beginning to think that she was beyond help."

"You two are disturbed. Like, seriously in need of major pills and years of counseling disturbed."

Crina looked over at Cynthia. "Are all Americans like this?"

Cynthia winked. "No, I think it's a Southern thing."

Jen cackled. "It's like I always say, us Southern belles give 'em hell!"

"Yee-haw!" Jacque and Sally hollered as they made their way into the hall.

"Way to not draw attention to us, ladies," Costin muttered as they passed other pack members.

"Costin, sweetie, there is no way to *not* draw attention to all this."

All the girls laughed as Costin rolled his eyes.

"Let's go -" Jacque started.

"Get our grub on. Yeah yeah, we know, wolf princess."

Vasile waited for everyone to be seated before he addressed them about the day's plans.

"I wanted to give you all an update on the situation with Decebel."

Jen sat up straighter, waiting to see what Vasile would say.

"Alina and I will be dining with the other Alphas tonight, and I plan to broach the subject of Decebel and Jen. Hopefully, once I explain things, they will be willing to allow Jen and Decebel to spend some time together without requiring them to participate in any more events."

Jen let out the breath she'd been holding. "Is Decebel going to be allowed out tonight?"

Vasile's eyes softened as he looked at Decebel's mate. "I don't know yet, Jen. If the Alphas don't agree, then it will probably be best to keep Decebel separate from everyone until we return home."

Jen just nodded her head in understanding.

"As for the rest of the day, our females will be having fencing lessons. Some of the older unmated males come from a time period when guns were not the method of warfare."

"No offense, Alpha," Jen spoke up, "but telling us that the males we should be looking for as mates are old enough to be considered exhibits in ancient museums doesn't do much for the ol' libido."

Crina and Marianna snickered while Sally rolled her eyes and covered her face in exasperation.

Vasile smiled. "So, then you will be happy to know that your mate is at least half a century away from being inducted into said exhibit."

Jen glared. "Not cool, V. So not cool."

Vasile chuckled and winked at her.

"Let's eat and be off. Oh, and one more thing, Jen," Vasile addressed her, face wiped clean of the smile. "Please refrain from stabbing some poor, unsuspecting wolf."

Jen blinked innocently. "Does that mean I can stab a suspecting fur ball?"

Vasile growled.

"I'll take that as a negative. Roger that, Alpha sir."

Chapter 27

Thad answered the cell phone that vibrated in his pocket.

"What?" he snapped at his contact. "So you have found a location to take her? Did you get the urine to pour on her?" He listened. "I understand that you think it's disgusting, but it would be pointless to hide her if they could sniff her out. The urine will mask it. Do as I ask. You know the price you will pay if you do not." He hit the end button and slipped the phone back into his pocket.

He stepped from the suite into the adjoining area that had been set up as a dining room, and watched as two of his mated females prepared the table for the dinner that would take place in less than an hour. He had made sure every detail had been taken care of, down to the moment he would hand Vasile, the greatest Alpha in two centuries, the fatal drink.

Thad smiled to himself as he thought about how the week had played out. Vasile's Beta was locked up, and they were all so distracted by the situation with him and the American they didn't have any idea there was a traitor amongst them.

He walked over to the mini bar and poured a drink. He lifted it into the air as he whispered under his breath, "Here's to a night to remember." He slung the liquor back, savoring the burn it caused in his throat.

A knock at the door brought him out of his reverie. He motioned for one of the females to open it. Dragomir and his mate Agnes walked in.

"Dragmoir," Thad inclined his head to the Hungary pack Alpha, then approached his mate. "Agnes. Looking ravishing, as always." He took her hand and gently laid a kiss on it.

"Thank you, Thad." Agnes smiled genuinely. "We feel honored to be your guests and honored to be included in this monumental event. It's time we stop fighting amongst the packs and join forces to help our species survive."

"Spoken like a true Alpha female."

They continued with small talk as each Alpha and his mate arrived. Vasile and Alina were last, both walking with the confidence that comes with reigning for two centuries. Thad made himself smile and gush over Alina just as he had the other females. He reminded himself that this would be the last time he would have to watch the pair cloaked in their own power. That thought was enough to bring about a sincere smile as he invited them all to sit around the table.

He planned for them to eat and relax, to give Vasile and his mate one more good meal before they left this life. Then he would personally hand each couple a glass of his oldest and most expensive wine. The poison would begin flooding Vasile's system within half an hour of consumption, and all hell would break loose.

"I can't believe that wuss bellyached when I nicked him with the tip of my sword," Jen growled as she and the other TFFs climbed the stairs to convene in her room. They'd finished dinner a couple of hours ago and had been sitting around, shooting the breeze when Jacque glanced at her phone and noticed it was only forty five minutes until Jen, Crina, and Marianna were supposed to meet the males in the gym.

"Jen, you slit his wrist. That's a little more than a nick," Sally pointed out.

"It healed in under a minute. I could understand his moaning if I had cut his hand off, but seriously."

Crina and Marianna laughed at Jen as they all piled into her room.

Jen immediately turned and pointed at Jacque and Sally. "Okay, you two are to meet Costin and Cynthia in," she glanced at her phone, "twenty minutes in Cynthia's office." She turned to Crina and Marianna. "I think we should wear bathing suits under our clothes. That way, if the top layer does come off, we aren't showing off our undies."

"Okay, we'll go and change and meet you back here in fifteen minutes," Crina told her as she and Marianna left. Jen gave them a nod, heading for her closet.

"Okay, Jen. We're out," Jacque hollered as she and Sally headed for the door.

"Wait, hold up." Jen stuck her head out from around the closet door. "What did you tell wolf-man you were doing this evening?"

"That I was spending quality time with Sally. Which isn't really a lie."

Jen smiled, but it was sad. "I'm sorry you've had to keep this from him."

Jacque shrugged. "I take comfort in knowing Decebel is going to beat your ass when it's all said and done."

Sally laughed.

"Thanks for that, Jac," Jen grumbled.

"Just keeping it real." Jacque waved as she and Sally left.

Jen stood in her closet, contemplating just how angry the Beta was going to be. "Won't be pretty, that's for sure," she muttered as she continued to search for her clothes.

Twenty minutes later, Jen, Crina, and Marianna sat in the middle of the gym with a deck of cards, glasses they had stolen at dinnertime, and some vodka Costin had somewhat shadily acquired. They had laid pillows from their beds around in a circle to lounge on, and Jen had set up her iPhone to play club music. Crina managed to figure out how to turn on only half the lights so it wasn't so bright, but a soft glow fell over the floor.

"Okay, now we just need the -" Before Crina could finish her sentence, the gym door opened and in walked four wolves.

"Where's the fifth man?" Jen asked with a wink.

"Alpha had business for him to take care of, so you ladies will have to make do with the four of us," Damion answered.

"I'm sure we'll manage somehow," Crina flirted.

Jen indicated where they should sit and Marianna passed out the shots.

"Okay, let's start this night out right." Jen lifted her glass filled with just enough vodka to throw back. "Here's to a night to remember!"

Everyone raised their glasses and clinks filled the room as they tapped them together and drank.

Jen watched the four wolves to see if there was any indication that they'd realized their drinks were laced. She grinned when they held their glasses out for another. Crina poured the shots as Jen began shuffling the deck.

"Okay, so you boys know how to play poker?"

"We looked up the specifics on the internet," Adrian informed her.

Jen looked at Crina and Marianna out of the corner of her eye. "Excellent," is what came from her lips, but she was thinking, *Like taking candy from a baby.*

She dealt out the cards. "We're going to keep it simple and play five card draw. Now, just like in a regular game, you can chose to fold, you can bluff, and you can call. Since we aren't playing for money, the easiest way to determine how the clothes come off are based on the bets. For example, if you bet a dollar that would equal a sock. If you were to bet five dollars that would be a shirt, so on and so forth. Make sense?"

"So the higher the bet the more intimate the apparel that is removed?" Damion asked.

"Exactly." Jen smiled.

"You've really put some thought into this, haven't you?" Josif asked.

"We Westerners take our poker very seriously, regardless of the method of pay." She set down the cards left in the deck and picked up her own. Everyone followed suit and looked at their hands.

"Okay. So, starting with the player to my left – Crina, place your bets." Jen looked at her expectantly.

Earlier, Jen had told them to only stay in the game when the bet was under five bucks, and fold any other time. She didn't like to brag, but she knew poker. She'd have these guys in their skivvies in no time. She would make the big bets to bait them, and regardless of the fact that they were wolves, they were men and she was just a little ol' girl. They wouldn't want to fold – it would make them appear unconfident and weak.

Jen had grinned at Crina and Marianna and made them laugh when she broke Kenny Rogers' "The Gambler." Marianna had asked, "Do you Americans have a song for everything?"

Her response had been, "You should see our reality TV."

Crina placed her bet.
And so it begins, Jen thought.

"Okay, let's go." Costin rubbed his hands together nervously.

"You okay Costin?" Sally asked. "You seem a little jumpy."

Costin looked at her and grinned. "Ask me after I survive this with my manhood intact."

Sally blushed and quickly followed Jacque.

They made it to the bottom of the staircase on the east side of the mansion. The Serbian pack's rooms were nearby.

"Okay." Costin pointed. "I'll come up with you and make sure the rooms are empty. Then Cynthia and I will go wait beneath the windows for you to start chucking out the goods."

Jacque nodded.

Sally cringed. "I think I'm going to be sick."

Jacque grabbed her by the shoulders. "Hold it together, Sal. We got this, okay?"

"We got this," Sally repeated, sounding anything but confident.

Costin tried the doorknob of the first room that he knew to be Damion and Adrian's. It opened smoothly into a dark interior. He grinned. "Good to go, ladies." He motioned them inside. "I'll check the other two and be on my way. You two hurry, alright?"

Sally and Jacque nodded as they began moving into the dark room.

Jacque made a beeline for the closet while Sally started stripping the beds.

"I really think we should be wearing gloves for this." Sally cringed as she pulled the sheets off and rolled them into a tight ball.

"Hey, leave one of those sheets unrolled. We can put all the clothes in a pile on the sheet and throw it out all together," Jacque hollered from the closet.

"Good call."

Jacque came out of the closet, arms full of clothes."Let's do this."

Sally laughed. She went to the window and pushed it open. Then she nudged the screen out and it fell three stories below, where Cynthia and Costin stood.

Costin waved and motioned for her to start throwing stuff down. Sally grinned and gave a thumbs up. She grabbed the first set of bedding and tossed it out. She looked down and saw Cynthia gather it up and put it in a wheelbarrow.

From there on out they worked like a well-oiled machine. Jacque ran around grabbing anything that could possibly cover a body part, Sally threw it out the window, and Costin and Cynthia stowed it in the wheelbarrow.

Five minutes later, they moved onto the next room.

Sally started pulling the sheets off the beds again as Jacque busted out a whispered version of "Heartless." Sally joined in as they worked.

On the third and final room, Sally leaned out the window as she dropped the final article of clothing. "How's the bonfire looking?" she whispered as loud as she could.

Costin grinned. "It's going to be epic!"

She giggled as Jacque pulled her back in. "Come on, Sal. We don't have time for flirting."

Sally's mouth dropped. "I so was not flirting."

"Just keep telling yourself that, sweetie. Maybe when Jen becomes a nun it will be true." She laughed as she tugged Sally out of the room and down the stairs. They hurried in the direction of the gym.

"I wonder how far they've gotten in the game?" Sally asked.

"It shouldn't take long. Jen said they were playing five card draw. That's a pretty quick game of poker." Jacque quickened her pace as she thought about how Jen might be sitting there, trying to keep naked werewolves occupied.

They made it to the gym and snuck up to the door windows. Jacque peeked up quietly and nearly died laughing.

"What? What's going on?" Sally yanked on Jacque's sleeve.

Shaking with silent giggles, she pointed to the window.

Sally quietly looked through the window's edge and quickly covered her mouth at what she saw. Marianna and Crina sat – looking rather put out – in their bathing suits. Across from them, four disgruntled males sat with nothing but socks on. They had taken the pillows and laid them across their laps. Jen didn't look much happier as she pulled her shirt over her head. Although, she still had her pants on.

Jacque jerked her phone out and texted Costin to get his butt here and help go door to door to announce the party. Sally and Jacque took off at a run and nearly collided with said wolf.

"Whoa! So we're good?" He held the fliers in his hands and handed each girl a stack.

Jacque nodded. "Let's hurry. Have you seen any sign of Decebel?"

Costin shook his head. "No, so we had better move our butts."

They all took off at a run, headed for the stairs. They made it to the second floor and immediately started knocking on doors. As they opened they smiled and pushed fliers into the hands of the occupants.

When they got to the end of the second floor and were on their way to the third, Jacque sent Jen a text, letting her know that the animals were on the move. Male and female wolves were already heading towards the gym. Then she quickly wrote Cynthia a text that said, "baby, light my fire," and snickered as she hit send.

Jacque and Sally had gone ahead of Costin, trying to get out as many fliers as possible before the inevitable happened.

Costin finally caught up with them and took the rest of the fliers. "You two go on and get out of here. I have a bad feeling."

Jacque looked alarmed. "What's wrong?"

He pushed them. "Just go. And hurry."

The girls didn't question him again, but joined the throngs of Canis lupis walking down the stairs.

Costin handed out the last flier and took off. He'd made it to the final staircase when a hand suddenly grabbed his collar.

"Why is there a fire on the front lawn?"

"Oh. Hey, Beta." Costin laughed nervously. "They let you out. Was it for good behavior, or -"

Decebel took a step towards him and growled, "Answer the question, Costin."

"The fire – okay, well. You see, what happened – what it is... Shit." He groaned and decided he'd be better off just giving it up. "Jen's burning the clothes, linens, and so on of the unmated Serbia males," Costin finally spit out.

Decebel stared at him like he had grown a second head.

"Where is my mate now?" Decebel's voice was calm, too calm.

"Um, getting the rest of their clothes."

"From where?"

"From, uh, the, um, males." Costin was trying to stall as long as he could, hoping Jen would already be out of the room.

"How is she getting the clothes from them, Costin." Decebel's eyes were glowing and his canines descended.

"It's kind of a funny story, actually. See, Jen, Sally, Crina, Marianna, and Jacque -"

"HOW!" Decebel growled.

"They're playing strip poker." Costin took several steps back as his Beta fought for control of his wolf. "If it makes you feel better, Jen is winning. I think." In hindsight, he decided that maybe that last part wasn't really helpful.

Decebel reached out and grabbed him by the scruff of his neck and pushed him forward. "Take me to her."

Jen heard her phone let out a little beep. She laid her current hand of cards face down on the floor in front of her, and started to stretch, lifting her arms above her head.

"Boys, I need a break for just a sec. How about another shot?"

The wolves across from her had their eyes glued to her frame as she arched and stretched. They all nodded in unison but didn't speak. Jen smirked at Crina, who simply chuckled as she poured another round of shots.

While Jen continued to stretch, she leaned towards Marianna. She got close to her ear and whispered, "The cavalry is on the way."

Marianna gave a slight nod of her head and smiled at the males as they tipped their shots back.

Jen glanced down at her half-clad body. *Man, that was close,* she thought.

As the gym door clanged open and her ears were met with ominous silence, she knew she had spoken too soon.

Decebel and Costin arrived at the gym door and Decebel had a sense of deja vu.

"If my mate is on the other side of that door..." He muttered the unfinished threat.

Several wolves had gathered and were looking in through the window. There was a murmur across the crowd of, "Are they naked?" along with giggles and laughter.

The Beta snarled and the crowd parted like the red sea. Decebel slowly stepped forward, and when he got to the window, he had to dig his claws into the palms of his hands to keep from phasing at what he saw. All the wolves around him fell to their knees as his power poured over them.

He turned back to the crowd. "Everyone return to their rooms. Now." His calm tone did not hide the rage inside him. Without a word, the wolves rose and left quickly.

Decebel looked down at Costin, who was still on his knees.

"Stand," he told him gruffly. "You knew she was going to do this? You knew how I would feel about it and you let her do it anyway?" His eyes were glowing and he was fighting with each breath to keep his wolf from striking out at the pup before him.

"I take full responsibility," Costin told him firmly.

"I will deal with you when I'm done with her." Decebel dismissed him.

He roughly pulled the gym door open and walked in. The scent of fear hit his nose as the four naked males turned and met his glowing eyes.

"Aww-kward," Jennifer sang as she watched Decebel storm in. She stood up, leaving the circle of naked males and half-naked females.

Decebel looked at Jennifer long enough to see that she was wearing tiny pieces of fabric that barely covered her essentials. Then he had to look away. He shook and fought for control, but nearly lost it when he noticed that his female pack mates weren't wearing much more. By the time his eyes landed on the males again, he was sure there was a puddle of blood on the floor from his claws digging into his hands.

Decebel was seeing red at this point.

"Phase to your wolves!" he snarled at them.

He waited and when nothing happened, he took large menacing steps forward. "You dare defy me as you sit naked in a room with *my* mate?"

Damion growled but lowered his eyes. "We can't phase. We've tried."

Decebel's eyes shot up to Jennifer's.

She shrugged innocently, biting her bottom lip. "Oops."

Now standing, Marianna and Crina backed slowly away as Decebel moved toward Jen.

"What did you do?" he asked her.

She glanced over at the Serbian males, then back at Decebel. "Do we have to do this here, in front of them?"

"Costin," Decebel called.

"Yes, Beta?"

"Please make sure these males get back to their rooms safely. As soon as Crina and Marianna are clothed, take them to their rooms as well."

Crina and Marianna had their clothes on before he finished speaking.

Decebel turned back Damion. "If you lay a hand on my pack mate, I will rip you limb from limb. I hope that this experience has taught you not to mess with our females."

Jen smirked but quickly wiped it clean when Decebel glared at her.

"You have my word we won't retaliate," Damion growled out.

Decebel nodded once and motioned to Costin to take the group out. He let out a slow breath. When Jen started to speak, he held up a hand to stop her.

"Get dressed, please." His voice was tight, his eyes narrowed.

Jen grabbed her shirt and slid it over her head, then slipped her shoes on.

"Let's go," he told her. Gently, but firmly, he took her hand.

Chapter 28

Decebel opened the door to Jennifer's room and motioned for her to enter. He hadn't spoken since the gym. He didn't trust himself. Not to mention, his wolf was making him bite his tongue because, although he was angry, he wouldn't allow Decebel to hurt Jennifer with his words.

Once inside, she walked over to the bed and slumped down. Her shoulders rolled over in defeat. He hated seeing her that way, but couldn't rid himself of the image of her barely dressed in front of those naked males.

"Why?" he asked her, his voice raspy as he tried to keep his wolf in check.

Jennifer looked up at him, no tears in her eyes, just simple resolve.

"They needed to learn not to mess with me and mine."

Decebel growled. "It's my job to protect you and defend your virtue."

"The hell it is!" She growled back. "It *my* virtue, Decebel. The key word is MY! I'm not going to sit back like some little obedient mate when someone takes a shot at me. Or you, for that matter."

Decebel snarled.

Jennifer stood up and walked towards him, but he turned away. He was too angry for her touch. His back did not deter her.

"I'm sorry that I kept this from you," she told him as she wrapped her arms around from behind. "I'm sorry that I hurt you. I'm sorry that I worried you. If it's any consolation, this will probably be the last time I take my clothes off in public."

Decebel's chest rumbled. "Probably?" he growled.

She smiled as she rubbed her face against his back. "Well, I'm not putting my dream of being a Vegas show girl on the back burner just yet."

Jen waited while Decebel's wolf slowly calmed down as she held him close. Finally, he turned to face her. He placed his hands on either side of her face, pushing stray strands of blonde hair out of the way. He ran his thumb gently along her bottom lip and Jen felt her breath catch.

"I've needed you, and missed you," Decebel whispered.

Jen didn't speak. She couldn't as he held her mesmerized by his glowing amber eyes. He leaned forward and inhaled deeply. Her eyes fell shut as his chest rumbled as he growled.

Then his lips were on hers. Gentle at first, but then he slipped his tongue through her lips and Jen gasped at the contact. Decebel started backing her up until Jen felt the bed against the back of her legs. He laid her back onto the bed, covering her body with his, never breaking the kiss. Jen's hands came up of their own accord and she ran her fingers through his hair, sighing at the softness.

Decebel pressed her more firmly into the mattress and she felt his hand on her calf. Slowly he ran his hand up to the back of her thigh, pulling her body closer until his hand cupped her bottom.

Jennifer groaned at the feel of his hand on her, not that she'd never had a guy put their hand on her butt, but this felt different. So much more intimate and possessive. Decebel trailed kisses from her cheeks, down her neck, up to her collarbone as Jen tried to catch her breath.

When he nipped her she gasped. The sound pushed through the fog of desire that had clouded Decebel's mind. He pulled back and looked into her eyes, gently caressing her face with his fingertips.

"We should stop," he whispered as he traced her red, moist lips in a trance-like state.

"Uh-uh," Jen muttered.

"Jennifer," Decebel growled. "Tell me to stop."

Jen closed her eyes in order to escape his soul-searing amber gaze. She took a deep breath and let it out slowly.

Clearing her throat, she was finally able to speak. "Decebel, I want you to stop." She opened one eye to peek at him. "How was that?"

A smile threatened to cross his face. "Almost convincing."

A thought hit Jen's mind as she considered what he was asking her to stop him from doing.

"Are you a virgin?"

Decebel shook his head and chuckled. "You're quite blunt, aren't you?"

Jen cocked an eyebrow at him.

"Jennifer, I'm 125 years old," he told her, as if that explained it all.

"That's not an answer," she growled. Then another thought hit her. "Should I be creeped out that you are so old?"

"If you want to break it down to a science, Canis lupis actually age one year to a human's six. I'm more like twenty in 'your years,' in a sense. If anyone should be creeped out it should be Jacque. Fane is only three."

That made Jen laugh. "Oh, that is just too rich. Definitely going to have to hold that one over her head." Then she got serious. "Okay, so twenty I can handle. Now, Captain Evader, answer the first question."

"No."

Jen looked taken aback. "No. You are refusing to answer?"

Decebel growled. "No, the answer to the question is no."

Jen just stared at him, not really sure how to respond. She knew she shouldn't be shocked, but she couldn't keep from feeling the hurt that flashed across her heart at his answer.

"Are you okay?" Decebel asked gently.

"When was the last time?" she asked him quietly

Decebel groaned. "Do you really want to do this?"

"When, Decebel?"

He tilted her head back up to look at him when she tried to shy away.

"It's been five years."

Jen's mouth fell open. "Oh." Her eyes moved to the ceiling.

Decebel caressed her cheek softly. "Are you okay?"

After a moment, she sucked a breath in through her teeth. "Well, I never thought I'd date such a loser... Five years?" Her eyes met his now, her mouth pulled up into a mocking smile. "I really overestimated your sexiness."

He rolled off of her and threw an arm over his face. "You are exasperating, woman."

"That's what you like about me."

Decebel grumbled noncommittally.

"So...does that mean you aren't mad at me anymore?" Jen asked hopefully.

He lifted his lip in a snarl, and she could see his canines were still descended.

"I'll take that as a 'not a chance in hell.' Good to know."

Then, randomly: "Did *Matty*," Decebel snarled the name, "touch you?"

She laughed. "You're seriously still hung up on that?"

When he didn't answer, she huffed and rolled her eyes. "We kissed, but that's it. And I only did it to keep him occupied so Sally could make a break for it."

Decebel took her by surprise when he was over her once more, his mouth covering hers.

Suddenly, the door to Jen's room flew open, and Decebel rolled off of Jen with a howl of pain and rage.

Jen sat up and saw a very panicked looking Costin in her doorway. She felt a sharp tug inside her, almost like a pulled ligament, but she wasn't in near the pain that Costin and Decebel obviously were.

Decebel snarled as he forced himself to his feet.

"What's happened to him?" he gritted through his teeth.

Costin shook his head, visibly fighting through his own pain. "He collapsed at the dinner he's having with the other Alphas. Alina fell next to him." The wolf's eyes were becoming wilder the more he talked.

Decebel grabbed Jen's hand and headed towards Costin.

"Where's Fane?"

"He's on his way with Jacque to the suite..." he gasped "...where the dinner is," Costin explained as they headed towards the stairs.

Jen stopped when two doors opened and Crina, Marianna, and Sally came into the hall.

Crina and Marianna were doubled over in pain.

Decebel snarled again, catching himself on the stair railing. Jen let go of his hand and ran over to help the girls.

"What's happened?" Crina cringed.

"Vasile has fallen," Decebel told them, still struggling in pain. "Jennifer, you and the other females need to get in a room and lock the door."

Jen looked him in the eye. "No, I'm going with you. We all are going with you." When he started to interrupt, she cut him off. "Sally might be able to help."

Decebel narrowed his eyes. "How?"

"She's a gypsy healer. She can heal werewolves."

Costin and Decebel's heads both snapped around to look at Sally, their mouths dropped open. Sally looked as if she wanted to crawl into a hole.

"How do you know this?" Decebel asked.

Sally started with, "It hasn't been conf -" but Jen spoke over her.

"She identified the herb that keeps wolves from phasing without looking it up. She just knew it. Cynthia said that's only a gift gypsy healers have and that there hasn't been one in a pack in over a century."

Decebel couldn't believe what he was hearing. What were the odds that a half blood, a dormant, and a gypsy healer would end up best friends and all in the same pack? The fates really had their hands in the Romanian Pack.

"Fine, let's go," he conceded. "But I don't want you out of my sight."

Jen nodded once, then began helping Crina forward. Sally and Marianna followed as Costin led the way.

Chapter 29

Two hours into dinner, Thad was finally ready to pass out the drinks. The attendees brought out two trays. He walked over and began handing them out. The last glass, he handed to Vasile.

Thad raised his drink. "I want to toast to a new era for our species. Our time is now. Hopefully many of our pack members will find their mates and we will be able to bear pups once again. To each of you."

A ripple of agreement flowed through the room as they each took a drink from their glasses. Thad kept an eye on Vasile to make sure the Alpha drank enough of the wine to be effective. When he saw him drain it, he had to school the smile that flashed across his face.

Vasile looked over at his mate and smiled. "You look beautiful, Mina."

Alina blushed. "Still the charmer, my Alpha."

"Alw -" Vasile tried to finish the sentence, but he suddenly felt a tightening in his chest and was finding it difficult to breathe.

"Vasile." Alina's voice was worried as she pulled her mate's face up to look at her. She gasped when she saw the wolf staring back at her.

"Poison," the wolf told her, and his eyes rolled back in his head as he collapsed.

Alina only had a moment to realize what had just happened before she herself couldn't breathe. It was like something was crushing her chest, bearing down on her. Everything went dark and she, too, fell to the floor.

Gasps and hollers broke throughout the room as Victor hurried to the fallen Alpha's side.

"There is a pulse but it's weak." Victor looked at Thad. "Quick, find the doctor Vasile brought with his pack."

Thad nodded once and turned to whisper in his pack member's ear, who then hurried out of the room.

Thad looked back to where Vasile and Alina lay motionless. He had to force himself into action so as to appear to care. He helped Victor and Dillon lift the Alpha and carry him into the adjoining suite. Dragomir picked up Alina's limp form and laid her gently beside her mate.

Agnes and Adrianna both had tears running down their cheeks as they looked on. The group watched as Vasile and Alina's forms began to convulse.

"Somebody help them," Agnes sobbed. Dragomir wrapped his mate in his arms and whispered gently to her.

Dillon, who had backed up to the door, was nearly knocked over when Fane, Decebel, Sorin, Cynthia, and a slew of females came rushing into the room.

Jen came to an abrupt stop when she saw Vasile and Alina lying on the large bed, their bodies convulsing. Her hand covered her mouth as her eyes filled with tears. Sally pulled away from Marianna – some invisible force pulled her towards the bed.

As Sally got closer, Fane turned and snarled, but Cynthia pushed him out of the way.

"Let her through," Cynthia growled.

The entire room plunged into silence as Sally, in a trance-like state, approached the bed. She climbed up beside Vasile and placed her hand over his heart. His body calmed immediately.

"What the..." Murmurs wound through the room as mouths dropped open and eyebrows rose.

Sally leaned over Vasile and placed her forehead against his. She closed her eyes and her breathing became deep and slow, as if she had fallen into a deep sleep.

"I guess we have confirmation," Jen whispered in Cynthia's direction.

"What is she doing?" Fane growled at the doctor as he watched Sally.

"She's a healer," Cynthia said in awe. "The first gypsy healer in over a century. In our pack."

Those old enough to understand the significance of her words lowered themselves to one knee.

Jen tugged on Decebel's sleeve. His eyes were glowing and she could see sweat had broken across his brow. "Why are they kneeling?"

"It is a great honor to be in the presence of a healer. Other packs will kneel out of respect."

After what felt like forever, Sally finally sat up. She turned to Decebel.

"His body has been poisoned with an herb. It's common in these parts. Moonseed." Her eyes were unfocused as she spoke.

"How? Who would do this?" Decebel snarled as he looked around the room. He wondered if he looked hard enough he'd be able to see their guilt.

"That doesn't matter right now," Sally continued in a low voice. "He needs the antidote. He is fading fast, and Alina even faster. He needs Wolfsbane. It will counteract the poison."

Marianna stepped forward. "I know what Wolfsbane looks like. I can go get some, it grows on the mountainside."

Jen looked at Jacque and Fane, saw the horror and fear in their eyes. She was so sick of people hurting those she loved. Decebel walked up to the bed as Sally climbed down to allow him closer. While he was distracted, Jen slid over to Marianna.

"Come on, I'll go with you," she whispered in her ear.

Marianna looked at her and a small smile appeared. "Okay." She nodded and they both backed slowly and quietly towards the door. Not one person glanced their way. All eyes were riveted on the fallen Alpha and his mate.

Marianna and Jen hurried through the mansion.

"We're going to need a flashlight for you," Marianna told her and made a quick detour.

"Where are we going to find flashlights?"

"There's a shed just out the far west doors. I'm crossing my fingers that there's one in there."

"Good call."

Marianna kept glancing at Jen from the corner of her eye, sure that she'd be able to pick up on her guilt. They made it out the door and headed straight for the shed, which had light glowing on the front of it, illuminating the entrance. They both hurried in and began rummaging through shelves.

"Gotchya." Jen grinned, holding up a large industrial flashlight. She flicked it on and shined it around the room.

"Perfect," Marianna agreed. "Okay, let's go before Decebel realizes you're gone."

They left the shed and headed to the front of the estate, hurrying to make it out of the gates and onto the dark mountainside. Both girls shivered as the cold hit them – neither had thought to grab a coat in their haste. Marianna knew that Thad made sure to have all the Wolfsbane close to the mansion destroyed, so they would have to walk a good ways out to find it.

"HEY! Wait up."

Jen's and Marianna's heads turned to find Sally running after them, her own flashlight in hand. Of course Sally would think to get a flash light – she was always prepared.

"Sally, what are you doing?" Jen asked in a rush.

"I saw you sneak out. I can help. I know what to do once we find the herb. It has to be ground up in a certain way."

Marianna squinted at her. "What do you mean?"

"The small leaves have to be separated and soaked in warm salt water to draw the healing properties out. If you just crush the plant and mix it in water it won't be worth anything."

"Fine, but be careful," Jen growled.

"Oh, you're one to talk about being careful," Sally snapped back.

Marianna started walking more quickly and Jen and Sally had to lengthen their strides to keep up.

"We're probably going to have to walk quite a ways. I'm thinking if we split up then we'll probably find it more quickly."

"Divide and conquer, sounds like a plan."

"Sally, you go far left," Marianna told her and pointed in the direction she meant. "Jen, you go far right, and I will go straight. You're looking for a plant with dusky green leaves and a purple bloom."

"Dusky and purple. Okay, let's do this." Jen headed in the direction Marianna had instructed.

She shined her flashlight across the ground, side to side, sweeping across the shrubbery. All the while muttering, "purple, purple, dusky, dusky," under her breath.

Jen had been walking for a half hour when she felt a shiver go down her spine. She stopped mid-stride and slowly turned in a circle. Looking into the trees, she shined the light into the foliage. Someone was following her. No, someone was stalking her.

"Who's there?" Jen continued to shine the light and she strained her eyes, trying to pierce the darkness.

Suddenly a dark form lunged at her. She dropped the flashlight to put her hands up and protect her face. She was hit roughly, knocking the breath from her lungs. Her head snapped back and she heard a crack as her skull struck something hard. The last thing she saw before blackness consumed her was sharp teeth and glowing eyes.

The wolf that was Marianna grabbed Jen's pant leg and began pulling her deeper into the mountains. She dragged her steadily for several miles to the deep cavern she had found. The wolf set Jen's supine form right at the edge of the cavern. Marianna then phased back to her human form.

Marianna shivered at the loss of her fur, but quickly shook it off and grabbed the buckets of wolf urine that Thad insisted she take, the ones she'd hidden the day before. She made it back to Jen's side just as Jen was beginning to moan and come to.

"Bloody hell," Jen groaned.

"I'm sorry, Jen. I'm sorry, but I have to do this." Marianna pushed Jen's legs over the edge of the cavern.

Jen gasped and her arms came flailing out as she reached to grab something, anything. Marianna gave another shove and Jen slid over the edge. Her stomach scraped against the stone as her shirt slid up; her nails tore as she scrambled to grab anything to keep her from falling.

Jen slid further and further, her feet pushing into any rock that might give her a foothold. Eventually she felt a protruding root and grabbed it, holding desperately onto the lifeline. She looked up and could just barely see Marianna in the darkness, leaning over the edge, a bucket of something in hand.

"Why are you doing this?" Jen asked, her voice tight with fear and the strain of holding on.

"You wouldn't understand." Marianna had tears streaming down her cheeks. "You have your mate. How could you possibly understand?"

"Try me," Jen snarled.

Marianna wiped her tears away. "I was in love. He was human."

Jen's mouth dropped open. "But what about your mate?"

"What about him," Marianna spat. "I don't see him. Do you, Jen? Who knows how long until I find him. It could take centuries, yet Vasile expects me to live alone, empty."

"He knows that only your mate will make the emptiness go away, Marianna," Jen said gently, trying to reason with the enraged she-wolf.

"I was happy with Drey. He made me laugh." Marianna's eyes clouded over as memories filled her mind. Then her face darkened. "Vasile found out and had Drey shipped off to the U.S. I was forbidden to see him, or any other human. The only way I can be with Drey is to no longer be under Vasile."

"Did you poison him?" Jen's eyes widened as her breath quickened.

"No. Thad did. Thad agreed to let me join his pack, and if I didn't find my mate among them, he agreed to let me go to the U.S. to find Drey. He told me I had to get rid of you. He figures getting rid of you will take care of the Beta as well. Decebel will either be killed by fighting Thad's pack or he will die searching for your body. He has plans for Fane, as well – they will be implemented in time."

Jen couldn't believe what she was hearing. Her arms were getting tired and beginning to shake. She had to try to get Marianna to change her mind somehow.

"Marianna, you don't have to do this. You could let me go and just leave. I won't tell anyone."

Marianna laughed. "Thad would kill me if I didn't finish the task he has given me. I'm sorry, Jen. I really liked you, but I love Drey and I won't spend my life hoping for a mate that I may never find."

She began to tip the bucket of liquid and Jen gagged as the stench hit her nose a second before the cold fluid drenched her. Jen sputtered and coughed, trying to keep it from her mouth.

"I am sorry about the urine, but Thad insisted," Marianna told her as she picked up another bucket and poured it. "He said it would cover your scent and it would take longer for them to find you."

Jen's hands began to slide as the root she was holding onto became slick from the urine. She tried to muffle the cry that came out when she slipped, only gaining her grasp at the last second.

"You would do anything to be with Decebel, Jen. That's what I have to do to be with Drey."

"Decebel is my mate, Marianna. It's not the same. You won't be satisfied with the human," Jen tried again, but knew it was hopeless as Marianna stood.

"I have to go, I don't want them to come looking for me. I pray your death will be quick so you won't suffer." And then she was gone.

Jen stared up into the darkness, realizing just before her hands slipped free that she was going to die. A tear slipped down her cheek as her grip loosened against her will. She cried out hoarsely as she fell. It wasn't as deep as she thought, the fall didn't last long, but it didn't soften the landing. She hit the ground hard and once again, darkness took over.

Chapter 30

Sally finally spotted the purple flower herb. She ran, her flashlight bobbing over the ground. She fell down next to the plant and began digging to pull the plant up by the root. She didn't know how she knew, but she knew it had to have the root attached in order for the antidote to be potent.

She dug and dug, her nails caked with dirt, and finally pulled up several plants. She tucked them into her shirt and began to run again. Faster and faster she pushed herself, the urgency for her to return riding her like a pack of angry wolves.

Sally didn't give thought to Marianna or Jen, she figured they were big girls and could make it back on their own. She finally spotted the estate's massive gated entrance. As she hurried through the gate and rushed up the steps to the front door, she nearly ran into Cynthia.

"Umph," Sally grunted as she forced herself to stop. She looked up at the doctor. "Is he still alive?"

"Yes, but only just," Cynthia told her darkly. "I want us to do this in my office. I don't want to tell anyone what we're doing, and when we go up to give him the antidote we will tell no one that we have it."

"Do you know who poisoned him?" Sally asked as her eyes grew wider.

"No, but it had to be somebody in that little dinner party. I will try to get Fane and Decebel to clear the room, but both of them are very volatile right now." Cynthia cocked her head to the side. "Decebel especially so since he just realized his mate was missing."

Sally looked sheepishly at the ground. "She's out with Marianna looking for Wolfsbane."

Cynthia nodded once and echoed Sally's thoughts, "Well, they're big girls. They'll make it back. Now, let's you and I get this antidote made."

Cynthia pulled Sally into the mansion and they hurried to her office.

Sally laid the plants out and told Cynthia to get her a container with warm water and some small vials.

Cynthia set the items on the lab table in front of Sally.

"This is so freaky," Sally muttered.

"What is?"

"Me knowing what I should do. It's like someone just turned on a switch."

Sally worked quickly, removing the leaves and soaking them in the warm water. She filled the container until all that could be seen were floating, dusky leaves. As soon as the water was room temperature, she knew it was ready. She took the two vials and filled them.

Something clicked as she held the vials in her hands. Sally closed her eyes and felt the magic – that's all she could possibly call it – flow through her as she called upon the healing properties of the plant. Her mouth began to move as she spoke the words that appeared in her mind.

"You are named the bane of the wolf when you actually heal.

I call to you this day to seek out the poison meant to steal.

Penetrate the wolf and pour life back into him all.

Give strength to my Alpha, don't let him fall."

Sally opened her eyes and a single tear slid into one of the vials. Suddenly the liquid began to glow pure white.

"It is done," Sally told Cynthia resolutely.

Cynthia nodded. She pulled out her cell and sent a text to Decebel.

Cynthia txt: On our way

"Let's go."

Decebel paced, his wolf was worried and hurt. Their Alpha was close to death. His Alpha's mate was close to death. And Decebel's mate had taken off without so much as a "bye, fur ball."

Cynthia had just texted him that she and Sally were coming up with the antidote. Now they just had to pray that it worked, that Sally really was a healer – though it seemed that she was. He asked for everyone to leave except for pack members, and the others stepped into the room where only hours ago the Alphas had laughed and toasted their packs.

Decebel continued to stare down the wolves through the open door, his wolf seeking out the one who would dare to hurt Vasile, but his mind was a mess, clouded with too many feelings. He would be calmer once Jennifer returned. Once she was by his side, he would sniff out the traitor.

Fane pulled Jacquelyn into his lap and wrapped his arms around her, trying to control her shaking. She was in shock – as was he.

"Who would do this, Fane?"

"I don't know, love. My father is very powerful, and with power comes enemies. I just didn't think there were any among us."

Jacque left Fane and walked to the bed, climbing up next to Alina. She took her hand and held it to her heart. Tears down her cheeks as she watched the woman she had come to think of as a mother struggle for every breath.

"She's the sweetest woman I've ever met, Fane. So selfless and loving." Jacque couldn't stop the sob that forced its way from her chest. She leaned down over Alina and prayed for her to be spared, for them both to be spared.

Fane slid his arms around her. A single tear escaped down his cheek, for his parents and for his mate. So many deaths in the past months, so many lives wasted. And now more would be taken. Either his parents' or the one guilty of attempted murder.

Sally and Cynthia entered the room and Decebel closed the door behind them, shutting out the others. Sally walked quietly to the bed and climbed up next to her Alpha, for as his pack healer, he truly was her Alpha. Tears threatened to spill over as she thought about how she'd felt the poison in his system when pressing her hand to him earlier. It was slow, seeping into his cells, killing, destroying.

She pulled the vials from her pocket and tuned the room out as she unscrewed the lids. Placing a hand behind Vasile's head, she leaned forward and pressed the vial to his lips. Just as before, the words she needed to say flowed through her mind and out her mouth. She whispered close to his ear as she held the vial to his mouth, waiting to pour until his lips parted.

"Alpha mine, hear my voice. I am Sally, gypsy healer to the Romanian pack. I call on your wolf. Come forward and take care of the man who houses your spirit and protects your pack. Come forth, Alpha wolf, and trust that what I give you is to heal and not to harm."

Sally watched as Vasile's lips parted, and she was able to tip the antidote into his mouth. She quickly poured the second vial and watched him swallow, close his mouth, and become still again.

Once again, she leaned forward and placed her forehead to his. She closed her eyes and slowed her breathing. She felt the wolf stirring beneath the man, hurting, afraid and angry. He feared for his mate, unable to feel her.

Sally whispered into his mind. *She is here beside you, Alpha. No harm will come to her if you will fight. Fight the poison, let the healing liquid move throughout your body. If you are healed, she will be.*

The wolf settled slightly. Sally could feel the Wolfsbane moving, seeking out the poison, almost as if it were a living being.

Rest now, Alpha. You are protected, you are loved. Sally pulled back and climbed down from the bed. She felt her body sag, not realizing how draining the healing had been. She looked at Decebel. "It's working. I don't know how long it will take until he wakes. They need to be protected and guarded."

"There will be no less than four wolves with them at all times. We will rotate in shifts so that everyone will get time to rest." Decebel turned to Fane. "I assume you want to stay?"

Fane nodded as he held his mate.

Decebel turned to the other pack members. "Skender, Boian, Sorin, you will take first watch with Fane. I have to figure out where the hell my mate is." He turned to Sally. "Come," he commanded gruffly.

Sally straightened, gathering her strength she followed the Beta out.

"Where is she?" Decebel asked her once they were in the hall, away from prying ears.

"She went with me and Marianna into the woods to find the Wolfsbane. We split up and I made it back first. I figured they would be right behind me," Sally explained quickly. She watched the Beta struggle to control his wolf.

"I'm going to check her room. Will you please get Cynthia and Crina and look for her as well?"

Not waiting for her answer, Decebel turned and quickly walked in the direction of Jennifer's room.

Decebel knew before he opened the door that Jennifer wasn't in her room. He entered anyway, needing her scent to surround him. He walked over to the bed and sat down on the edge.

Only hours ago he had lain in this bed, holding her, kissing her, showing her how much he loved her and wanted her. How had this day gotten so screwed up so quickly? He felt his chest tighten as darkness seeped in. His Alpha was sick and the pack was weaker for it, his mate was missing, and his wolf was on the verge of rage.

Decebel's hands shook as he took Jennifer's pillow and pulled it to his face. He pulled in a deep breath and took a small amount of comfort from the warm vanilla and cinnamon that seeped into his very being.

His mind wandered to a time long ago when his heart had been held by another woman, young and full of life and spunk just like his mate. Cosmina had been a joy to all around her and he had lost her. He hadn't thought his heart would ever heal from the loss of his sister. But then he'd met Jennifer, his mate. She filled the hole in him and poured life where death had slowly begun to take over. Now he didn't know where she was, didn't know if she was okay.

Decebel's heart broke and his wolf pushed forward as a mournful howl poured from the very depths of his soul. As he took slow breaths, trying to calm his wolf and pull himself together, he could feel his wolf reaching, seeking the bond between them that had yet to truly solidify. His shoulders slumped.

"Have you any idea how long I've waited for you?" His mind reached of its own accord.

Then in the silence Decebel heard her.

Chapter 31

Jen could feel something warm and sticky running into her eyes. She reached up to wipe it away and a sharp pain pulled a gasp out of her.

"Crap," she growled. She realized then that she'd probably broken her arm. She moved experimentally and felt a stabbing pain in her side. Jennifer thought for a second, trying to remember what little she could from *ER*.

Okay, pain in the side, hard to breath. Probably broke a rib, maybe punctured a lung. Excellent.

She rolled to the side and was able to raise her other arm to her head. She felt a gaping wound, one that was pouring blood down her face and into her eyes. She tried to apply pressure, knowing she needed to try to stop the flow. She was weak, and getting weaker.

"Have you any idea how long I've waited for you?"

Abruptly, Jen sat up and nearly screamed from the pain that ripped through her body. *Not possible*, she thought.

"I did not just hear that," she spoke into the darkness. She closed her eyes and waited to see if she would hear more of the voice that she needed to hear as much as she needed air to breathe. Her heart pounded in her chest, her breathing was shallow, and despite the cold, she could feel sweat trickle down her neck.

"I've only just found you and now I'm losing you."

She let out a slow breath, savoring the sound in her mind. *Finally*, she thought as tears streamed down her cold cheeks, mingling with the blood that continued to flow. *Finally.*

"Decebel?" she sent hesitantly.

"Jennifer?" Decebel's voice was urgent, firm.

"You can hear me?" she asked him, still unable to believe that they were speaking through their thoughts. She had dreamed, wished, hoped, and longed for this to happen.

"Bloody hell. Yes, I can hear you. Where are you? What happened?"

"I don't know where I am," she told him, trying to remember what had happened. *"It's dark...and cold. The ground feels like rocks and dirt."*

"Jennifer, what happened?" he asked her again.

"It's Marianna, Decebel. She made some sort of deal with Thad. Decebel –" her voice grew stronger as she began to remember what happened, *"Fane and Jacque, they're in danger. Thad wants them all dead. You have to protect them."*

"I have to find you," Decebel insisted.

"No! You have to protect them. If something happens to Fane, Jacque will die. The same with Vasile and Alina. Decebel, you have to make sure they are safe," Jen pleaded.

"I WILL NOT LEAVE YOU TO DIE!" he roared at her through their bond. *"Do*

not ask this of me, Jennifer. I will not lose you. I can't." The last came out as a near whisper.

"Decebel, we aren't bonded. If something happens to me you can go on and have a life. Jacque can't. If Fane dies, she goes with him. That's not acceptable. I will not take her life for mine, do you hear me?"

Tears streamed relentlessly down her face as she tried to make him understand that she wouldn't be able to live with herself if something happened to Jacque or Sally.

"Bonded or not, Jennifer, you are my mate. What you ask goes against everything I am. I cannot put others in front of your well being. You ask for a river to reverse its flow, and the fires of hell to freeze over. It isn't possible."

Decebel's voice was becoming more and more of a growl as *he* tried to make *her* understand that as her mate, he would not abandon her.

"I understand. This is hard for me, too. I love you, Decebel. I've loved you from the moment I met you. I love you bossy, mad, gentle, affectionate... I love you any way you come to me. I want us to have a chance, and I have to believe that the fates aren't so cruel as to only give us this one. I have to believe that if we aren't together in this life, then in the next."

Jen tried hard to make her voice strong. She wasn't going to pretend that the idea of never seeing Decebel again didn't hurt worse than any pain she had ever experienced. She would rather be back in that burning car, feeling her flesh be seared, than think there was no chance to be with him. *"If I have to, then I will believe enough for the both of us. But Decebel, if you come for me, I will never forgive you, mate or not. If you love me, clichéd as that is, you will protect those I love. And if this life is over for me, then live for both of us, and I will wait for you. I will see you again. I will kiss you, I will touch you, I will love you, Decebel. If not on this side, then on the other."*

Decebel's shoulders shook at the force of emotion that rolled through him. Not since his sister had died had he felt such grief. Only this was worse, a thousand times worse. Jennifer didn't get it. Though they weren't yet bonded by blood, their connection was strong. Already he felt his soul tearing in two at knowing there was a possibility he would lose his mate.

"How can you ask this of me? Please, Jennifer. Don't."

"To late," he heard her whisper.

Decebel took a deep breath. He hated himself for it, but he relented, knowing she would accept nothing less.

"I love you. I will keep them safe, but I will come for you. You will live, do you hear me? You will live. LIVE ! Pentru mine, iubitule. Te rog traiesc (For me, baby. Please live)."

"It's so cold... Decebel? Take care of those I love. That means you."

Decebel felt her growing weaker, could feel her mind shutting down. He felt so helpless. Once again he was unable to save the one he loved. He squeezed his eyes shut and fell to the floor. Their bond had finally opened, and for a few brief moments he had felt her. Felt all of her. Now there was only darkness.

He momentarily gave himself over to the wolf that pushed and snarled to come forward. His eyes glowed, his claws extended from his hands. His canines lengthened as he tilted his head back and howled.

Standing, he shook with rage and wrenched the door open and walked out into the hall. He caught a scent that nearly made him phase. *Marianna*, he thought. *Welcome home, pack mate.*

Decebel took off at a run, following her scent. It led him straight to the room where his Alpha and his mate laid at death's door. The wolves in the adjoining suite separated as Decebel stormed through. He ripped the door from its hinges as he pulled it open.

Fane, Skender, Boian, and Sorin all came forward, snarling, preparing to defend their Alpha. When they realized it was Decebel and saw the look in his eyes, they all backed down and bared their necks. His eyes scanned the room and fell on his prey.

Marianna stood next to Sally, tears streaming down her cheeks. He walked over to her slowly, letting her watch her fate come near.

Decebel grabbed her around the throat and lifted her from the floor, her back against the wall.

"WHERE. IS. SHE!" he growled into her face.

Marianna squeezed her eyes shut as she tried to fight the compulsion in her Beta's voice.

Marianna knew if she told Decebel what he wanted to know, Thad's wolves would tear her limb from limb. She knew because that's exactly what Thad had told her would happen. She didn't know why she had come back – she should've just left – but she thought that would make her look guilty. It obviously hadn't mattered.

She knew Decebel would kill her, but he would be merciful and make it quick. Thad would torture her. She bit her lip until it started to bleed, struggling to breathe as her Beta's hand tightened.

"Answer me, Marianna."

"I can't, Beta. He'll kill me," she whispered.

"You are already dead. You were dead the moment you hurt my mate, the moment you dared to touch what is mine. You were dead the moment you agreed to lead her to death."

"You won't torture me. Please." Marianna opened her eyes and looked into Decebel's. "I just wanted to be with him. Vasile wouldn't let me."

Decebel's eyes widened as her words sunk in. "You did this for a human? For a man who is nothing to you?"

"I LOVE HIM. He is *something* to me." Marianna shook with her pain and grief.

"If you will not speak, then I have no further use for you," Decebel told her calmly.

Marianna nodded, accepting the fate she had chosen. She looked into Decebel's eyes once more, knowing it was the last thing she would ever see.

"Let it be known this day Marianna broke pack law and hurt one of her own. Attempted to murder my mate and betrayed her Alpha.

That is why she dies this day," Decebel looked at the female he had watched grow from just a pup." Decebe's eyes softened briefly, "This is not easy for me. We cannot allow betrayal in the pack. A pack is only as strong as the loyalty that holds it together. "

"I'm sorry."

He jerked his hand sharply to the side, breaking her neck before she could continue. He wouldn't drag her death out and he didn't want to hear her excuses. Not while his mate lay dying.

"Is everything okay? I thought I heard -"

Decebel turned at the sound of Thad's voice. Thad's eyes widened in shock as he looked from Decebel to the crumpled body at his feet. In that moment, he knew he'd been found out. As Decebel snarled and lunged, Thad phased in mid air and ran straight for the glass window, throwing himself through it.

Decebel stopped mid-stride when power wrapped around him.

"Decebel, come to me."

Decebel felt his Alpha's power surrounding him, offering him strength and comfort. He tried to fight it, but even in Vasile's weakened state he was strong. He turned, legs moving without his permission. He approached Vasile's bedside and lowered himself on one knee.

"Alpha." Decebel bared his neck as he trembled for control.

"Open yourself to me," Vasile instructed.

Vasile and Decebel had done this only one other time. It was an ability only an Alpha and Beta shared, a way to pass on the memories if the other should fall. Decebel closed his eyes and forced his breathing to calm. Vasile placed his hand on Decebel's forehead and watched the images and sounds the poured from his Beta's mind into his own.

The room was silent as the rest of the pack looked on, frozen by the events that had just unfolded, that they didn't yet understand.

When it was done, Vasile opened his eyes and met Decebel's.

"She is alive."

"Only just." Decebel's voice was barely above a whisper.

"You can hear her thoughts?" Vasile's lips curved ever so slightly, happy that his Beta's bond with his mate had finally formed.

"I did. But now it's silent, dark."

"That could mean she is unconscious."

Decebel nodded, unable to even consider the alternative.

"We will find her, Beta," Vasile told him firmly.

Decebel stood. His wolf was still at the forefront, unable to rest, unable to think about anything but finding their mate.

"If..." Decebel had to clear his throat before he could continue. "If she dies, you will have to kill me."

Vasile nodded once, then added, "She will not die."

Decebel closed his eyes. "How can you be so sure?"

Vasile chuckled lightly. "No one as fierce as Jennifer Adams will go quietly into the night."

Epilogue

Decebel gathered rope, flashlights, and water. Costin was waiting along with Fane, Skender, and Sorin.

"Thad's pack bailed with him," Fane announced.

Decebel growled. "We will deal with him once Jennifer is safe."

"Vasile and Alina are under guard. They should be safe enough here, for now." Sorin's words were torn apart as screams erupted from down the hall.

The five males took off at a run towards the shouts and screams. Crina was running towards them.

"FIRE! They've set the mansion on fire."

Decebel kept moving toward the rooms that now had smoke billowing from them.

"Go through the rooms make sure everyone is out," he yelled over the roar of the flames. The fire was engulfing everything in its path quickly, too quickly, as if something gave it power.

More screams filled the mansion and, once the upper rooms had been checked, they tore through the rest of the house.

"Get everyone out now! Fane, you come with me. We'll get Vasile and Alina."

Decebel was running while shouting his commands. He snarled as flames crawled like demons from hell up the walls.

"Something about this is wrong, Beta," Fane spoke Decebel's thoughts aloud.

"Magic," Decebel muttered. "Dark magic."

Jen struggled to breathe, fading in and out of consciousness. She tried moving at one point, but the pain was so great that she had passed out. Something had just awoken her – a noise, maybe. It was dark, and so cold.

She heard scuffling far above her. An animal? A person?

"Hello?" Her voice was hoarse. "Please help me."

"What is your name?"

Jen heard the female voice some from somewhere up above and nearly sobbed at the sound.

"I'm Jen."

"Hello, Jen." The voice was so soothing and comforting – it made her want to curl up in a ball and sleep. "My name is Rachel…"

**Please enjoy this excerpt from
"The Legacy of Kilkenny"
by Devyn Dawson**

Chapter 1. Sleep
ABEL

Rolling over in bed, pulling the pillow over my head, didn't help to muffle the noise that assaulted me awake. I sail across the room to bang my hand on my alarm clock until it is silenced, nice way to start my day. Not any day, my first day of my junior year. If things work out right, I'll have enough money saved up to buy a car by the end of this semester. Until then, I get to ride with my mom. Lame right? It's six in the morning, usually I'd be dragging ass since I didn't fall asleep until four, but the first day jitters have me amped awake.

Last night I was almost asleep, and then I heard the neighbors' dogs barking, which kept me up. Not to mention, before that happened, I saw the crazy lady across the street sneaking to water her lawn. It had been another dry summer in Oklahoma; a water rationing ordinance is in place. If anyone is caught watering their lawn, they are slapped with a hundred dollar fine. It is beyond me how she isn't caught, being she is the only one with green grass on our street. Why risk a ticket for green grass? I never saw what caused the dogs to bark, but I was amazed that no one even bothered shushing them. No lights. No yelling. Nothing.

BOOM! BOOM! BOOM! I just love the wonderful sounds of the broom stick banging on the ceiling, which happens to be the floor to my room. It is one of my mom's wonderful ideas to make sure I was awake, it sounded like a sonic boom went off under the bed. "I'm up!" I yell down to her as I bang my baseball bat on the floor. BOOM! "Mom, I'm up!" Scrambling across the room to yell out from my bedroom door, I stub my big toe on my hand weight I forgot to put away. "Shit," I grumble under my breath.

As I do every morning, I send a text to my sister Allie, telling her to get up. I know for a fact she sleeps with the phone by her head so she can see status updates as they come across the phone. We're both insomniacs, so mornings always come too soon. I've been her personal alarm clock for the last year when our mom suggested I start calling her to wake her up. So, she gets to go away and I'm still responsible to make sure she is responsible. She starts her second year at college, and I'm stuck here to entertain the parents.

The silence after she moved out was deafening. In the beginning, I would get up and walk around my room trying to make my mind shut up and let me sleep. I would hear the mumbling of my mom and dad talking, or whatever it is parents do behind closed doors when they think their kids are sleeping. I miss having Allie just a wall away, now there's no one tapping on the wall checking if I'm awake. I don't miss her dramatic attitude, but I do miss her driving me to school. For someone that is 5'3" and weighs next to nothing, she has enough attitude to put Chelsea Handler to shame.

The kitchen still smells of fresh paint and sawdust from the recent renovation. I've logged hours and hours of being in home improvement stores, staring at colors of paint. Yellow apparently isn't just yellow anymore, it is *sweet buttery cream* not to be confused with *buttery cream*. I think it took my mom about a month to pick a color, just the other night I heard her talking about changing it. Argh. My usual backpack parking place is on the counter by the barstools.... not anymore. I might scratch the granite and I'll be reminded how long it took her and dad to save up to have a nice kitchen. I drop my stuff by the back door for our frantic escape to get to school on time.

At breakfast, mom pours herself a cup of coffee, her big mop of black curly hair looking especially wild. Sometimes it is hard to discern between freshly fixed up hair or morning bed-head. I know better than to ask. Mom is just mom, sorta on the weird side but strangely likeable. She isn't overly fond of her given name of Natalie, she prefers to go by Nat. She is telling me something about the cost of eggs and how it only cost her five dollars to fill up her tank when she was in high school, blah blah blah. Another morning of her non-stop chatter, a good indication she had too much caffeine.

"Is dad working tonight?" I ask as I reach around her to grab a Pop Tart and napkin.

"Abel, have you ever known your dad to miss a day of work?" Mom said as she dabbed at the coffee she dribbled on the table.

"I dunno, maybe. Hey, I've got a FBLA meeting after school; I'm catching a ride home with Shane so you don't need to bother with car pool today. Okay?"

"If it gets me out of dodging crazed high school drivers, I'm good with it, just make sure you're home by six."

"We probably should go, don't want to be late on my first day and all." I shove another Pop Tart in my backpack as we both head to the car.

The car pool lane is moving so slow, move already! I can't wait until I get a car; riding with my mom is so lame.

"Don't forget to call me when you get home, I'll have my cell on me. Oh, in case I'm not home there are some enchilada's in the freezer, just heat them up in the microwave." Mom reached in her purse handing me a fifty. "That is lunch money, so be sure to give it to the cafeteria lady."

"It's all good. Bye mom, I'll see you later." I hurried up out of the car before she started getting emotional like every year on my first day of school.

I look up at the picture perfect school. The architect must have modeled it after a story book, with its pitched roof, canopy covered walkway and crimson red bricks. Water rationing doesn't pertain to schools, they want them to look pretty and inviting so the kids are proud of their school. I learned all that from my mom's unquenchable thirst of news. The Daily Pied (pronounced pee'd) is her source of news that would never make it to the paper if it were one of the big hitters like The Oklahoman.

Catching up to Shane we fist bumped and strolled in as if we own the place.

"You going to the meeting after school?" Shane asks.

"Yeah, is it still cool if I get ride from you?" Like he'd say no, I think to myself.

"No problem. I gotta go, see you at lunch."

Second hour I'm sitting in English Comp III thinking about how this room didn't make it when they were going for kids being proud of school. The prison cell gray cinder block walls have two windows that look out over the dumpsters. I see the secretary sneak out and huddle behind one of the dumpsters having a smoke, totally breaking the no tolerance rule. I turn my attention back to class when I notice everyone is whispering like a swarm of bees. Gossip.

It is impossible not to turn my head and see what everyone is talking about. She is the hottest girl that has graced my school's hallways since Allison Chambers, class of 2009. Now *that* girl was hot.

Julie Tidsdale, the one girl that drove most everyone crazy, is sitting directly in front of me. Julie is the queen of girls at school, and you can almost see her back arch and her fangs come out as she notices the girl that walks in. Mrs. Horn comes over and introduces the class to Prudence Phelan.

"Please call me Pru." Her gray eyes look confident as she stands there in front of the class for everyone to gawk at. The curves of her body not hidden under the navy blue baby-tee, it just so happens to make her red hair look amazing. Her voice, oh man her voice is incredibly sexy, husky but not in a boy way. I knew at that moment what my dad meant when he said a girl that has everything you could ever dream of was trouble... and *trouble* just walked into my English Comp III class.

My next class is US History, my least favorite subject. The teacher is new to the school and looks just like Jack Black. Actually, he looks so much like him I practically died waiting for him to talk. Sadly, he isn't J.B., I think to myself. He has the most monotone voice I've ever heard in my life. My brain is fading in and out and I struggle my best not to fall asleep.

The woods were so thick, I could hear them gaining on me. She kept telling me to go left and once I hit the clearing skirt around the edges to the right for about 30 feet and head back into the woods. A hiking trail is there so it will be easier to gain speed. I was getting hot but I had to keep going. I lost them at the clearing so that gave me a little time. I heard a warning shot, I knew it was a ploy though there were three of them and the one with the gun went another direction. I could hear the brush moving behind me so I knew the guy with the bow was back there. Her voice, I heard it again (in my head), *Run! There is a cave close to where you are.* She was talking but I could see the image of what she was telling me. It sounded just like Pru. Damn, the devil's thorn was thick and growing over the path, I knew I was bleeding but I couldn't stop yet. That voice again, *hurry, get in the cave, they won't see it, you'll be safe. I'll be there soon. Don't move.* I jumped over two fallen trees and climbed into the cave just in time to hear the hunter stop, I peered out, he didn't see me... but I took a mental picture so I'd remember his face. I lay down, the ground was cool and I was so hot. I needed water.

I feel someone shaking me, I jump sitting straight up. "Whoa! What the?" I turn to see everyone looking at me. I hate it when I fall asleep in class. Thankfully I didn't drool all over myself.

During lunch, I see Julie trying to take pictures of her and Pru. I notice Julie is the only one making the kissy face, Pru looks bored out of her mind, which I admire. Every time I look in their direction, Julie has her arm stretched out as far as it will go taking self portraits. I don't think I'll ever understand the point. I mean seriously, is it really necessary to document your look, minute by minute?

Girls in high school have their own set of rules. One, keep track of the competition, from what she wears to who she knows. Two, what does she drive? Three, who has she done? Four, who are her parents? The list goes on and on. Guys, well we don't get that deep, we just want to know what's for lunch? I'm not what you'd call the ladies man, sad but true. I haven't had a steady girlfriend since eighth grade and I'm not totally sure if two weeks is considered a steady relationship. Our school is so small that we are environmentally friendly, relationships are frequently recycled yet Julie Tidsdale isn't worth recycling to me.

"Hey Shane, did you see Julie trying to get the new girl to be her new bestie?" I say as I shove a French fry in my mouth.

"She's just dumb, I can't stand that girl. I can't believe I'm friends with someone that had their lips on that pain in the ass," Shane says as he digs frantically through his backpack. He pulls out permission slips for his home economics class.

"Being you're the only guy in school who hasn't made out with her, don't hate. It was eighth grade; I've raised my standards since then. Is that a home ec slip?" I ask pointing at the paper in his hand.

"Oh, *don't hate* Abe, I'm sure not taking cooking classes from my mom, if you know what I mean?" Shane says as he laughs to himself.

Even though I agree with him about his mom's cooking, I'm not going to admit to it. "I'll see you at the meeting. I've got to stop by my locker before math so I'll catch you on the flip side."

The rest of the day is full of the same crap every day is filled with. By the end of the day, every guy had taken a pic of Pru's assets and shared it with all of their friends; their friends shared it with theirs and so on and so on. Everyone had the nerve to sneak a pic, except me. I luckily have friends that feel it their personal responsibility to make sure I have copies of the pics too.

Where to find Devyn Dawson Books
http://www.amazon.com/Legacy-Kilkenny-ebook/dp/B0055JCFDQ
http://www.devyndawson.com/

Lightning Source UK Ltd.
Milton Keynes UK
UKOW04f1932081113

220724UK00001B/37/P